Loving Naomi

Meghan Newkirk

WESTBOW
P R E S S®
A DIVISION OF THOMAS NELSON
& ZONDERVAN

WestBow Press books may be ordered through booksellers or by contacting:

WestBow Press
A Division of Thomas Nelson & Zondervan
1663 Liberty Drive
Bloomington, IN 47403
www.westbowpress.com
844-714-3454

ISBN: 978-1-6642-2112-3 (sc)
ISBN: 978-1-6642-2111-6 (hc)
ISBN: 978-1-6642-2113-0 (e)

Library of Congress Control Number: 2021901248

Printed in the United States of America.

WestBow Press rev. date: 03/26/2021

To Scott, Ellis, Daphne, and Betsy
This book is for you.

One

I DIDN'T MEAN to be a bad friend. I really didn't.

I didn't want to make people feel like I didn't care about them, but my inability to not feel guilty about every little comment likely made other people feel self-conscious or criticized.

I was driving home from a lunch date with a couple friends from school who wanted me to live with them when we finished college that spring. I told them repeatedly that I liked the idea of rooming together in our own super cool apartment off campus, but truthfully, the thought of living with other people gave me nervous sweats and constant nausea.

"Sounds great!" I said.

"I'd love to!" I gritted my teeth.

"We will have *so* much fun!" I choked out.

All the faked enthusiasm was because I needed to please people, and it was about to bite me right where it hurt—my brain.

It was a typical January afternoon in Raleigh, North Carolina, and even though the local meteorologist promised it was supposed to be warming up outside, the air had a chill to it that stung my skin when the wind blew. I was driving back to my apartment after a future roommate get together where we were supposed to talk about how we'd save our money to rent an amazing chick-pad and all the ways we wanted to decorate it. I should have been stoked, but instead I spent the cloudy drive home reflecting on how I'd let everyone down by anxiously telling them that I just couldn't live with them. I didn't have a legitimate reason.

I just kept saying, "Girls, I just can't. I'm sorry."

We were all seniors in the Communication Department at NC State University, and everyone else was thrilled about our impending graduation. But I wasn't. I was twenty-one years old and lived alone in an apartment above my parents' garage.

Anxiety was an evil pet—it lived inside of me and followed me everywhere. Sometimes it was quiet, but most of the time anxiety was an internal whisper that grew louder and more intense depending on the day. It was always there, and I couldn't separate the anxious lies it whispered in my ear from the truth based in reality. When irrational thoughts invaded my mind, I couldn't accurately remember conversations or recall situations. These unwanted thoughts kidnapped reality.

In my driveway I heard the familiar popping sound of acorns being flattened under my truck tires. Soon I would be able to hide myself away in 600 square feet of my own thoughts and concentrate on the fears of the day without interruption. Well, not completely without interruption, because I still saw my parents every day.

I liked the idea of living on my own with a group of girls, but having my parents close by gave me the control that I felt I needed to survive. Change in any form was not something I welcomed. I had been deeply afraid of change since I was a child, and it was a characteristic I was stuck with.

My mom was gardening in the side yard beside the house. "How'd it go, Naomi? Did the girls understand why you wanted to live at home this spring?"

Nurse by day, gardener at heart, my mom was my friend, my confidante, and one of the only people I felt comfortable opening up to about my brain games. I walked around the car slowly and she stood up from behind a shrub to straighten her sun hat. She was covered in soil, and her luscious silver bob was full of leaves and little bits of pine straw.

What gardening chores there were to do in the middle of January was a mystery to me, but there she was with her gloves and rake, working the soil once again. My parking spot was on the other side of the house, so often I was able to sneak into my oasis unseen. Not this time.

"Fine, I guess. I'm sure the girls totally don't get why I wouldn't want to live with them. I couldn't even really give them a decent reason why." I slapped the keys against my hand as I spoke. The sting of the impact kept me from hearing my rowdy thoughts.

"Well, all you can do is trust your gut, sweetie. Do what's best for you, and don't worry about what they think. Trouble was, you kept saying you would live with them. You have to learn how to set your boundaries and stick—"

"*Stick* to them!" I finished for her.

I'd heard the boundaries talk more than I cared to remember. I had heard it all my life, along with the talk on how if I organized my binders correctly, I would get better grades. *Ha! I wish.* It didn't seem to matter how many tabs or files I had. By the end of every semester, my bookbag looked like a paper war had gone down inside, and there were no survivors.

"Honey, I'm just trying to help you get more organized. That includes how you communicate in relationships. Don't say yes to something unless you're prepared to follow through." She shadowed me up the stairs that led to my front door.

"I know, I know, Mom. Easier said than done. Trust me." I closed my door before she could follow after me. Once alone, I could relive the conversation with my friends over and over, detail by detail, facial expression by facial expression.

I sat on the edge of my bed, bouncing up and down as I picked my cuticles while turning over the lunch conversation like stones in my head. The dreaded "what if" game seeped up from the deep crevices of my mind. My friends acted like they understood why

I wanted to live at home, but *what if they don't understand because I didn't really give a good reason? What if they think it's because I don't like them? What if they think I'm immature because I'd rather live at home? I mean so close to home. What if they can't find another person to room with them, and it's all my fault? It's all my fault... It's all my fault...*

I washed my hands and took out my phone to send a group text to apologize to them. I needed to see if they were upset with me. I felt vulnerable doing that, but it would give me the short-lived relief I needed just to make sure they weren't mad.

Hey ladies. So sorry again for not rooming with y'all this spring. I really appreciate your understanding and friendship. I feel so bad!

Momentary relief washed over me after I pressed the send button and washed my hands again to remove any germs that may have transferred from my phone back to my freshly cleaned hands. There was no immediate response from them, and the rapid-fire obsessive thoughts once again took root.

After many sweaty minutes passed, Beth, my oldest friend from high school, finally responded.

That's okay. We'll figure it out!

Wow. That answer sure didn't provide much relief. I read and reread her text about a hundred times and realized I would have to walk away from this situation feeling uncomfortable and let the anxiety pass...eventually. I was used to stomaching the tension, the jittery heart, and the one-track thought waves. It wasn't fun, but that seemed to be how I was meant to live.

I love people. I love being with people, and I most definitely enjoy making people laugh. It felt odd to be such a mix of a person— my brain could go to such serious, even dark, places, and yet my heart was addicted to fun. One day in high school, I left math class, went to the bathroom, and made myself a toga out of toilet paper. Acting completely normal, I went back into class while the entire class erupted in laughter at my ridiculous transformation. Those were the moments I lived for. Even with all the fears that gripped me, *that* girl was always inside, struggling to get out.

I decided that I needed a distraction for the afternoon, so I grabbed my phone and some sweet tea and headed downstairs to see what Mom was up to. Maybe she could help me find a part-time job on Craigslist that would distract me from the spinning inside my brain.

I shouted from the top of the apartment stairs, "Hey Mom? Where you at?"

"Out here visiting with my Japanese maple, dear! What do you need?" She answered from somewhere amidst the many bare branches of her favorite tree.

"I'm job searching on my phone. Mind if I keep you company, look for jobs, and freeze my tail off while you work?"

I never liked to do anything by myself because the quiet allowed in too much extra internal noise. I tried to keep my mind off the day's stressful lunch, but every so often comments my friends had made during lunch would rise up in my head, and I would let myself relive them—only five times…or six…or maybe seven if it helped me feel calmer.

"Sure honey! You just take a look on your phone and read me any job descriptions you want help analyzing. Oh! You should check the church website. Sometimes people will post part-time and temporary work there. That would be a great place to start since you know so many people there already. Might be fun to work for someone you already know."

I cringed at the thought of working for someone from church. My parents brought us up to go to church, to believe in Jesus, and to love others well. I wanted to believe deeply in an all-loving God, but the thought stuck in my head that I never believed enough to make the cut into heaven. I asked Jesus into my heart probably eight hundred times by the time I was thirteen, and in middle school I had a journal where I'd written down my prayers ending with the phrase "In Jesus' Name, Amen" over and over.

I used to make myself write "In Jesus' Name, amen" in perfect handwriting, then repeat it out loud with a "perfect heart"—I don't think there is such a thing, but I sure tried—so that my prayers would actually count. It was silly, but like all my other odd rituals, it brought temporary peace to my fear that I wasn't one of God's children.

Intense worries could only occupy my brain one at a time. They took turns. And on this particular day, I wasn't obsessing about whether or not I'd go to heaven, so I went to the church website without much stress.

There was a choice on the main menu called "'Job Opportunities for the Church Body.'" I clicked on it and pulled up a list of jobs that church-folks were searching to fill. There weren't a ton of jobs to choose from, so I wasn't optimistic.

"Wanted: Leaf and stick removal from yard. May also need light pruning and weeding."

Nope. Not for me. Don't like getting dirty or being outside.

"Needed: Someone to drive my grandmother to her doctor's appointment once a week. She is 82 and may need to be lifted in and out of the car." *Nope. Totally not my jam. Driving people in my car is too much responsibility. I would be afraid of unintentionally hurting them by getting into an accident. And then worry that the accident was intentional. Pass.*

"Dental office receptionist needed a few hours a week. Good people skills required as patient communications will be frequent." *Maybe. I love working with people, but I hate the dentist. I'll have to think on this one.*

The last ad was worded differently than the rest, and it caught my eye because of how creatively it had been written.

"Too much stuff! I have too much stuff, and I need help sorting it. I am a recovering pack rat in need of someone who can help me sift, sort, and decide what to keep. You can set your own hours and would not need to deep clean anything, I don't think. I am old but not nearly as old as I may look. I've had a busy life...hence all the stuff. Cordially, Corrie Dean."

I yelled out since I could no longer see my mom from where I sat on our garden swing. "Hey Mom! Do you know a Corrie Dean at church?"

Her head popped up from behind her giant *Daphne odora* bush. "Corrie Dean? That name sounds familiar. If memory serves me, she's the wife of a deceased missionary our church used to support. That's all I know though. Why?"

"Well, it seems she needs some help sorting through her things. Sounds like she has quite a collection of junk. Think that would be a good job for me? I don't like caring for older people. It makes me majorly uncomfortable, but I think this could be a good compromise, right?" I always liked having my mother's stamp of approval on my decisions...even at twenty-one. It was unnecessary, but I got a sense of peace knowing she concurred with my plans.

"Yeah. Why not? You can always meet with her and see how you feel about the job. It sounds like she could be an interesting person to work for. You may learn about different communication styles in other cultures from her experience as an overseas missionary. Consider it research for your major."

She was stretching with that, but her points were valid. I suddenly realized it had been a while since I'd washed my hands. I could feel the nasty, grimy film building on my scaly and dry hands. Surely they were contaminated. I mean, I *had* been handling my filthy phone a lot.

Feeling the tension rising in my gut to make them clean again, I jolted up from the swing and called out, "I'm going to go upstairs and call her right now. See if I can get an interview. I'll see you at dinner."

"Okay dear!" Mom called back, unaware of the real reason for my quick departure.

I closed the door behind me in my apartment, squirted thirteen pumps of soap in my hands, and scrubbed until my heart felt clean. I didn't call Mrs. Dean like I said I would. It would probably take me three days to muster up the courage to give her a ring and request an interview.

Two

"WHO ARE YOU interviewing with again?" my big sister Shana asked me with heavy breath during our Saturday run.

My sister and I were close. She could tolerate my complications and my sometimes-inconsistent ability to love the people in my life well. She was my only friend, period. We fought, like most sisters do, but we forgave, forgot and moved on. She couldn't understand my personal battles, but she at least tried. We called each other "Silsta," which is far better than "Stinky." That's what Shana called me for a while in elementary school.

"She's an old widow from church who needs some help going through her 'house of junk,' as she calls it. Her name is Corrie Dean. She sounds really nice, actually. She told me she had heard of me from pastor Don and felt like I'd be a great fit for the job. I meet her on Tuesday."

We slowed our pace mid-run to get in more talking time. I chose each step carefully, only letting my feet land where the road looked squeaky clean out of fear that I would accidentally step on someone's vomit, contract the Norovirus, and die of dehydration. It made running a little awkward, but even so, our run was my favorite time of the week and not just because I got to catch up with my Silsta. Running cleared my mind and by the end, difficult situations made a lot more sense. And I loved the rush of endorphins at the end of a good run. I didn't do it for weight loss because I was already skinny enough, even too skinny according to some. Shana, on the other hand, made running look easy. She was tall with chestnut-colored curly locks that flowed to the middle of her back. It never seemed like she had to style her hair because it was always fixed beautifully, even when she was covered in sweat. Her eyes were a striking blue that everyone noticed, especially boys. She was an elementary school teacher who was beyond gifted with young people, particularly with kids who had challenging backgrounds or difficult home situations.

"Third graders are just little sponges! I tell you!" She puffed, "They are so impressionable and love to hear stories about what's going on in the world. Plus, they ask so many curious questions!" Her passion for teaching was obvious.

I wished that I was that passionate about my communication degree, but my knowledge was general at best, and I was going to have to do a lot of brainstorming to figure out how I would use my education. How I was going to use talking as a way to benefit the world and support myself was a baffling question for me with no real answer at the moment.

"It's great that you love what you're doing so much. I envy your commitment."

At the end of our run, we stopped for water at a local café where we'd parked before our run. We sat in our usual spot, in the booth closest to the window, while the place filled up with people arriving to get coffee and hang out. I watched a pair of bluebirds flutter around a nearby birdfeeder as Shana sipped her ice water.

"You'll figure this career thing out, Silsta. I can't wait to hear about this eccentric old lady you're going to work for too. I wonder what kind of stuff she has. Maybe old artifacts that are worth a lot. Maybe she'll share with you some of the money she gets from selling them because you helped her sort through them." Shana wiggled her eyebrows with excitement.

"Or maybe it's just a bunch of junk that's going to make me have to take a shower when I get home every day after work. I'm such a germaphobe, I'll likely have to use bleach on myself," I said, only partially kidding.

"Do you know anything about where she lived or what her and her husband did overseas?" Shana never acknowledged or laughed at my self-deprecating jokes because she said it was cruel of me to make them. Cruel to whom, I'm not sure.

"No, not really. All I know is her husband died in some sort of work-related accident, and then she moved back here about five years ago."

"Hey! Maybe you could show her your toilet paper toga sometime and see if she's ever seen anything more authentic in Greece." Shana chuckled. She had heard rumors of my high school math class escapade and never let me forget it. She even hunted down a few photos people had taken and had the photos blown up for my high school graduation party.

I laughed back. "You know what? That was my finest work, if I do say so myself. Saturday Night Live would be lucky to have me. You know I'm right too!"

"Haha! You wish, Silsta! Ah, well. On that note, and with that awesome image in my head, I guess I better get going. I've got lesson plans to write. Where you headed today?"

"Eh, nowhere special. I'm gonna go home, take a shower, and then work on my paper for World History. I don't know how I made it almost four years without taking that class, but evidently, I can't escape it. I mean, a three-to-five-page paper every week? It's outrageous!"

The café door was pull-to-open, so I would normally walk through it behind whoever I was with to avoid touching the disgusting, germ-laden handle. But this time, right as we were about to reach the door, Shana realized she had forgotten her keys and called out, "You go ahead. I'll see you next week, but text me after your interview Tuesday. Love you!"

I could barely make out what she was saying as my brain whirled with what to do next. *Do I wait for her to finish, then let her go ahead of me so she can get the door? Would that be too obvious? Of course, it would be too obvious, and she will certainly think I'm not thinking right. Here come the what ifs...What if she already thinks I'm not thinking right? Of course, I'm not thinking right! Who wouldn't think that? What if I touch the door and get a nasty stomach bug and am laid up for days? What if I...barf! People are now waiting for me to open the door. I have to do it. Take a deep breath... Okay, pull your sleeve down so you don't have to touch the handle. Here goes...*

I braved the door and made my way outside. Perspiration beaded under my arms, and as I got in my car, I pulled the hand sanitizer from my backpack, squirting it all over my hands along with the sleeve of my shirt. I felt the panic lessening but could tell it would take some time to ease, even with the endorphins from my run still on board. *Why couldn't I just open the door? Why can't I act normal?*

I took a breath, squirted on a little more sanitizer, then started driving as fast as I could with the windows rolled down, hoping that the whooshing air in my ears would drown out the racket of the worries in my head. I realized far too late that I had accidentally run a stop sign because I was all caught up in my head. With a sigh of relief that nothing serious happened, I shot up a quick flare prayer to God,

"God, could you please, please just let these worries in my brain lift?"

I didn't talk to God often, but when I did, it was usually with desperate prayers like this one.

I made it home only to notice my seatbelt dangling next to me. I had been so distracted by fear that I had driven home with no seatbelt. Once again, my self-imposed dread caused me to frantically ignore the safety measures I normally care to follow. I was only partially present sometimes because of the agony brought on by the churning ocean in my mind.

Three

TUESDAY MORNING BUSTED in fast like a toddler having a tantrum. I wandered around my house as I got myself ready to go to class and then over to Mrs. Dean's house right after lunch. I was looking forward to meeting her, but more importantly I was looking forward to adding to my bank account. There was a knock at the door as I was grabbing my purse off the counter. It had to be my dad. He was the early bird of the family, and he enjoyed coming to say hi before I left for school.

Dad loved his job as a public speaking professor and academic advisor at the local community college. He enjoyed getting to know people through their college experience. And he, like me, loved to entertain people. With short salt and pepper hair, a husky build, and a beyond genuine smile, he was a rather handsome guy. And he was, hands down, my biggest fan, even if we did fight like the dickens sometimes.

"Hey Dad. You can come in!" I called out without even asking who it was.

"Hey Naomi! How ya doing sweetie? Ready for your first day on the job?"

"Yeah! I think so. I mean, it's just a part time job. It's not like, a career."

"Doesn't matter, sweetie! You still have to go in there and be yourself. Be reliable. Ask questions. Know the expectations. Think leadership," he chanted.

"I'm helping a lady clean out her house, Dad, not running for office. I'm sure it'll be fine." I tried not to let my irritation show in my voice. I appreciated him, but I resented how much I needed both him and my mom to cope with life.

"Listen, don't get upset with me. I'm just trying to help you know how to approach this opportunity. I'm not criticizing you, so ease up on your old man." He shook his head.

"I gotta run. I've got class at nine, but I can't wait to hear about your time today! Text me later." He kissed my head and ran out the door before I could respond.

I wondered if most twenty-one-year-old adults had parents who were so invested in their lives. Maybe my parents were so involved in my life because I lived close, or because they knew I was a homebody. Granted, I let them into my life with ease, but I also wondered if it was time to cut the cord a bit.

Maybe I should've moved out like I planned to. Maybe that's healthier. What if I'm not mentally healthy? I probably hurt Dad's feelings when I told him I had everything under control. Maybe I should go find him and make sure. He probably thinks I'm ungrateful. I can be so selfish. I should go after him. I don't have time! I'll just text him. Okay thoughts, you gotta go. I don't have time for this.

I put down my phone, grabbed my coffee, keys, and bag, and slammed the door while mumbling "'please God, no'" under my breath like I often did to keep the awful images in their place.

Better not mutter under your breath in front of Mrs. Dean. She'll wonder who in the world you're talking to...

I slowly turned onto a rough gravel driveway lined with ceramic cat statues that led to a house with a giant American flag hanging proudly by the front door.

"Oh my." I counted all the pieces of "'art'" that lined her driveway. "Fifteen, sixteen…wow… eighteen cat statues? Who has *this* many cat statues?"

I started to get a little nervous about exactly how much stuff I would be sorting through. I parked behind a beat-up old VW bug whose burnt orange color looked more like a patchwork of rust than actual paint. There were bumper stickers of all different kinds covering the back window and door of the dilapidated punch buggy.

"'I love my Calico.'" Of course, a cat sticker. *Makes sense.*

"'Thank you Jesus.'"

"'Honk if you love Jesus!'" This one made me laugh out loud as I envisioned her driving down the road asking to be honked at.

There were a lot of funny stickers, but it was a serious one that caught my eye. Beautifully painted across the back hatch, just above the license plate was the phrase, "'This too shall pass.'"

I don't know why those words stirred me up inside. I didn't even know this woman, and already her bumper sticker made me feel completely exposed. Things didn't always pass. My thoughts didn't ever stop. Nor did my guilt or the constant invasion of unwanted extreme fear bombs that came out of nowhere.

What if I stepped on the gas and slammed into the back of her car? It wouldn't take much. I totally could. Do it. Just do it. Just do it. Just do it. Just do it.

I frantically put the car in park and turned off the engine. Unwanted thought alert! Sometimes I called these random, unwanted thoughts "spikes" because that's what they felt like in my brain — a grenade of a thought thrown down on to my gray matter, exploding and leaving nothing but shrapnel in its path.

I muttered a quick, "please, God no" to myself to try to get rid of the intrusive thought, but images of me slamming her car to bits kept coming. I was digging my nails into the back of my hand to make them quit when a face appeared at the front door. *Better get out of the car quickly.*

Another quick "please, God no" under my breath, and I opened the door.

"Well, hello there. You must be Naomi Lang. You are such a pretty young thing," the woman at the door said.

This couldn't be the widow, Mrs. Dean. She was younger than I pictured, likely in her early sixties, at most. She had short cinnamon colored hair pulled back into a half ponytail. Her nails were painted a funky turquoise blue color, and she had on bright red lipstick. She was attractive at first glance, but close inspection revealed a face marked all over with the remnants of either adventure or tragedy.

"Hi." I gave her a warm smile. "It's so nice to finally meet you. I wasn't expecting... Well, I mean, I was expecting... I mean, I didn't know...what I should expect... I mean, you don't look like..."

What am I saying? She must think I'm so insensitive.

"An old hag? I bet you were expecting to see some old lady who needed help going through her household. Well, the joke is on you! I'm a spry chicken." She cackled to herself at an inappropriate volume.

"Oh no! I didn't mean that! I just meant I didn't know what to expect. I'm so sorry. I'm really sorry," I stuttered back to her. I walked into her house smothered in embarrassment and clearly off to a rocky start. I dug my nails into the back of my hand to keep from getting too stressed and then covered the marks with my long sleeve.

"Come on in and cop a squat. Let's have some tea and get acquainted." Mrs. Dean moved like a sloth as she reached for the teapot and opened drawers to retrieve utensils.

Her kitchen was wildly decorated with colors so bright they hurt my eyes, postcards from families all over the world on her refrigerator, and piles of papers stacked on every counter. I tried to hide my surprise at the overwhelming visual stimuli. I shouldn't have been surprised since my job was to help her declutter but seeing it in person was a whole different experience. She was in no way filthy, but there was no sense of organization anywhere. There was mess in every corner and on every surface.

"Tell me about yourself, Naomi. What's important for me to know about you?" She turned on the teapot she snuck out from behind a giant stack of manila envelopes.

I laughed nervously. "I really am so sorry about what I said before. I didn't mean to sound so... thoughtless. Well, stuff about myself, uh... I mean, I don't know, really. What do you want to know?"

"What makes you tick? Who *is* Naomi Lang? I must know a little bit about you before you learn all my secrets as we go through my entire life! But no more apologizing," she said confidently. "It simply isn't necessary."

"Yes ma'am. Let me think. Who is Naomi? I guess I'd say I don't really know yet. I'm twenty-one, about to graduate from college. I love my family and well, God, too, I guess. I enjoy being with people and making them laugh. Still trying to figure out the rest of it though. I feel like a complicated ball of feelings and thoughts, if that makes any sense at all."

She gave me uninterrupted eye contact the whole time I spoke. I felt like she was looking into my soul, and it was borderline terrifying.

"Great answer! I was nervous about meeting you and showing you inside my web of disorganization from years of collecting. But I can tell already we're going to get along just fine. So, the job is a simple one. I need your help cleaning up the mass of things I've gathered over the years. You'll do different things every day. Some days I may have you shred a stack of papers, and on another I might have you polishing silver. That sound stimulating enough for you?"

"Sure! Will you need me to decide what to throw away and what to keep, or will you be helping me with that? The job sounds great though, really." I tried to sound like organizing was something I found pleasure in.

"Good question, my dear! I like where your mind goes. It will depend on the types of items that need going through. Sometimes I'll need you to help me be decisive. All of the things I've collected are valuable to me. They're each a memory of times gone by and remind me of my sweet husband, George. These items represent our life together, and I'd hope you'd be willing to listen to me jabber on about our time together as I let some of these things go." She rubbed her hand lightly over her heart as she closed her eyes for a moment. "You ready to be fly paper? I'm gonna be stickin' memories to you constantly."

I chuckled and nodded my head. The idea of helping her seemed fun. I was surprised how quickly I felt comfortable with her and how much I liked her already.

"What do you want to get out of our time together?" she asked, out of the blue.

I stopped mid chuckle and looked up at her. She was giving me the dreaded soul-searching stare again, and I felt exposed in the same way that silly bumper sticker had exposed me.

"Uh, I don't really know. I guess I'm excited to help you get organized and feel better about your life?" I shrugged. *Real smooth.*

"I'll take it. Sounds good. Welp, let's get started then!" She grabbed the pile of manila envelopes and slammed them down in front of me. "Let's get these puppies shredded!"

Mrs. Dean, or Miss Corrie as I was instructed to call her, showed me where the shredder was, and for the next hour, I sat shredding documents that looked like a bunch of graphs and charts. I had no idea what they were, but I kept on shredding like a good little worker bee.

I worked in the kitchen while Miss Corrie read in the other room. There was a window right next to where I sat, and pretty soon I heard a leaf blower blaring right beside me. I figured it was a neighbor, so I didn't pay much attention to who was operating the blower.

Just as the noise started to get distracting, I called out to Miss Corrie. "I'm done shredding. What do you need me to do next?" I was hoping she would move me to a quieter part of the house for my next job.

"Oh, you know what? That's plenty for today. When would you like to come back? Does Thursday after lunch work for you?"

"Yup! Sounds great! I'll come around the same time I came today."

She ushered me to the side door by the kitchen. Right by the door on the counter was a toolbox with a mess of nails and screws spilling out, covered by a giant hammer. I immediately received an unwanted mental picture that would occupy my mind for days. *Pick up the hammer. Hit something. Hit someone.* Awful visual images of me picking up that hammer were in my head, and before I could stop myself, I frantically whispered, "Please, *God no!*"

"What's that dear? Did you say something?"

"Uh…uh…no. Sorry, I started to say something then changed my mind." I dug my nails into the back of my hand while I fought with all the muscles in my body to make myself walk past the dreaded hammer. I even closed one eye as I went by it so I wouldn't have to look at it one more time.

Her brows furrowed in curiosity. "I'll look forward to our time together day after tomorrow, Naomi."

"Bye!" I bolted to my car, almost tripping over the twenty-something male landscaper working right next to my truck. I flew past him and slammed my car door, starting the engine as fast as I could and muttering "please God, no" repeatedly to keep from imagining myself smashing into her VW again.

I spent the next month with Miss Corrie shredding papers, cleaning out the fridge, organizing her sock drawer, and decluttering the bathroom cabinets. They were easy, mindless tasks that would've been torture for me to do in silence. Thankfully, Miss Corrie had a chatty and upbeat nature which took care of that.

She followed me around while I worked and asked questions about school or my family. I loved her company, so I had no trouble answering her questions. She filled our days with her stories of time spent in unique and far-away places. She'd recall restaurants and cuisines from around the world where she and George shared meals with special people they met during their travels.

The stories of her life didn't piece together all at once, but in bits and pieces as she narrated our time together. Miss Corrie either ignored my occasional self-talk brought on by intrusive thoughts or pretended not to notice, but I'm almost positive she heard me. She never again asked me to repeat myself, almost as though she understood that I wouldn't know how to explain to her what I was saying or why.

We had a good rhythm that worked for us. Like me, she was an extrovert. I could tell she enjoyed the time we spent together by the way she received me each week. She would have tea or coffee ready for us to share while I worked, and she talked. I always felt welcomed by her, and it was refreshing for my soul.

As chatty as we both were, we never got super deep or spiritual in our conversations. Maybe that was because I didn't want to go there, or perhaps it was because she didn't want to go there. Or maybe both. We found more than enough topics to cover, just the same.

I was due to work on Valentine's Day, so I decided to bring Miss Corrie some flowers to celebrate. She called herself "the stereotypical woman" because she had a weakness for roses. I chose pink to show my gratitude for the job and our time together.

I struggled to hold them as I got out of the car, and a deep, sultry voice called out, "Are those for me?"

I let out a startled yelp, as who I could only guess was Miss Corrie's yard man waved politely to let me know he was the friendly caller.

I opened my mouth to respond, but no words came out, just a little air that hissed as I exhaled.

"I didn't mean to scare you, but I just figured you brought those beautiful flowers for me, being the resident landscaper and all." He pointed to my roses with a faint grin.

At first I was frozen, but then I found some courage to joke with him back. "Well, they would be for you, but you'd likely kill them by the time you got them home. I mean, seeing your work around here, I can predict what would become of these beauties... Yeah, so, I decided to give them to someone who would appreciate them...and *not* let them wilt."

He laughed as he made his way toward my truck. As he got closer, I noticed how handsome he was. Bright hazel eyes, short brown hair, and super tall, almost lanky. He was my age, if not a little older. His face was clean, no sign of a beard at all—a true baby face. I was unfamiliar with the courage I was experiencing. No spikes. No fears. No impending doom. I wasn't used to being so mentally relaxed. It was new.

"Considering those flowers are already dead since you cut them, I guess it wouldn't matter how I cared for them, now would it?" His voice cracked and squeaked slightly.

"I'm off the hook. I didn't cut them. I just bought them." I smiled with a shrug.

He laughed. "You're an accomplice then."

"Alright, alright. You can have the roses. I mean, you must be pretty desperate for a Valentine if you're gonna steal these from sweet Miss Corrie."

"Sweet Miss Corrie? Ha! That tough old broad? I wouldn't ever cross her..."

"Hey Hey Hey! Now I resemble that remark!" Miss Corrie shouted from the open kitchen window. "Get in here, Naomi, and give me my flowers!"

"I'm coming!" I shouted up toward her shadow in the window. "Nice to meet you there, Mr. Landscaper man. Happy Valentine's Day."

"I do love to be called Mr. Landscaper man, but you can also call me Joshua. Just never, ever call me Joshie."

"I'm Naomi, which you obviously just heard since Miss Corrie kindly broadcasted it to the neighborhood. Nice joshing with you." I took a few backward steps toward the side door and promptly tripped on one of her many ridiculous cat statues. I wobbled but managed to magically catch myself.

"I'm okay! I think," I called back as Joshua turned around to hide his laugh.

"You know me well already, my dear. These are gorgeous. Thank you! Does this mean you're my Valentine?" Miss Corrie said and immediately lifted the flowers to her nose to take in a giant sniff.

"Sure! My dad thinks Valentine's Day is the perfect time to give all us girls a gift. He's surrounded by women, so he's learned that making us feel special always works in his favor."

As I walked toward the hook on the wall to hang up my purse, I noticed that hammer still sitting in the same spot on the counter. I did my usual ritual of closing the eye closest to the hammer and cringing to myself to avoid mental spikes as I passed it. I had to prepare for that trip by the hammer every day I worked, so I thought I'd gotten really good at hiding that it disturbed me so much.

"Why do you always close one eye when you walk by that side of the kitchen? Is there something there that bothers you?" Miss Corrie studied me with her hands in her pockets.

It looked like she wasn't going to let me off the hook with the hammer routine like she did by ignoring me talking to myself abnormally.

"Oh, you know, hammers just kind of give me the willies. I don't really know why. I know, it's a peculiar thing. Sorry."

"No need to apologize, dearie. As you can see, I have my fair share of...let's say, unique qualities." And that was the end of it. She didn't pry anymore and shockingly didn't make me feel at all strange for my bizarre answer.

"Since it's Valentine's Day, I was thinking we could go through some photos together, and you could put them in dated envelopes for me. Might be a fun thing to do today...or incredibly unwise. I'll get the tissues while you put those flowers in a vase. Grab the one on the top of the fridge, the blue one. It's the one George gave me on our first anniversary when we were living in France." She shuffled to the other room.

As mysterious as I thought I was to her, she was equally mysterious so to me. Some days she would be chipper, quick, and jolly, while other days she would keep to herself a bit more and move very deliberately. I finished putting the flowers in the correct vase just in time to hear her call out, "Bring those flowers in here! I want to look at them while we work."

"On my way," I sang back, but right as I was about to turn around, I saw Josh through the window getting something out of his truck.

I lost my breath at the sight of him, which threw me into a tizzy yet again. I needed to get myself together. I felt this strange swirl of excitement when I saw him that caught me off guard and unnerved me.

"Okay, I'm here. Flowers can go right...there." I placed them on the piano and sat down next to Miss Corrie slowly. I felt the need to be careful and gentle around her, though I had no reason to feel that way.

She had two unorganized stacks of pictures. Some were black and white. Others were worn from age.

"Let's dive right in. Why don't we each grab a stack of photos, and I'll divide them into piles based on the year it was taken as best I can. Feel free to ask any questions about who you're looking at. Maybe we should divide the piles into decades, instead. What do you think?"

"By decade sounds good to me. I think they'll be easier to sort that way. I'll go ahead and label them starting with the 1970s."

We began dividing the giant stacks of photos into organized piles that I put into envelopes labeled by decade. There were pictures of Miss Corrie and George together in France when they were first married, kissing under the Eiffel Tower. Then more photos of them kissing on beaches in Southern California. I didn't ask too many questions, and there weren't too many other people in the photos other than she and George, so most of the snapshots spoke for themselves. I didn't know how sensitive she would be if I asked specific questions about George, since he had passed away recently. I kept my thoughts to myself while letting her chatter on.

"There were many parts of our life and marriage that George and I didn't get an opportunity to photograph. We were either too poor in the very beginning, too busy during the years of doing mission work, or having too much fun adventuring to find time to take pictures. Most of these photos were taken by friends or family. I'm grateful we have as many as we do." Miss Corrie touched a photo of George as though she were caressing his face.

"It sounds like you and George had a very happy marriage."

"Very happy, but of course, there were hard times too. We spent most of our marriage moving around a lot. It was exhilarating, deeply challenging, and always sanctifying."

"Sanctifying? What does that mean?" It was a church term that I'd heard before, but I'd never heard it used in real life. It sounded like something reserved for the saints.

"It's the everyday ways God uses to make us more like Jesus. It's like a peeling away of sin. Or modeling of clay. It is usually uncomfortable, but in the end, it's quite beautiful. We won't be fully sanctified until we're with Him in Heaven, but we can trust He's working in us until that day."

"Huh. I guess I've never heard it quite like that before. Interesting perspective."

"It's not my perspective, dear. It's the truth."

I wasn't sure how to respond to her bold opinion, so I just kept on questioning her about the experiences she had while living in other places. "Where was your favorite place to live? And why?"

"Boy, *that* is a tough one. I loved something about everywhere we lived. In the 1970s, we lived in France, the 1980s in California, the 1990s in Africa, and then when we retired we moved to Raleigh. Not as many places as you probably thought, I'm guessing. I liked something about each place. In France, I loved the food! Oh man, it's clear why Julia Child fell in love with French cooking. I think I gained fifteen pounds the first six months we lived there. California had beautiful landscapes—beaches one direction, mountains the other. Very fun. Then in Africa, it was the people. That's pretty general, but I think I answered your question."

As she was talking, I pulled out a tattered black and white photo from the bottom of the pile. It was a picture of a man wearing overalls, a white collared shirt, a dark wool fedora, and muddy boots. He had one foot up on the edge of a tractor and was smiling with a soft, kind, and an almost amused grin. He had a pleasant looking face and he smiled as though he knew it.

"Who is this?" I held the photo up to Corrie.

She had gotten up to get herself a glass of water, so as she cautiously sat back down she took the photo from my hand.

"Who?" she asked in a puff as she lowered to the cushion. "This guy? That's my father. Handsome, right? Rugged guy, for sure. He had his fair share of lady callers. Worked on a farm in Germany, so he wasn't hurting for muscles. He's about nineteen in this photo, I believe. He always looked older than he was." As she reminisced, she began shuffling through the other photos as if she were looking for something specific. Eventually, she found the one she was looking for and stuck the photo under her thigh.

"My father, Henry, or Tank as his friends called him, lived during an unfortunate time in Germany. A time when to go against the grain was the equivalent to putting a knife in your own back. He was young but bright, with his own opinions about religion, family, and most damaging, politics. Adolf Hitler was supposed to save Germany from ruin, build up the economy, and give them back the pride that had supposedly been taken from World War one. Many of my past family members thought Hitler could save them from poverty and bought into his psychotic ideas, but my father knew better. He refused to support the new leader with the same gusto the rest of the country was eager to give."

Corrie shifted in her seat and bit the corner of her lip. "When World War II officially began, my father lived in fear of having to fight. He stayed locked in a horse stall for weeks, desperate not to be discovered by the enemy, his own people. He couldn't bring himself to fight in a war that he felt nothing but hatred for. My aunt would bring him food secretly, not wanting to draw attention to his hiding place. But the war was not going well for them, and they began to draft all healthy young men. Despite his best efforts, he was drafted to become a Nazi."

"He was a Nazi?" I shuddered.

"Yes, dear. He was. You have to understand, many of these boys didn't want to participate in the war. They didn't believe in the propaganda being spoon fed to the German people. The ideas they promoted made my father sick. He hated them. He loved his family and didn't want to leave them, but he had no choice but to serve. At nineteen, shortly after this picture was taken, he went to war. Nothing but a boy, out there fighting for a cause he despised. As a messenger, his job was to carry notes back and forth between battle lines on a motorcycle. Sometimes he would even transport prisoners from one location to another."

She swallowed hard and continued with a quivering voice. "One time, he made himself sick by drinking rancid milk as a desperate attempt to escape the evil around him. It was a brave and futile effort. My mother once told me that Pa let one of the prisoners he was supposed to be transporting go free. I remember wanting details about who the prisoner was and what happened to him, but my mother knew nothing more than what she shared with me. Pa was a private man who carried with him the awful things he saw during those early years of his life, things far too heavy for any man to carry. It wore on him."

She took the picture from under her leg and handed it to me. It was the shell of an older man, about the same age as Miss Corrie. He looked leathery, ancient, exhausted, and defeated.

"When the war ended, my father went back to work on the farm. There, he met my mother. They married and moved to the States not knowing any English at all. He worked as a maintenance man while Mama took care of my brother and me during the day and worked nights as a waitress in a nearby diner. They taught me what it means to work hard and be diligent. My parents were genuine people, and I miss them every day." Tears gathered in her eyes. "Are you close with your parents, Naomi?"

I was absorbing her story inside and out. "Yes ma'am. Very close to them. They take good care of me. I'm thankful for how they love me, even when I'm not very loveable. I'm sure your parents knew how much you loved them too. Is there a picture of your mother?"

"Sadly, no. My brother has most of the photos of my parents, which are few and far between as it is." She exhaled a heavy breath. "Well, I think I'm emotionally spent. Aren't you, dear? Let's go rustle up a snack. I'm pretty sure I have a cheesecake from Costco in the freezer. Can't go wrong with Costco cheesecake! Am I right?" She pushed herself up from the couch and ambled out of the room.

I didn't get up immediately because I wanted to complete the job of sorting all the pictures into the dated envelopes. I held the two pictures of Tank as I examined them closely. He went from being an energetic, handsome young man to worn out, wounded, and old by the end of his short life. *Is that what happens to everybody?* With the amount I worried in my life, I was sure to look like a wrinkled and worn-out piece of leather by the time I was Miss Corrie's age. I probably wouldn't even live that long. And I wouldn't go to Heaven either, with my lack of faith.

God doesn't know what He's doing at all!!!! Uh-oh. Don't think things like that about God. He'll hear me, and I'll get punished. I'll never be forgiven for the awful things I think about Him. My car will likely run off the road today, or I'll get a debilitating disease. But maybe I want to hate God. He's never helped me with my brain, just like he never helped Miss Corrie's father.

My hands moved like lightning as I finished stuffing the envelopes and filed them away in Miss Corrie's mahogany desk. I muttered a quick, "Please God, *stop*," hoping it would push away any more weedy thoughts from taking root and growing into the dark places of my brain. No matter how hard I tried to keep them at bay, various unwanted images of throwing the photos across the room festered. My thoughts were tornados, spinning out of control.

"You coming, Naomi? I'm about to devour this whole cheesecake, and honey, it ain't gonna be pretty if I do," Miss Corrie hollered from the kitchen.

"I'm coming!" I took a quick step into the bathroom to wash my hands...again. When I washed my hands, I felt a cascade of relief and inner peace that lasted for a few fleeting moments. Everything I touched contaminated my hands. These imaginary marks and sensations of contamination would build up and washing them properly was the only way to regain a sense of control. I washed thoroughly and often but rarely felt clean.

When I entered the kitchen, Miss Corrie was sitting at her little red table with two plates of cheesecake served up and a kettle of water on the stove.

"I tell you something, girl. You do spend a lot of time all wrapped up in thinking, don't you?"

Once again I felt exposed by her, emotionally torn up and called out for being the eccentric that I was. I didn't know how to answer. *Should I try to be vulnerable and tell her my secret thoughts or pretend I have no idea what she's talking about?* I decided to compromise since she had just shared so much of her life with me.

"Ha ha. Yeah, I guess I do. I've always struggled with anxiety, ever since I was a little girl. When I was eight, my appendix ruptured. I was septic and never the same after I recovered. I spent seven days in the hospital getting antibiotics. My mom says I was always a cautious youngster, but after that happened, I entered the 'self-tortured' category of fear." *What am I doing?! This is way deeper than I had intended to go.* I couldn't take back what I'd said, so I downplayed it instead.

"I mean, my fears aren't *that* outrageous. I'm a deep thinker, so that's more of it, I think."

"Your truth is safe with me. Thank you for opening up about that. I'm sure it wasn't easy for you to do. Anxiety is a common problem in this world. God even talks about it in His word. 'Do not worry about tomorrow, for tomorrow has enough worries of its own.'" As she spoke the scripture, she closed her eyes like she was saying the words back to God.

"I'm sure that's true for you, Miss Corrie, but I know for a fact that I can't *not* worry about tomorrow. It's impossible."

"Oh, nothing is impossible with God, girl. He doesn't expect you to carry these troubles on your own. He sent His son to take those burdens away. His Holy Spirit is with you, in you, helping you give all those troubles to Him. Lay them at His feet."

"You don't understand, though. I've tried that. It *does not* work! Even my prayers are laced with fears that strangle me. They

29

suffocate me, intrude on my mind, and infect my heart. If He could help me with those, I think He would have by now." And then I completely lost it. I was standing up, shouting, and shaking. The teapot whistled in the background, but Miss Corrie sat planted in her chair, giving me the same direct eye contact she always did, and at that moment I loathed it.

She spoke tenderly, almost in a whisper. "Sweet child, God loves you, but He never promises a life without struggle, pain, or hurt. His ways aren't ours, and whatever happens to us is for our good and His glory. It doesn't *feel* good. Trust me, I know. But we can trust Him, because He promises to love us and ultimately save us from our own sin."

"That may be true, but I definitely don't feel like it is!" I grabbed my bag and fled out the door.

I couldn't hold back the tears as I ran past the hammer down the steps to my truck. Joshua was there blowing leaves—I could hear him by the corner of the yard. I didn't look back so he wouldn't see my giant tears. I couldn't face another person. I knew he saw me because I heard him turn the blower off and I could faintly hear him call my name through the window as I started up the engine. I pulled out before he could get remotely close to me.

Four

SHANA AND I were an odd mixture of similar and completely opposite. We were both extroverts, we loved being around a variety of people, and could talk to a tree like it was our friend. We were, however, polar opposites in the way we coped with life. Shana took challenges head on—she was like a matador, facing headlong a challenge like it was a bull to trick into submission.

Despite our differences, growing up with her as my older sister was easy. She was my protector, my Great Wall of support, and sometimes my trumpet of defense. That isn't to say I didn't argue with her or resent her for being all that I wished I could be. Everything seemed easy for her. I never saw her do a lick of homework, yet she was at the top of her class. It was as if she didn't have to tackle giants every day, like I did. I knew that was false, but secretly resenting her for how fantastic she was gave me some sense of control.

But I hated myself for thinking bad things about my sister, and it only made me feel insecure and defeated when I was with her. I knew she sensed the trouble in my heart and at times, suffered under my stinging remarks, but for the most part, she was gracious to me despite my immaturity. I knew that I needed her support to survive the hurricane that was my brain. She filled up my tank with encouragement but most of all with the relief of her laughter.

I could make Shana laugh better than anyone else in my life. She loved hearing the exaggerated tales of my life while we were running. She shared a little of her confidence every time I saw her, just by being herself and loving me.

Shana was engaged to a strapping, slightly older guy named Beau Hinton. They met in college in a biology class where he was a graduate student TA who taught the entire semester while the professor was playing hooky. Story goes, Shana sat in the front row next to a loud-mouthed classmate who befriended Shana and they would get in trouble with their chatty antics distracting the class. Beau asked to speak with her after class one afternoon. She was certain she was going to get a talking to, but instead he asked her to have dinner with him at the diner inside the bowling alley near campus. The rest is history, and now they were engaged to be married in May.

Her car was parked in my parents' driveway when I came careening down the road after my explosive chat with Miss Dean. I knew if I went in to see my folks, she and Beau would be there, and I had to consider whether that was something I wanted to face. I sat in the car to mull it over, still hot from the stress, when my dad came around the corner wearing his apron that read, "'Grill Master—Born to be on Fire'" and carrying a plate of raw hamburgers. It made me chuckle that he insisted on grilling even when it was frigid outside and only 4:30 in the afternoon. Dad saw me and I had no choice but to face him and everyone else.

"Hey Naomi! How's it going? Want to eat some Valentine's Day burgers with us? That is unless you have a hot date I don't know about in which case he better be coming here anyway to meet your old man."

"Sure Dad." I wiped my cheeks and eyes with my sleeve to make sure there were no makeup smudges. "I'd love to come have dinner with y'all. I'm right behind you."

When we got inside, I could tell that Shana sensed something had happened because she looked at me with a furrowed brow, awkwardly mouthing, "Are you okay?" She looked like a fish trying to grab a pellet of food, lips wide open.

I nodded that I was fine, but when I looked down, I saw that I still had a prominent red rash on my chest, my souvenir of stressful, embarrassing, or anxiety-producing situations. Today had been all three, and the rash was taking an eternity to fade.

Beau was out of the room for a while but returned and greeted me with a hug. He was a country boy and dressed the part in his blue jeans, flannel shirt combination. He had super short black hair, crooked smile, and was built strong like a farm hand. He had a little twang to his voice, the Tennessee in him, which gave him a pleasant twang. I hated I couldn't just relate to people the way he did without being petrified my thoughts would become as contaminated as my hands. He was naturally an easy person to talk to and I wished I could be the same way.

"How's that ole' job of yours going?" He gently patted my back as he winked.

"It's good. Fine. Yeah, I mean, it's fun working with Miss Corrie. She's really fun to be with, and it's fun getting to be with her ...so, yeah," I stuttered as my mind tried to press pause.

"Sounds...fun, fun, fun!" Beau gave me a jab with his elbow.

He and I liked to razz each other. Since I never had a brother, he was the testosterone I missed out on terrorizing. He was equally as ruthless with me. I'd give him wet willies, and he would steal my food during dinner if I got up from the table and would either hide it or eat it—most of the time he just ate it. It was an ideal brother-sister relationship of combined respect, sarcasm, and teasing.

The timer on the oven beeped, and Beau yelled with his Tennessee twang, "somethin's ready!"

"Come and get it, guys!" Mom called from the kitchen.

"Told ya! I'm starvin'." Beau rubbed his hands together. "Mrs. Lang, your food is by far the best I've ever had."

"Her head is sure to grow with all your compliments," I whispered loudly as I passed behind him to get to my chair.

"Let's give thanks for the food." Dad prayed, "Dear Lord, we thank You for Your kindness and goodness to us. We know that You have blessed us richly, in more ways than we realize from moment to moment. May we always remember Your hand upon us each day. Oh, and bless this food to our bodies. In Jesus' name we pray, amen."

Suddenly the words Miss Corrie said that afternoon shot through me like an arrow. *Do not worry about tomorrow.* Her words kept haunting me, floating back into my psyche. I wanted to ask my family what they thought about her advice, but I didn't want it to be obvious something had happened during my time with her.

There was a lull in the conversation, so I went for it. "So, I've got a deep question for y'all. Do y'all think it's possible to not worry about what will happen tomorrow?"

Silence. Not one person answered right away.

"I mean, just thoughts, comments, beliefs. Anything," I threw it out to them.

"I'd have to say yes. It *is* possible to not worry about tomorrow," Shana answered. *Of course, she would answer that way. She has nothing to worry about, like, ever.*

"I don't know. I mean, I'd like to say I don't worry about what's going to happen the next day or the one after, but it sure does seem impossible at times. Sometimes I feel my concerns for the future creeping in like kudzu, and I can't make it stop growing. I think God wants us to give it to Him though." Beau shrugged.

"Honey, this is such an interesting question," my mom said sweetly. I can count on her to offer a compliment or encouragement to lift me up. "I would answer yes, you can face each day with confidence and not fear, but God has to help us give our worries to Him. We can't do it on our own, or we would fail every time."

"I agree with your Mom. God doesn't expect us to face challenges alone, and God doesn't guarantee our lives will always be smooth like peanut butter. We can trust that He will give us what we need to be resilient. We must not face each day with fear. We have to try to face it with faith." Dad lowered his head and placed his hand on top of her soft pillowy head.

I started feeling a hot feeling. *Did they really believe God would grant them the ability to not worry? What had I done so horribly wrong that He was just gonna skip over me on this one? If I could yell and scream at God, I would right now. Stop it, Naomi! Those thoughts can get a person thrown in the wrong direction for eternity.*

I dug my nails in the back of my hand again as I tensed up, as I used all my willpower to shove the evil images into submission. Nothing seemed to be working.

"What do you think, Naomi?" Shana asked back.

"Um...honestly? I think it's a load of lies! I don't think it's remotely possible to face the future without worry! I mean, how can we not worry? There are diseases! We could hit someone with our car or kill someone by accident! Or worse, kill them on purpose! People could hate us for no reason at all! I mean, it just seems like there is far too much to be afraid of to *not* wake up each day with crippling worry and a huge pit in the gut."

The room felt hollow after I finished. Everyone kept eating, but I felt my dad's eyes on me. I stared at my plate the whole time—I was afraid of who was looking at me during my wild confession. My toes tingled as the adrenaline surged.

"Sweet girl, I'm always praying for God to give you faith to believe that He will never leave you. Even on your worst day." He acted like he was praying with his hands pressed together and eyes closed.

What they didn't understand was that my brain couldn't be wrangled like a cow with a rope. It wasn't a fire that could be put out with a lot of water. It was a river flowing out of control through me at top speed. Some of my biggest and most crippling fears revolved around my faith, my eternity. Why would God help someone who thought such awful things about Him? Surely those offenses added up to a sum of scary consequences.

The first thing I did when I returned to work the following Tuesday was apologize to Miss Corrie for my outrageous behavior. She forgave me and kindly asked for no further explanation. She even asked *me* for forgiveness for how forcefully she had spoken her beliefs. Our conversation ended with a hug that felt full of mercy and love, instead of an immaturely slammed door. I could tell in that moment that Miss Corrie loved me, not just as a friend, but as a mentor.

I still wrestled with my feelings about all the things she and my family had thrown at me, but I knew I could discuss anything with her now, especially after she so graciously comforted me the week before. I tried to apologize a few more times during our time together, but she finally got stern and demanded that I "knock it off already." I wrestled with feeling guilty about hurting her but was also relieved that she adamantly insisted I stop apologizing.

Over the next two months, I cleaned every counter, organized every drawer, and shredded every unwanted paper while filing the ones that were needed. Before long, there wasn't much left for me to straighten. I still showed up for work because we both appreciated the companionship. I helped her with grocery shopping, light cleaning, and sorting the mail—doing the jobs most daughters would readily do for their parents.

One afternoon in March, I was at Miss Corrie's house folding her laundry when I looked out the window to discover a few small lavender flower buds on the trees. The weather was finally warming up, and I desperately wanted to get outside to take in the delightful season change.

"Hey, Miss Corrie, are you in the mood to take a walk?" I tossed a pair of wrinkled shorts back into the pile of unfolded clothes.

"Why, you just read my mind." She grabbed her shawl from the hanger on the wall.

We started down the trail slowly—it seemed everything Miss Corrie did was careful and methodical. With the bright sun shining on us, we were both quiet, absorbing the beauty around us. Ever since the incident weeks before, Miss Corrie had been more guarded with her words about her faith and life. I found myself missing her wisdom. Her insights were scary, yet oddly comforting. A lot of what she shared, I had already heard from my parents or at church, but when it came from her, it soaked in like water into the cracks of dry earth. When she stumbled on a tree root, I took her arm and wrapped it through mine.

"Miss Corrie? Can I ask you something? Or maybe two somethings?"

"Mm mm?"

"What ever happened to your dad...and to George?" I asked with trepidation.

"Two devastating somethings, but for very different reasons. My dad lived a full life, haunted by his own nineteen-year-old shadow. He raised his children, provided for his family, loved his job, but always felt the weight of his past. He had a humbling life that brought many challenges, but he faced them bravely. He died at eighty-five of a broken heart after my mother passed away from cancer."

She gazed up at the trees above us and squinted. "Now, when George died it was a shock to everyone. He was only fifty-two when he died. We were living here in Raleigh at the time, and he was on a trip to see one of the men he worked with to plant a church during the 1990s. George had a passion for church planting. He wanted people everywhere to experience being part of a church body that worships together, learns together, and points others to Christ. As you know, we started planting churches in France when we first married, I was only twenty-one, and he a whopping twenty-five years old."

She slowed her steps and looked down as she kicked a stray pinecone. "He worked closely with a church planter there who mentored him and helped him graduate from a small theological school close by. They then began church planting in small towns surrounding Paris. We lived there for almost ten years, making friends while helping other young people plant churches all over France. George was then called to Los Angeles to basically do the same work, only in a very secular part of the United States. He became the touch point for many church planters. He listened to their difficulties, heard their dilemmas, fed their souls."

A family of geese honked loudly as they flew over us, we both looked up, but Miss Corrie didn't stop her story even with the noise. "During those years, we wanted so much to have a family of our own, but God had other plans. We were never able to conceive. I worked at a local homeless shelter as the secretary to help keep our finances manageable, even though I would have rather been home with a baby."

"Wow, that sounds challenging."

"Yes, those were hard years. Many of them were full of yelling and turmoil. I was angry at George for not being more present with me. He was helping everyone else but didn't grieve our lack of children with me. I thought his ministry was his mistress. I resented him. I resented God."

"*You!* Resented God? But your faith seems so…unshakeable."

"No one's faith is built on perfection. I used to shake my fist at God many nights, so angry that He wasn't giving me what I wanted, because I knew best, of course."

"I sense sarcasm." I chuckled.

"You got that right. I had no idea what God had planned for us but soon discovered His plans were far harder yet more amazing than I could've ever guessed. You want to hear more?" Before I could answer, she said, "Well, of course you do. I still haven't told you what happened to George. Plus, by the look on your face, I've got you hooked."

"You're a piece of work, you know that?"

"You're certainly not the first one who's ever told me that, I know that much. Okay, so here's what happened. George was asked by another pastor in our denomination to move to Rwanda to assist with a church plant, but this time he would also be working for the US Embassy to help with translation. George spoke fluent French and was gifted at learning languages quickly. They were hoping he could work with the Embassy to keep missionaries safe and be a resource for them. This job would be much harder for him and for me, considering the volatile political atmosphere at the time. We moved there when tensions were high among the people. We had no idea the genocide was about to begin, and millions would be killed all around us."

A cold breeze began to blow toward us, so we turned around on the trail headed back to her house. She started to adjust her shawl and dropped it. I picked it up and brushed the leaves off before helping her wrap back up in it. "We both worked tirelessly over those years. We stayed protected during wartime, but it was not an easy place to live in the midst of the massive terror around us. Hundreds of people I loved were viciously murdered. George was a huge help to his church family during those years. He translated for refugees and shared the Gospel with countless people. How he learned all those languages is a mystery to me. The man never slept. After the war, he did his best to teach Christ's message of forgiveness to the people of Rwanda. There were so many sins committed during the war, and many people were desperate to feel forgiven for the things they had done. Little did I know how much forgiveness I, myself, would have to extend later on."

She stopped walking to hold my hands in hers while she looked into my eyes as she spoke. "At the end of those years, we were both exhausted and ready for some rest. We moved to Raleigh in the year 2000, but George continued traveling to various church plants all over the world to offer his suggestions, strategies, and wisdom. I went with him as often as I could, but it became hard to keep up with him. One Friday afternoon, I got a call from our good friend Thomas, a fellow church planter, who worked closely with George throughout his travels. George was supposed to have stopped at Tom's church in Dallas that day but had not yet arrived. He was scheduled to fly in from Miami, but according to the airline, he never actually boarded the plane."

Her lower lip began to quiver, and her voice vibrated. "He'd disappeared! His disappearance became a full-blown investigation within a few hours. Police said that he left his hotel in the morning, obviously headed to the airport, but never made it there. Long story short, George felt compelled to take a homeless man to breakfast on his way to the airport. He first met the man outside the hotel when he arrived in Miami, and they started to become friends. George had already given him food a couple times, along with the Gospel, but wanted to take him out for a proper meal before he left town. Well, apparently, this gentleman wanted money more than a meal. Investigators told me George had already given the boy hundreds of dollars, but that wasn't enough. The young man shot him in the back as George walked away from him outside the Waffle House where they had just finished eating."

Miss Corrie's shoulders fell, and she let go of my hands to wipe the tears that quietly slid down her face. She didn't make a sound as she wept in front of me.

I couldn't utter a word of apology or sadness. My mouth would not move. I tried my best not to imagine the scene of how and where George died. They were images I didn't want to focus on, but my brain wouldn't let me avoid. I shuddered as the images came rushing in, and I picked my thumbnail in an attempt to distract myself from the visions of violence in my mind.

She took a deliberate, loud breath and raised her head to look at me again. Then she linked her arm around mine and started walking. "I don't live in an angry place, dear. I wrote the young man who killed George a letter a few years back telling him that I forgave him. I don't know how I mustered up the courage or the words to actually execute that, but once I did, I felt a hundred pounds lighter. George loved me, but he loved Jesus more. Telling other people about God was his passion. He'd seen a lot of ugly in this world, but his goal was to pour out truth to others. That's what he was trying to do for this young man, but God had other plans."

"How, I mean, how did you...?"

"Wake up every morning? Well, not intentionally, I can tell you that. God forced my eyes awake every day. Made me put my two feet on the floor. Pulled me out the door to my job as church secretary and then met my needs along the way every stubborn moment. Some days, breathing took all my energy, my heart hurt so bad. But what I learned is that God gave what I needed in those aching times. It wasn't easy, but I'm thankful for how He provided."

Boom. The bombs began again. Her words were exploding in my heart. Breaking down walls I didn't even realize I had built.

Tears filled my eyes. "Could you help me to learn like that, Miss Corrie?"

"You've been learning this whole time, young lady. God is gonna teach you whether you like it or not."

As I walked to my truck to leave, I couldn't stop picturing George on the road walking away from the man who killed him. It disturbed me that I couldn't seem to shake the image from entering and reentering my brain. I was talking quietly to myself when I heard footsteps coming up behind me. It was Joshua. It had to be. I spun around to see him standing there awkwardly, almost like he knew he had just interrupted me. He was completely covered in dirt, and his boots were soaking wet.

"You know, you're gonna get toe fungus if you keep letting your boots get so wet all the time." *Filter is down, I guess. Is that suggestion or a joke?*

"Nice to see you too. Thanks for the tip."

I immediately regretted my comment, turning red. *What am I saying? Great, I probably hurt his feelings.*

"I'm sorry. That was really tacky," I stammered.

"I'm so insulted." He teased. He looked down as he brushed the dirt with his feet.

"So, what's up?" I desperately tried to change the subject to something other than my awkwardness. Joshua and I saw each other in passing when we worked at the same time but hadn't really talked all that much. He still made me nervous, but not in the usual way. I was nervous *and* excited.

"Yeah, so…" He looked up once then kept his gaze locked on the ground. "I wasn't sure if you'd be interested in going out sometime. Like maybe we could go grab some dinner? What are you doing tomorrow night?"

I stood there with my mouth hanging open. *He's asking me out? He's asking me out on a date! After I mentioned toe fungus! Toe fungus! What do I say? What do I say?*

"This is the time you say 'yes,' Naomi!" Miss Corrie hollered from her front window.

"Thanks, Mrs. D! I appreciate the support!" Joshua called back. She blew him a kiss. "I got your back!"

I laughed at her antics and loyalty to those she loved.

"You know what? That would be fun. I could use a night out. Want to pick me up at seven?" *I can't believe I'm saying yes to him.*

"You're actually going to give me your for real address?"

"Maybe I will. Maybe I won't. I guess you'll find out tomorrow!" I threw him a wink and climbed in the truck.

I pulled away, realizing I had totally forgotten to give him my phone number. By the time I got home I knew I'd completely blown it when I got a text.

> *Good thing Miss Corrie has your digits and your address.*
> *Sorry I forgot to ask for it! See you tomorrow at 7.*

Five

I FLEW THROUGH my front door the next afternoon after a long day in class, grabbed my phone, and texted Shana immediately.

SOS! I have a date!!!! TONIGHT! GET OVER HERE! STAT!

I knew she had arrived when I heard the sound of tires peeling in the driveway.

Dad came running outside yelling, "What on earth is going on out here?"

"Can't talk now! Naomi has a date tonight!" she blared.

Before Shana even made it to the front door, my mom started blasting me with texts.

Your dad says you have a date? -mom

Is this true? -mom

Can we meet him? -mom and dad

"Why does Mom insist on ending all her texts with her name? Doesn't she know we can see it's from her?" I chuckled.

Dad did hear from the town crier I have a date. -Me

Yes it's true. -Me

Sure. You can meet him. Come over at 6:30. -Me

Very funny -mom

Shana helped me pick out my outfit, jeans with a navy-blue tunic. I could feel my system flooding with adrenaline. My hands were shaky, and I was beginning to feel slightly nauseated — a fantastic way to start a first date.

"Who is this guy? How'd you meet him?" Shana prodded.

"He's Miss Corrie's landscaper. I don't know much about him, but he's just…"

"*Perfectly perfect?*" Shana squealed.

"Dreamy is a better way to describe him. He's got this calm way about him. A quiet confidence that makes him really approachable. I assumed he was taken, so when he asked me out, I think I stood there for what felt like an hour just mentally processing the question." I was styling my hair with my straightening iron while spraying hairspray on all the fly away baby hairs that constantly got in my face.

Shana was standing in the door jamb watching me. Suddenly, she noticed the red nail marks on the backs of my hands, the outward sign of my inward battle. I caught her staring and pulled my sleeve down.

"Are you doing okay?" she asked worriedly.

"Yeah. Of course. Why? You know Mabel scratches my hands sometimes when I wrestle with her." Mabel was our family cat who had major people problems. She scratched, bit, and hissed at everyone but my beloved father, the cat whisperer.

"Okay, just checking. I know you can sometimes…"

"Look, I'm fine! No need to worry about me. I worry enough for everyone." Right about that time, I heard the door open.

"Hello! Anybody home?" Mom called through the screen door.

"Back here, Mom! In the bathroom. I'm getting ready."

"Isn't this so exciting? I can't wait to meet this young man. Who is he?" she asked as she jumped up on the bed and sat crossed legged like a junior high girl at a slumber party.

"I'll catch you up. He likes plants, he's dreamy, and Miss Corrie likes him," Shana gushed as she flopped on the bed with her head in my mom's lap.

"What time is it?"

Mom glanced at her watch. "It's 6:55. He's coming at 7:00, right?"

I could feel the bile rising in my throat. Panic was beginning to boil. *I can't do this. I cannot do this. I'm going to say everything wrong. I'll make lame jokes and probably hurt his feelings somehow. Where is God? Isn't He supposed to help me? Some help He is.*

I abruptly shut the bathroom door and proceeded to dry heave into the trash can. Right about this time, I heard men's voices...as in more than one man. First, I heard my dad. Then I heard someone else I didn't recognize, then Joshua. Meanwhile I continue to hurl, horrified I wasn't welcoming my date but relieved he wasn't seeing me like this.

Outside my door, mom started knocking and whispered, "I have closed your bedroom door so no one will hear you. Your sister and father are kindly entertaining your guests. Let me just say, I wonder if you are really ready for this. Honey, I'm so sorry. I think you're *not* ready. If you can't go on a first date without retching... I mean, I'm sorry. I might have to put my foot down here and say you shouldn't go..."

As she rambled on, I got myself together. I wiped my eyes, brushed my teeth, and prayed. An actual real prayer, not just a flare prayer. I asked God to carry me through this fear and help me survive the date without barfing.

I want to be normal. I want to be normal. I want to be normal. What really is normal?

My mom was still uttering, "I pray you're ready" as I opened the door and walked right past her to the kitchen.

Shana, Dad, Joshua, and some other guy I had never laid eyes on stood in my kitchen. I froze with confusion when Joshua blurted out, "This is my friend Stephen. He's gonna come hang out with us tonight if that's okay."

All eyes were on me for an answer.

I swallowed the hard knot in my throat to find my answer. "Sure. Sounds good? I mean, yes. Hi, Stephen. Nice to meet you. Let's get going...guys." I waved goodbye to my family and shrugged.

Mom hung in the corner looking distressed by my meltdown. She was shaking her head, likely still muttering about my lack of readiness.

"Bye guys! Have fun!" Dad yelled out.

"Nice to meet you, Mr. Lang!" Joshua called as we walked out.

"Oh, please, call me Bill!" He offered eagerly.

I could tell Dad wanted Joshua to like him too.

My date trio decided to go to a well-known Mom and Pop restaurant downtown called Uncle Joe's Place. It had a hippie vibe and served all local, homegrown cuisine. The whole drive I kept wondering what was happening. *Had I misunderstood him earlier? Did he ask me to bring a friend, and I just didn't hear him, so now I'm stuck on this unexpected outing with two guys instead of just one?*

I sat in the front seat next to Joshua, riding quietly, except when Stephen would pop his head in between us every so often with commentary. I found myself wishing I was playing Whack-a-mole instead. Considering I wasn't a fan of hammers, I tried not to visualize it, but I was at a loss for how to make him stop.

"So, what's your major?" Stephen shot out way louder than necessary.

"I'm a communications major at State," I said flatly to the air behind me.

"That's cool. I'm a model at the mall," he stretched his neck upward to catch a look at himself in the rearview mirror.

"A model at the mall? I didn't know they had models at the mall. What do you do? Like runway shows?" I couldn't believe what I was hearing. *Is this guy for real?*

"I'm one of those people who wears clothes from a store, like American Eagle, and stands in the front window so everyone can see what the clothes are supposed to look like. Then they'll buy them, of course." He flung his head back with a jolt.

"Huh. Like a live mannequin. Who knew?" I looked out the window at the moon gliding by.

"You should come see me sometime. I mean, I work every Friday and Saturday night, so you could totally come then. I could get you a discount on some clothes." Stephen's voice was low, almost a whisper.

Is he flirting with me? I couldn't help but wonder who I was supposed to be on this date with. Joshua was pretty much silent the whole drive to the restaurant. He commented on the weather and traffic, but that was about the extent of it. I was stumped. *This amazing guy asks me out, but then can't bear to go on a date with just me? Maybe he decided I'm not worth his time, and this was his way of giving me the hint.* My palms were sweating profusely, and I still felt slightly nauseous. When I realized he might be giving me the shaft, they got even sweatier, and I checked out.

Dinner was spent with Stephen talking about himself to me or talking to Joshua about the sports coverage on the seven hundred television screens that surrounded us. I ate a little bit of my salad but couldn't get much down. I pushed the food around my plate to make it look like I had eaten, like a child would.

I never ate with my hands in public because my hands were away from a clean sink and the number of germs on my skin skyrocketed. Every surface was contaminated. Anything I touched left a grimy film on my hand to haunt me. The door handle, the menu, the tabletop, were all vessels for diseases. The thought of eating food with my bare hands was the equivalent to taking a bullet. I did my best to avoid the bread and appetizers without being noticed by my two dates.

At the end of the night, Stephen asked to see the garden, so I took them on a tour of the backyard. Mom was an amazing horticulturist. She was a Master Gardener, friend of the local arboretum, and an HGTV junky. Her garden was spectacular all year, but in the spring, new blooms and infant growth was a feast for the eyes. Mom strategically placed timed spotlights along the path to make it easy to see the garden, even when it was dark.

"Your mom must spend hours working in this garden. It's just amazing." Joshua gently touched the tip of a Japanese maple leaf. "I'll have to come get a tour sometime when it's daylight so I can really appreciate it."

What in the world? Now he's talking about coming back here? I was beyond baffled. Right as Joshua was finally starting to talk to me, Stephen grabbed me by the waist and started doing the conga. *Yup, he is flirting.*

"Come on. Let's go up here and see what's around that dark corner." He put his arm slyly around my shoulder and attempted to guide me up the stone steps. I weaseled my way out of his grasp and walked the other way.

"Um, actually, I'm pretty tired, so I think I'll head to bed. Thanks for dinner though...ya'll. It was...nice." I gave Stephen, then Joshua, unnatural side hugs. I could tell Joshua wanted to say something, but he stood there with his mouth open like he was on the verge of speaking, but nothing came out.

"Cool! Let's do this again sometime," Stephen blurted out.

I gave him an awkward thumbs up then went inside. I watched from my window as they sauntered back to his car. Joshua was hanging his head as Stephen skipped ahead. Maybe he was disappointed or embarrassed? I couldn't tell, and I had no idea what to think about seeing him in the future.

I scarfed down some peanut butter toast, and I had just sat down on the couch to mentally decompress when Shana knocked at the door. She and Beau had hung around at my folks' waiting to see how the date went and were coming to check in.

"How'd it go? What was the deal with door number 1 and number 2? Was that guy his bodyguard?" She whacked her hand on her forehead with a thud.

"I have absolutely no idea what to make of this whole evening. Joshua was quiet all night, and Stephen was so...forward. I don't get what Joshua sees in him as a friend. He flirted with me the whole time. It was uncomfortable. Maybe Joshua didn't really mean to ask me out? Either that or he got cold feet and needed a wingman."

"What do you think, Beau?" Shana asked. "Why does a guy bring another guy along on a date?"

"I've never done that before, so..." Beau put his hands up in defense.

"Oh, get over yourself. I know you've never done that, but why would a guy do that? Can you come up with some reasonable reason?"

"Uh, well, I guess a guy might do it if he thought it was just a hang out and not an actual date. Did y'all discuss how you'd go out?" He was digging deep.

"No, we didn't discuss *how* we'd go out. I mean, he asked me to go to dinner with *him*. He didn't say, 'would you like to go out with *us*?' I'm sure he's just not interested. It's fine, guys. I'm really okay. I'm not super experienced with this whole dating scene, but I'm smart enough to know when someone isn't interested. Y'all can go. I'm gonna take a shower and fall into bed. I'll be fine, trust me. My heart hasn't been broken," I muttered.

"Okay then, we'll let you be. Love you, sis. Text me tomorrow." Shana hugged me from behind as I put a lone dish in the dishwasher.

"See you, girl. Be good," Beau said sweetly. I could tell he wanted to say more, but there wasn't much anyone could say to fix my disaster of an evening.

I lay in bed that night rolling the events of the day over and over in my mind like marbles from hand to hand. *I thought he wanted to go out with me, but I guess I misread his intentions. Typical me.*

An image popped in my head of Joshua crashing his car on his way home.

I sat bolt upright. *"Noooo!"*

The unwanted thought kept growing on itself, like ivy strangles a tree. *If I think this thought, maybe he'll get in an actual car accident. I'll be responsible.*

"Please, Lord, no," I dug my nails into my hand. *I cannot possibly be this powerful. It's not logical but feels like it could be true.*

Every fear, unwanted thought, and image felt like a real concern that demanded my attention. Each one had power to take over my logic, my feelings, and ultimately my discernment. After a few minutes of intrusive thoughts, I could no longer see the truth in anything, only the lies my mind created.

I tossed and turned for forty-five minutes. The image of his car crashing and flaming wreckage hijacked my mind as I frantically tried to make it stop fearing I could cause Joshua to die just by envisioning it. I looked at the clock. It was midnight. I had to text him to make sure he made it home and I didn't cause his death.

You make it home okay? I texted. Followed immediately by,
I wanted to make sure you were okay. I'm sorry. I know it's late.
Within less than a minute he texted back.
Yes, I made it home. I've been up since I got back here. Can't sleep.
I can't sleep either. Why can't you?'
I've been feeling terrible for how awful that date was. I'm so sorry. I'm sure it wasn't what you expected. My friend Stephen is a little pushy, and I didn't have the heart to tell him this was a date. He was at my apartment all afternoon, and when I told him I was going to dinner with a friend, he just assumed he could come along. I never meant to make it confusing. Can I get a do over?

I read and reread this text almost twenty times in total disbelief. *He didn't get it right? He messed up? Can I forgive him? Of course I can!*

Now Joshua only seemed even more attractive to me. He admitted he was wrong. He explained himself and gave reassurance, my brain's drug of choice.

It's okay. I totally get it. What would you like to do next?
How about putt-putt this Saturday? I'm a mean golfer. Probably not as good as I think, but you can practice if you want to.
You're on.

I went to sleep feeling better about the whole situation, but with fresh nerves about our next date... when I'd actually have to go out with Joshua alone. Having Stephen on our first date was a bust, but it gave me the buffer I needed. I was protected by the third wheel filling in the gaps of silence this time, but next time it would be all me. I knew I needed to let it go and get some sleep, but I had to wait until I ran out of energy and my brain finally petered out.

The next morning as I headed out to class, I found a note on my car along with a balloon on my side mirror. The balloon said, 'Get well soon' and had golf balls all over it. The note read, "'I hope you recovered from our last date quickly. I'm looking forward to taking you down in putt-putt Saturday. Rest up. You're gonna need it!'"

"Nice balloon! Are you having a birthday I forgot about?" Dad hollered from the front stoop and began to head my way.

"Ha. Isn't it hilarious?"

"Are they from your boyfriend...I mean boyfriends?" he teased.

"Good one...Daaaaaad," I sassed back.

"You going to have another date with this young man?"

"Yeah, this Saturday. I'm looking forward to it. Should be fun."

"Hey, so I wanted to follow up with you about something you brought up a few weeks ago at dinner. The question you asked. I've been kinda thinking about it since that night."

"Dad, that was weeks ago. Why are you bringing it up now?"

"It's hard to see your daughter struggling and not know what to say to help, so sometimes I end up not saying anything. That night, I spoke strongly about my views, and I hope I didn't make you feel dismissed." He sat down on the garden swing and patted on the seat for me to join him.

I sat down while I fidgeted with my keys. I had no idea what he was going to say, and I was nervous I'd have to share more than I wanted to.

"I know I do a terrible job hiding my feelings. I'm sorry I sprayed my insecurities on the family that day. It was immature and inappropriate." I jiggled my knees up and down.

"Hey, we're a family. That's what we do sometimes, spray insecurities at one another." He chuckled. "In all seriousness, we don't just listen to the words we say. We try to actually hear and see the deeper things behind what's shared. My answer that night was a declaration that didn't offer much help to you in your struggle. But I truly believe that God doesn't leave us out to dry in this difficult world, even when it feels that way. Do you remember reading the book *The Hiding Place*, by Corrie Ten Boom?"

"I read it a long time ago. Mom made me I think."

"Remember, Corrie and her sister Betsie hid Jews during World War Two and shared their faith with many people along the way, even when taken as prisoners in a concentration camp. She told a story about a time during her childhood when her father tried to help her understand hard circumstances in life, particularly death. Her father reminded her that when they traveled, he always gave her the train ticket just as they were about to board, not before. Just like God knows when we're going to need things. We can't run ahead of Him. He always gives us the strength we need just in time."

My eyes filled with tears. He had listened to me and heard I was struggling to trust God in the moments when things were out of control, when the world felt harder than I could take.

Dad put his arm around me. "You are loved by Him, Naomi. You're not just a pawn in some game He created. He loves you more than I do, which seems impossible since I love you more than peanut butter, but..."

I chuckled. My dad always knew how to make me laugh.

"No matter what happens in this life, He'll give you what you need in every moment...especially the difficult ones. Even if you don't feel Him with you all the time, you can trust that He is because His word promises that."

"Now *that* seems impossible."

"Well, believe your old man. It's true. I've lived it." He stood and kissed me on the temple. "Have a great day. I love you, and don't you forget it."

"Thanks for following up with me, Dad."

The rest of the day, I thought about what he told me. I let it steep into my heart. Could he be right? Did God really meet us where we are and give us what we need in the *exact* moment we need it? In all those moments when my brain filled with unwanted thoughts, God could help me stop them? Well, if that were true, He would've done it by now, right? Or maybe God was handing me my ticket in time, I just wasn't seeing it. It felt good to percolate on this without feeling completely unraveled. That day, I called it progress.

Six

MISS CORRIE COULDN'T wait to hear all about my first date with Joshua, so when I stopped over to tell her how it went, she spent at least five minutes laughing hysterically at our mixed-up evening. I'm not sure why she found it so comical, but I definitely loved to tell a funny story to an eager audience, so I exaggerated the tale to keep her entertained.

"Oh boy, I feel like I was there with you." Miss Corrie laughed.

"It was an experience, to say the least. I'm just hoping our date this weekend will go smoother. I'm not sure why I haven't asked before, but how did you meet Joshua?" I got the tea pot off the stove and poured two cups.

I wasn't officially working this visit. Instead, I had stopped over for her company. Sometimes, when I did this, she would still pay me if I helped her around the house, but some days she invited me to come for the sheer fun of it. We were both rejuvenated by our conversations, full of thoughtful topics or sometimes just everyday musings.

"Let me see...if memory serves me right, he and I first met when he came to interview to work for me. He's the son of one of George's church planting friends. George mentored his father off and on as they planted a church in San Diego. Joshua came to college at North Carolina State for a landscape design degree and a couple of years ago began his own business. When I met him, he was soft spoken, articulate, and kind. I appreciated his gentle nature and tender heart. I needed him to begin working here since I couldn't keep up with all the yard work after George died. I hated to give it up, but once I met Joshua, I knew it was in better hands with him anyway. He's a catch. That's for sure. I'd be lying if I said I wasn't on my knees praying the two of you really fall for each other."

"Don't get too excited. I'm a handful. I'm not so sure he'll want to take that on." I shook my head to myself.

"I know the feeling. Trust me. I couldn't believe George picked me. When we met, I was covered in acne, shy, and incredibly insecure. I was sunning myself on the beach, white as a sheet, when a strong, young lifeguard came over and asked if I had any extra sunscreen he could borrow. I sat there just staring at his rippling muscles and couldn't even speak."

"Are you kidding me? You just stared at him? I mean, I get it. Sometimes I swear I have words, but they just won't make their way out."

"There's something about a good-looking man that makes you appreciate God's creation. Wouldn't you say?" She swooned.

"Miss Corrie! I can't believe you're talking like this!" I snorted. "I mean, I can't believe you're talking to *me* like this! I've never even kissed a guy, not really anyway. Once, in high school, a guy kissed *me*, but to be honest, I thought it was gross." I shuddered.

"Let me share some truth, dear. Brace yourself. You want to know the *most* attractive quality about a guy?" She leaned into me like she was going to tell me a big secret.

"Um, of course! Don't keep that from me!"

"The most incredible and attractive quality a man can have is his love for God. I mean, when George talked about his faith or prayed, whoo whee, I would come unglued. After that afternoon at the beach, he invited me to a Bible study, and I knew from the moment I heard him share his faith that he was the guy for me and would be forever. So, listen to what is in Joshua's heart, dear. When you see what's in it, you'll know if he's for you. He may not be the godly man for you, but if he is, you'll know."

"I feel like I might be too... Well, never mind."

"Too what, dear?"

"I'm afraid I may be too dysfunctional for him. I mean, he's got his stuff together, and I'm just a bundle of nerves all the time. I'm worried that once he figures that out, he won't like me anymore. I don't know. Maybe it'll all be fine. Even if it's just the one date, it'll be a good experience."

"The sooner you realize we are *all* dysfunctional, the better. George may have been my dream guy, but he was in no way perfect. Nor was I! He had just as many shortcomings as I did, and believe me, everyone needs to give grace to one another."

Miss Corrie had an eloquent way of saying hard things to me that left me feeling incredibly encouraged and enlightened rather than scared or condemned. I left her house feeling even more thrilled about my date with Joshua. I was hopeful but wasn't sure in what way. I felt this excitement in my heart, a stirring, and desire for peace I hadn't felt before. It was odd and compelling all at once.

I heard birds chirping outside my window early Saturday morning. *Today is the day. I'll probably mess the whole thing up—say something awful or fall on my face. I'm not made for this. I'm an evil-minded person who wants to hurt people and hates God. I'll never make it work with anyone. I'm broken. God is terrible. I'll end up missing out on heaven for all these evil thoughts. If I write a perfect prayer to God, maybe I can save myself. I can save myself.* Those negative thoughts pulsed through my being with every heartbeat. I tried to quiet them by writing perfect prayers to God, in perfect handwriting, to offset my bad thoughts.

Shana had assisted in the critical task of picking out my outfit the night before, so I felt at ease with that step of preparation at least. Joshua was coming to pick me up around 10 o'clock, so I had plenty of time to thoroughly clean my room while I thought about what lay ahead, especially since it was 5:30 a.m. My stomach felt like a small animal was trying to eat its way out, but not like the heaving drama prior to our first date. I paced around the apartment with my cup of warm coffee and sipped it in rhythm with my steps. I tried to read my Bible, but the words only danced fitfully on the page. I still changed my outfit about fifty times before I finally settled on one. I wore a pair of distressed jeans with a red shirt and my black converse sneakers.

Before I knew it ten rolled around, and Joshua was right on time.

"Morning! Are you ready to get your sport on?" He wore a collared Nike golf shirt and an enthusiastic smile.

"I hope it doesn't require too much skill. I'm not very athletic. I mean, besides running. That's not really a sport though, not the way I do it anyway."

"You'll be alright. Considering we're going to a place where there are pretend animals all around and birthday parties for kids, I'm guessing you'll do fine. I like your place. Do you like living so close to your family?"

"I guess yes and no. My parents are fantastic, but there are times I wish I had more independence." I glanced around my living room quickly to avoid eye contact.

"I get that. My parents are pretty great too. They live in San Diego, but my sister lives here. She's got two little kids I get to spoil." He grinned big when talking about them. "All set to go?"

"Sounds good to me. Let me grab my purse." I yanked my purse from one of the hooks by the door so hard the surrounding jackets careened to the floor. My face immediately turned as red as my shirt as Joshua helped me gather them back up.

"Oh man, I'm sorry about that." I felt myself begin to sweat. His eyes met mine for a brief second as we squatted together on the floor. He looked like he was a little red himself.

"Oh no worries. Stuff like that happens to me all the time. I'm so excited I'll probably hit the ball wonky and knock somebody out." I saw his dimples make a brief appearance as he grinned.

We headed down the steps when we heard my dad bellowing from the back porch. "Have fun, you two! Have her back by eleven! Oh wait, that would be in an hour, so let's say midnight!" He slapped his thigh as he laughed at himself.

"Will do, Mr. Lang!" Joshua happily bantered back.

The putt-putt place wasn't too busy, but there was one family ahead of us on the course. I chose a purple ball and Joshua a NC State red ball, fitting for a diehard fan like him.

"Okay, here we go...ladies first." He gestured toward the first hole which had a giant elephant ride beside it. I hit the ball, and it ricocheted off the side of the wall, bounced into the air, hit the elephant's trunk, and landed in a giant pool of water just below the bridge we were standing on.

"Huh...that was a little hard." I peered over the side, just catching the splash of my ball as it plopped into the bright blue water. "I guess I'll need another ball." My face felt hot again, but Joshua was already halfway to get me a new one.

"Here." He handed me a Carolina Tarheel blue ball.

No way! I chuckled. "No way am I using a Carolina blue ball. Nuh, uh. It ain't happening."

"Alright. Good answer. That was a test, my friend, and you just passed."

"Great, but who's going to use that disgusting blue ball? It certainly isn't me. I'll take this one right here." I picked up Joshua's red ball and crossed my arms, refusing to exchange them.

"I guess this is when my brilliant plan unravels. I'll use the reject ball. Why don't you hit yours again? Maybe you'll keep it in the state of North Carolina this time."

"Ha. Ha," I laughed, flirting back.

When I hit the ball the second time, it rolled gently down the hill but didn't land where I aimed. Joshua took his turn, and his ball hit mine, knocking me even farther away, but landing himself right beside the hole. He got it so close, a strong breeze would have blown it in, while I had to hit mine two more times to get it in. This pattern continued for the remainder of the game. I would hit my ball with amateur precision, then he would blow past me and land himself within centimeters of the hole. It was no contest who was going to win, and we both knew it pretty early on.

"You sure are competitive. I mean, do you just play putt-putt well, or do you dominate at other sports too?" I leaned on my club as I stared at him while he putted.

"Is it that obvious that I love sports?" He cringed with embarrassment.

"I'd say it's more than crystal clear you like sports. You're critiquing the four-year-old's stroke in front of us, for crying out loud!"

"His grip was totally off. His dad should've been helping him with that."

"Oh, come on! You can't be serious? He's four!" I shook my head.

Joshua steadied himself for a shot as his tongue slightly stuck out with concentration. His feet shifted his weight back and forth while he regripped the club.

"Watch it, or I won't buy your lunch, and you'll have to go hungry," I teased. He answered with a wink in my direction before he concentrated intently on the ball again.

Right after he finished his shot, I got a sinking feeling in my gut, like you get on the downhill side of a roller coaster, a dropping feeling that something bad was about to happen. It was my clue that an unwanted image might be coming in hot, and I'd better be ready. My muscles tightened as I visualized a golf club cracking down hard on Joshua's head. I tightened my grip on my club as I fought the fear that I could possibly be the one to swing the club at him.

Why would I imagine something evil like that? I must be a violent person. How terrible am I?

I closed my eyes for a second, feeling disgusted and fearful all at once. *Please God, no.* I chanted in my mind over and over as I tried to stop the tidal wave of images that flooded my being. I must've looked stunned when I came to, because Joshua was looking at me with a puzzled brow.

"Yeah, I don't want to miss out on lunch." I sputtered.

"Are you okay? I thought I lost you there for a second." He put his hand on my shoulder gently. His touch surged through my arm, tingling.

I couldn't even make it through the first hour of our date without my mental nemesis showing. *Why can't I just be normal?*

I did my best to move on, hiding my horror by acting like nothing had happened. "Oh yeah! I'm great. Just trying to visualize the next hole." I blinked rapidly a few times to clear away any leftover images.

We were almost to the eighteenth hole, and I had mentally checked out, lost in the waterfall of worry that started to flow two holes earlier. I needed to turn off the fear of using the golf club to hurt someone. It felt like a hot iron in my hand. It was actually burning my skin. I wanted to drop it and run away so I could stop visualizing all the awful things a person could do with one.

Who thinks about these things? I must be some kind of evil person to have thoughts like this. Could God even love someone like me? Joshua must think I'm ...Or worse.

These thoughts shackled me, held me captive, kept me from leading a normal life. I hated them and in that moment I hated myself. I felt completely insane.

My phone started vibrating on the last hole as Joshua took his final stroke. It was a text from Miss Corrie,

I hope y'all are having fun! Remember, you're just as dysfunctional as the rest of us, so worry NOT!

How did she know what to say at the exact moment I needed it? I read and reread her text, doing my best to soak in her words, desperate to find myself again and salvage this date. I craved reassurance when deep irrationality hit but encouraging words could only fill me for a moment before bizarre, illogical reasoning overcame the reassurance. Despite that, her text seemed like more than the usual reassurance I craved. She was trying to point me to a new technique for coping. She was urging me to worry *not*. She believed I was capable of overcoming my fears.

"Are you ready to go to lunch?" Joshua prodded with a hesitation in his voice.

"Of course. Hey, sorry for my silence back there. Sometimes, I dunno, my mind just gets stuck. I don't really know how else to explain it, but yeah…sorry about that." I winced and pushed a few stray hairs behind my ears.

His face lightened. "Oh, well, that's okay. I get it. I just assumed you were thinking about something important. Don't worry about it." He took the flaming hot golf club from my hand to set it back on the counter. I sighed with relief. He seemed unflappable, despite my odd behavior.

During the first part of lunch, we chatted cordially, almost like the date had only just begun. I wasn't very hungry, but my stomach was completely empty to the point where I could feel the acid in my gut rising to my throat. I took small bites, easing my way into the meal.

"Tell me about yourself, Joshua. What are your likes? Dislikes? We already know you're addicted to sports of all kinds, and you are a killer putt-putt golfer. What else is there?" I smirked over the rim of my very sweet tea.

"That's a big question! I don't even know where to start with that one…. okay…let me think. I don't like… wait for it…brussels sprouts! I'm pretty sure that's genetic though, and—"

"Genetic? Wait what? You're out of your mind. I love Brussels sprouts! They're my favorite vegetable!"

"Then this can never work," he razzed. "I'm kidding of course. *Anyway*, I do love all sports. I enjoy watching basketball, tennis, football, golf…. I guess whatever is on. Mostly, I play basketball and tennis, but I'm up for playing any sport if the opportunity presents itself. I hate running for the sake of running. I'd much rather be playing a game while I run. Makes it more fun."

"I love running! Are you kidding? It's so relaxing. That rush of endorphins afterward…. man, makes me feel like I could accomplish anything. Playing sports is too much pressure. I always feel like I'm going to mess it up for the whole team…. nope, can't do it." I shuddered.

"Really? That's interesting. We've determined I don't like stinky sprouts. What food don't you like?" He took a dramatic bite of burger and eyed me with soulful hazel eyes.

"Food… Okay…I don't like…brace yourself…pie."

"Pie? You don't like pie? Now that's like not liking an entire food group! How can you not like pie?" He put his hands on the top of his head in disbelief.

"I just don't?" I shrugged. "I also don't like fireworks. Are you going to call me un-American for not liking fireworks *or* pie? Pie is just so, bleh. With the crust that has no flavor, to the weird squishy fruit or nut filling… ew, it just does nothing for me. And fireworks? What's the fuss about? Ooooo, ahhhh… I feel nothing." I poked at my fries with my fork.

"I just don't believe what I'm hearing. Alright, so I'll know who not to call on the Fourth of July to go to the fairgrounds to see the fireworks." He set his burger down and took on a more serious tone. "Now, tell me something about *yourself*. Like, what's something that most people don't know about you?"

"I mean, I'm not that interesting, really. I'm a communications major, which means I should be really good at talking to people. Ironic because I sometimes feel completely deficient at it. I'm finishing my senior year at NC State and have no idea what to do for a career. I certainly can't work for Miss Corrie forever. I can tell you that." I repositioned my napkin neatly in my lap. "What about you? How do you like the landscaping biz?"

"I like working in landscaping, I think. I don't always feel like I do a perfect job on things, but I'm improving, so I guess that's something. I enjoy being my own boss, setting my own hours, managing my own people, keeping the clients I want and stuff. Right now, it's just me and a couple of part time employees. I'm not making a ton of money yet, so I'm still living pretty frugally as I try to save and grow the business. Eventually, I'd like to hire more people, but right now, I have to juggle it myself."

I could tell his heart was in his work, not in the actual work of landscaping, but the ethic of doing any job well.

"Would you say you're a perfectionist then?" I looked into his eyes deeply for the first time the entire date. I asked a hard question, one that I was eager to know the answer to.

"I guess so. I definitely don't like leaving things undone or not done as well as they could be. It's hard for me to let things go when I'm responsible for them, but I'm learning. Miss Corrie started demanding I eat lunch with her when I worked on her house because she figured out I wasn't stopping to eat most days. That's how we got to be friends. She fed me."

"She is something else, isn't she? I enjoy her so much." My heart relaxed at the thought of her.

"Me too. How has it been working for her? She filled you in on her interesting past?" He wiped an extra dollop of ketchup off the side of his lip.

"Some of it, yes. She's got so many stories. I'm sure more will come out as time goes on. I don't know how much longer she'll have work for me, though. She'll probably try to pay me to do laundry or dishes she could do herself. I think she keeps me on just to keep paying me because she has a heart for helping the poor college student."

"I think she loves the company. I have to make sure all my jobs are done before I knock on her door. She'll talk to me for an hour if I let her!" He laughed. "So, do you go to church with her? I thought I heard her mention it."

"We go to the same church, yeah, the one I grew up going to."

"Do you not go there…now?" He leaned towards me with his elbows on the table like he was eager to hear my answer.

"No. I mean, yes. I go there now. I guess. I go when I can, anyway."

"It can be hard to get motivated to go to church on Sundays, but I'm always so happy when I do. It's the only place I can really rest spiritually, let go of my shortcomings and lay them down. I can actually feel the weight of my sin lifted off my shoulders and placed on Christ." Joshua looked the most serious I had ever seen him in that moment.

I suddenly felt intimidated by him. I was in no way craving church right now. Church only welcomed unwanted thoughts, and if Joshua only knew some of the awful things I'd thought about God, he'd say I was lost for sure. I envied his confidence and the comfort he seemed to receive from going to worship services.

I was saved when Joshua's text message notification chimed. He jumped when it went off, lost in our conversation.

"Uh, oh. It looks like my sister needs to take my nephew to the doctor. He may have broken his foot jumping off the bed. She's wondering if I can babysit my niece so she can run him up to the pediatrician. Do you want me to drop you off back home or…are you brave enough to tag along?"

I wasn't sure how to answer him because I definitely liked kids, but when it came to babysitting I worried the children might get hurt on my watch. It's wasn't my favorite thing to do, even though I had plenty of experience babysitting through high school. And despite my insecurities, I was pretty great at it. I loved making kids laugh with my ridiculous antics and felt honored when children asked me to come back with big puppy dog eyes. To say I had mixed feelings about babysitting was an understatement.

"Sure! Why not? We had a third wheel on our other date, so why not have one on this date too? Maybe she'll drool less than Stephen did."

"Wow. Aren't you hilarious? I'm going to track down our waitress and get our check. I don't want my sister waiting around too long with my poor nephew in so much pain."

Joshua was so intentional about everything he said and did. I had absolutely no filter most days, so my foot spent a lot of time in my mouth. His quiet nature was calming for me, peaceful to my soul. I wasn't sure how, but simply being near him made me feel more relaxed and comforted. I got this feeling deep down, the kind I think Miss Corrie tried to tell me about, a deep whisper that said, *he's good for you.*

It took me by surprise, and for a brief moment, I felt a glimmer of hope that maybe I found someone who complemented all my quirks. Was it too good to be true? *Probably*, another voice scorned.

———————

"Uncle Josh! Uncle Josh!" a tiny voice called from inside the living room as we let ourselves in to the modest home of his sister Maria and her husband Andy.

"Hey bud! What did you do to yourself?" Joshua said as we rounded the corner into a bright and cheerful living room painted a welcoming blue with striped wallpaper on one wall. Joshua's nephew, James, was lying with his foot propped up on a pillow, craning his neck over the back of the couch to see his uncle.

"I was Superman saving baby Gita from the evil vacuum Umma was using in the other room. It was coming for her, and I needed to jump off the bed in time to save her!" he exaggerated with big hand gestures. At no more than four years old, he had an impressive vocabulary for his age.

Joshua sat on the edge of the couch where James lay and put his hand on his foot gently. "Where does it hurt, bud? Your foot or your ankle?"

"My foot. Umma said I may have killed it," he said matter-of-factly.

"You can't kill your foot, dude. I think she meant you may have broken it. Or you might have just sprained it. Inside your body we have muscles that attach to our bones to keep them in place, and you know your muscles are what make you stronger." He lifted his arms and pretended to flex his muscles. "Sometimes the bones inside can break when we're too rough on them. You'll go to the doctor and he'll take a picture to see if any of the bones in your foot are broken or if it's just a sore muscle. It'll be easy-peasy. Speaking of your mom, where is she?" He looked around, surprised we hadn't seen her yet.

"Umma is upstairs puttin' Gita down for a nap. She told me to talk to you until she comes down."

I leaned over and quietly whispered in Joshua's ear. "So, who's Umma? I thought your sister's name was Maria?"

Right as I asked, a gorgeous young Asian woman entered the room. Her hair was black and thick, about shoulder length but pulled back in a messy bun. It was then I noticed how little her son James looked like Joshua.

"Umma means 'mom' in Korean," Maria answered kindly as she walked in.

"I forgot to mention my sister is adopted. She's actually just a few months younger than me. We're practically twins. Can't you see the resemblance?" Joshua put his face right next to hers before he hugged her.

"It's nice to meet you, Naomi, is it? I'm really sorry to interrupt your date. Andy had a big meeting today and couldn't get out of it. These things always seem to happen when he has important work events or is out of town. Hopefully it won't take too long. Gita just went down for a nap, so when she gets up, you should only have to play with her a bit before we're back. James, are you ready to get going? There's a bottle in the fridge for Gita if she gets up. She'll wake up hungry. I have no idea how long or short she'll sleep either. Come on J." Maria gestured to James, and Joshua jumped up, scooping him off the couch in one swift motion.

"It's nice to meet you too!" I yelled behind them as they walked out the front door.

Maria was obviously in a hurry, and I didn't want to keep her by talking too much, so I stood awkwardly at the door while Joshua patiently hooked James into his car seat, gentle and kind, like he was a precious and fragile package.

I wanted to have kids but never felt like I'd do a proper job raising them, so it seemed like an impossible dream. As I witnessed Joshua and his nurturing gestures, it became clear to me that I wanted to end up with someone like him and ultimately have a family. I was momentarily shaken by the epiphany but also exhilarated at the sudden revelation. He skipped up the stoop with enough time to turn and wave to Maria and James as they drove off.

"What now?" I turned to see him waving wildly until the car was out of view.

"Well, we can go inside and chat while we wait for Gita to wake up, or we could just go home. She'll probably be fine on her own. She's almost one." He shrugged with a smirk.

"I opt for staying and chatting. I think that's the wiser choice." As I turned around to go inside, he nonchalantly put his arm around my shoulder. I turned to look up at him.

Standing quite a bit taller than me at six foot three, he looked back with a deep, penetrating gaze. His hazel eyes glimmered with anticipation, but what he was so excited for, I wasn't sure. I sort of froze in place with his arm draped over my back, unsure what to do next. I took a step forward, which he matched, walking by my side. I took another only to have him follow me again, grinning.

"I'm only trying to make sure you get to the couch safely."

"I appreciate that, good sir. I might have gotten lost without you walking with me." I laughed.

This whole situation was completely new to me. We made it all the way to the couch, and his arm never left my shoulder, nor did I release a breath the entire journey. We sat down next to each other on the navy leather couch as if we were moving in slow motion. I gingerly twisted my neck to look at him and found him staring directly at the side of my face.

"So. What do you want to do now?" he asked with an innocent shrug.

"Sounds like the baby will sleep for a little while at least, so, maybe we could just chat? Or if you know how to work their television, we could watch something." I tried to avoid eye contact.

I began to fidget, a tingle starting in my toes and moving its way through me. My muscles started to tense up as I waited for the dreaded unwanted thoughts to begin, but they held off this time. No inappropriate or uncomfortable image intruded at this particular moment. I suddenly felt safe in his slight embrace, comfortable in my own skin while pressed up against this new person I hadn't even let into my life yet. The whole experience felt like a contradiction I didn't want to overthink in fear it might end, so I just started talking.

"I remember when I was a kid, I loved playing Barbies. It was the one thing Shana didn't like to play, so I got to imagine whatever scenarios I wanted and enjoyed every second creating my own make-believe worlds. Granted, the one childhood friend who would play Barbies with me was allowed to watch soap operas, so a lot of our plot lines were based on the overly dramatized lives from *All My Children*. What's something you remember from growing up?"

"Maria tells me I don't have a fantastic memory, but I'll do my best. Let me see… I'll confess I wasn't a huge Barbie guy. I know, that's shocking for you."

I cackled. "Very, but also a relief."

"I remember playing basketball on the back patio for hours as a kid. Growing up in San Diego was awesome for many reasons, but the weather there makes it easy to play outside pretty much all hours of the day. I'd have pick-up games with kids in the neighborhood or friends from school almost every day. I'd say that's one of my fondest memories. Good question, Naomi. Now I'll go. Let me think a second about what I can ask you." He took his arm off my shoulder and peered at me like he was pondering what to ask while tapping his finger lightly over his mouth.

"What's your biggest fear?" he finally asked with a gentle smile.

It was like a cannon went off. My heart pounded, he had to have been able to hear it. His question was simple, but for me it was a loaded gun.

I was sure his goal wasn't to go super deep or make me uncomfortable. He probably figured I'd say I was most afraid of spiders or cockroaches or thunderstorms. Wrong. My fears were out of his league. I wanted to generalize, but I was still experiencing an emotional hug from him, so I felt safe to share a little more than I typically would.

"That's kind of a heavy question, wouldn't you say? Especially on a second date?"

"I figure I already broke all the dating rules when I brought another guy on our first date and now making you babysit on our second. What's a serious question compared to those mood crushers, right?" He bumped his shoulder into mine flirtatiously.

"I don't know if you can handle my answer. Can you put it in the vault and never let it out?"

"You can tell me anything." Joshua spoke with a seriousness that showed he was really listening.

I was shocked when I felt no temptation to back out of the conversation or flee the scene of a potential confession. I leaned close to his ear, and he lifted his arm back up over my shoulder, pulling me close.

"I'm afraid," I whispered then took a deep breath and let it out. "Of...myself." I let my words just hang there like a horrible smell in the air.

He drew his face back to look at me more intently, confusion in his eyes. "What about yourself are you afraid of?"

I sensed my guard going up, but for whatever reason I felt the need to let him know this part of me. If we were ever to become more than just a short-term fling, I had to let him hear at least *some* pieces of truth about what I really feared. If he couldn't handle this answer, then he could never handle me. I had no earthly idea where this brief moment of bravery came from.

"I'm afraid of everything about myself. I'm afraid of what I'm capable of. I'm afraid of what can happen to me. I'm afraid of what I could do. I'm afraid of what people think. I'm also afraid of germs, because they're just nasty. Have I scared you off yet?"

"So, wait. You're truly afraid of all that?" He swallowed hard.

"Truth? Yes. I don't know how else to articulate it, and I've honestly never shared quite like this with anyone but my mom and sister. Even with them, it never comes out how I want it to. I'm sure I'll relive this conversation in my head for the next three days until something worse comes along to worry about." I was shaking a little bit at this point, not heavily but it was almost like my muscles were releasing a toxin along with the truth held in my words. "Okay, your turn. What are you most afraid of?"

"Well, I was going to say clowns, but that'll just sound insensitive after everything you just shared. I'd say I'm most afraid of failure. I want so badly to be successful and do things perfectly, sometimes it's paralyzing for me. I know I have to let that all go, but...yeah... It's not an easy thing to do." My jaw clenched tightly pressing my teeth hard into each other.

"Wow. Look at us having a real adult conversation. I'm impressed. Thanks for sharing that with me. I don't fully understand all you meant by your answer, but I promise I appreciate your honesty. I hope you didn't feel like I put you on the spot." He patted my knee, then rubbed it before pulling his hand away.

"You know what's strange? I didn't feel nervous telling you. Being anxious is a big part of who I am, but I keep it well hidden, or at least I try to. It feels strange that with you I haven't felt such a severe need to hide it. I'm not quite sure what that means exactly."

Joshua pulled me closer as I spoke, and I rotated my body so I could rest my head on his shoulder. He leaned his cheek against the top of my head then softly kissed it. It gave me goosebumps all over.

"I'm glad you feel like you can talk to me." We sat in comfortable silence for a good while until we heard a slight whimper as though someone had been in the room with us the whole time. My head shot up off his shoulder, and we both looked at the other, confused.

"What is *that?*"

"Oh man! That must be Gita on the monitor. Aw, that was a short nap." Joshua shot off the couch up the stairs.

Pretty soon I could hear him through the monitor speaking in a mellow, sing song voice. "Hey there, pumpkin. Uncle Josh came to take care of you today."

Gita was whimpering slightly as he spoke. He grunted as he picked her up out of the crib. "Umma will be back soon. Don't worry. Miss Naomi and I will take good care of you, okay sweetie? Do you want to meet my friend? She's really nice and pretty like you. Come on…let's go see her." His voice faded from the monitor, followed by his heavy steps coming cautiously down the stairs.

As he entered the room, holding her on his hip while still supporting her back with his other hand, I was blushing from overhearing the accidental compliment he likely didn't intend for my ears. The way he conversed with Gita made my heart go up and down in my throat like it wanted to come out entirely.

"Gita, this is Naomi. Say, 'Hi Miss Naomi!'" He grabbed Gita's hand and made it wave toward me.

Gita giggled a hearty laugh that filled the room.

He did it again. "Did you like that? Say, 'Hi Miss Naomi!'" He waved her hand a little rougher this time, causing her to erupt into a sweet cackle once again. He repeated this about ten times until her laughter faded, and she started whimpering again.

"I bet she's hungry. Does she need a bottle or something?" Even with my limited knowledge of children, I knew she was old enough to eat big people food, but I also didn't know what she could have, so I was praying Joshua would know.

"Oh yeah! She's got a bottle in the fridge. Could you hold her while I get it?" He plopped her on my lap before I could even answer him. *Don't hurt her. Don't hurt her. Don't hurt her.*

I bounced her tamely on my knee. She started to giggle again, so I bounced slightly harder. Again, she erupted in laughter, so I did it a little harder. Her head was moving back and forth, hair flying from one side to the next. I stopped bouncing when Joshua came back in with the bottle all warmed up and handed it to me while gesturing to go ahead and start feeding her. She took the bottle and began to suck it down ferociously. Poor girl was hungry.

"I'm going to run to the bathroom while she's happy. Are you cool with that?" Joshua asked as he slid out of the room in a hurry.

I looked down at Gita and smiled. "Sure. We're all good here, I think." I couldn't believe how nicely this day was going and how few fears I had had all day, for the most part. All of a sudden, I got a sinking feeling in my gut, a void that signaled me to notice that I wasn't worrying and take it as a sign that I should be. What had I missed? I looked down at Gita. She looked so peaceful while she ate.

I sure hope I didn't hurt her when I was bouncing her. What if I gave her, like, shaken baby syndrome from shaking her head so hard back and forth? Isn't that how that happens? What if she has brain damage, and I have to fess up to Joshua and Maria that I'm the one to blame? They'll hate me forever, and I'll probably go to jail. How will anyone forgive me? What if I wanted to hurt her? Did I want to see how hard I could shake her? I bet I hurt her. She looks like she's hurt.

Hot panic starting pulsing in my core and moved its way through my extremities. My neck and shoulder muscles were seizing while the air in the room was sucked out. *It can't be possible. I couldn't have hurt her just by bouncing. Could I?*

I couldn't stop the waterfall of fear from coming this time. I must've looked paralyzed with terror because Joshua noticed something was wrong the moment he walked back in.

"Are you okay? You look like you've seen a ghost."

"Yeah yeah. I'm fine. Could you take her? I'm going to run to the bathroom too." I almost threw Gita into his lap in an attempt to flee the curse that was myself.

I shut the door to the bathroom forcefully and put the top down on the toilet. I sat on the lid and replayed the bouncing over and over and over in my head while whispering the sequence of events to myself. In moments like this, I was prosecutor, defense attorney, and criminal all in one. I made a case against myself then worked feverishly to find any solution to prove to myself I wasn't the evil person I feared I was. I put my arms over my head and my head in my lap and rocked back and forth, letting the images play in my mind like a broken record.

Suddenly I heard a female voice echo from the living room— Maria. *I guess they're back. I'll have to wait and see if Gita is okay or if she ends up having that shaken baby condition I've heard about. I'll have to confess to them. Better to keep it to myself until she shows signs.*

I mustered up the courage to leave the bathroom, and when I opened the door, Joshua was standing right there as though he was bracing himself to knock.

"Hey. Are you okay? You disappeared. Maria and James are back, the doc could easily tell it wasn't broken, so we can go. You sure you're okay?" He put his hand on the small of my back as I walked ahead of him.

"Yeah, sorry. I'm fine. Just had a little moment of panic. It's all good."

"Alright. If you say so." He sighed.

Maria thanked us for helping her and reported that James had only bruised his heel, no broken bones. I was only half participating in the conversation because my insides were still swimming in an intrusive brainstorm.

As we left their house, Joshua was silent. He didn't even attempt to venture into the depths of where I was mentally. Finally, the tension in his truck was suffocating me more than the shaken baby fear, and I began to feel overwhelmed with embarrassment.

Oftentimes when I had an episode of cascading panic, I would hear a faint voice that I called my "gut whisper." This voice offered a second of clarity where I could sense reality and begin to get a peek at the truth amidst my internal storm. It was the light at the end of the tunnel telling me that deep down I knew the truth, so I didn't need to be so scared. Sadly, when I heard my "gut whisper," it would fill me with sadness, embarrassment, and shame that I could let some unlikely fear occupy my time and energy. That moment came on the ride home with Joshua, and I knew I had to start the conversation despite my terror to open my mouth.

"So...yeah... I'm sorry I kind of...well, got lost in myself back there. I can't really explain what happened, but I'll be honest, it happens to me a lot, so if you want to stop getting to know me, I completely get it. I don't know what to say, but I'm sorry. I know it doesn't make much sense. I'm sure Maria thinks I'm a bizarre person. I'm so sorry." I was word vomiting. I just wanted to keep him from rejecting me, so the words kept flowing from my face.

He finally put his hand over top of mine and said, "Look. I may not get it right now, but please don't assume I'm just going to give up on getting to know you. Sound good?"

I had never heard him speak so directly...or sternly. It took me off guard yet made me feel confident he truly meant what he said.

That was the end of our second date. No hugs, no kiss, just an open car door and brief farewell. I spent the rest of the night soaking in the tub and marinating in every interaction of the day. My mind never stopped until I finally passed out from sheer mental and physical exhaustion. God knew what I needed after that day—sleep.

Seven

MISS CORRIE ASKED me to pick her up for church the next morning, probably to insure I actually went. As she got in the truck, she hit me with the question I was dreading most.

"How was your date yesterday?" She was almost bellowing at me, little bits of spit flying with excitement.

I couldn't break it to her that I had pretty much blown the whole thing, so I played it cool instead. I choked out, "It was fine!"

"Fine? I need some better adjectives than that, dear. Give me a spicy, give me a marvelous, give me an unbelievable, but do *not* give me a fine."

"Honestly, Miss Corrie? I blew it. I blew it! I just could *not* be normal, and I think I scared him off."

"Stop the car," Miss Corrie demanded.

"What? You want me to…?"

"Pull the car over right now," Miss Corrie ordered again.

We were driving on a four-lane road, of which I was in the left lane, so I had to change lanes, then turn onto the next available street, which took me a moment to do.

The whole time, she just kept muttering, "Pull it over. Just pull it over."

I had just barely gotten the truck into park when she turned toward me and grabbed my face with both of her hands. Her fingers were ice cold, but her palms were rich with warmth.

"Look at me. You have got to *stop* saying you're not normal. You, my dearest dear heart, are created in the image of God, the image of a God who loves you. You have struggles. Well, who doesn't? You need to realize your self-hatred does nothing but allow Satan to take control of your insides. Don't give him that much power." She gave a confident nod.

"Today, at church, I want you to replace those repetitive thoughts that strangle you, with the phrase, 'Help my unbelief. Jesus. Help my unbelief.' He'll help you embrace who you were made to be, His broken child, healed in Jesus." She let go of my face and sat back in her seat. "Okay, you can go now."

She waved her hand toward the road in front of us, leaving me no time for rebuttal. "Go ahead." I sat frozen. "I said, get going."

I took her suggestion during the service and chose to repeat the phrase she recommended to myself. As I did, they changed from being rote words into a prayer, then into an intimate conversation with God. I got an overwhelming, almost suffocating, feeling of peace. Pastor Don spoke about the "good news of the Gospel." His eyes filled with tears as he explained the peace that comes with placing our sins at the foot of the cross because of God's complete love for us.

God was using Pastor Don to make the scriptures come alive to me. A warmth began to grow in my heart that day as I absorbed the truths being preached from the Word. *Do I really find comfort in Christ? Could I really believe this? I think I can. I think I do.*

I realized that morning that God wasn't surprised by who I was, and He wasn't disappointed with how He had created me. I couldn't keep putting my value in what other people thought or how I appeared to those around me. The only opinion that mattered was God's, period. I had never felt this content at church before, never this quiet in my spirit. I repented to Him without fear of rejection, bathed in God's words of forgiveness, and flew on the wings of the choruses as we sang of God's love for us.

I had no idea where God would take me, but I was finally ready to embrace God as my Heavenly Father again. My fears were far too large for me to fight alone, but they were not too big for God. I clearly wasn't handling my life well solo. It was time to turn the reins over to their rightful owner. I was, at last, His.

Hot tears welled in my eyes, and a sensation of urgency rose up from my stomach. I sensed panic coming, even though I had no reason for it. Feelings of emptiness and concern were tempting me, urging me like a siren in the ocean, beckoning me to fill up the open chasm with worry, about anything, anything to fill the void. Time not spent worrying was wasted time.

I rose before the final song was finished, rushing outside. I took a deep breath. The air smelled like dead fish, thanks to the Bradford Pear trees in bloom on the corner. Why people planted them was a mystery to me. I'd have to ask Mom sometime why they were so popular.

I began to pray again, *help my unbelief,* in my head. I knew it was only a bandage for a weeping wound, but for the moment, this new routine brought me some peace. I didn't know how to progress in my journey, but as I looked up at the pillow like clouds floating effortlessly by, I knew I wasn't alone in the battle. It was a momentary gift.

As a child, I gave Pastor Don a hug after the service, but I hadn't hugged him in years as my anxieties grew into rebellion. That morning, however, I ran to give him an extra tight hug, leaving a few wet tear stains on the shoulder of his crisp shirt.

Shana and I went shopping together the week following that monumental Sunday service. My mind didn't stop racing, but I felt the hope that came with trusting in God in spite of my continued struggles. I experienced moments of doubt in my faith, but for once I could let those fears go more quickly. I guess God had finally decided to have mercy on me with at least one group of fears.

"So are you going to at least text him?" Shana's eyes bore into me while she placed a hot pink polka-dotted bathing suit back on the rack.

"No. I don't think so. He knows how to get in touch with me, and I don't want to seem desperate. If he wants to go out again, he'll let me know."

"What if he's just waiting for you to give him a little tidbit of something, or what if he's just thinking—"

"Look, Silsta. I don't need any assistance playing the 'what if' game. Let me just rest in my choice, do it my way."

"Fine. Are you buying anything you tried on for the beach this weekend, or are you passing on it all? I'm so thrilled to get back to the beach house, see the island again, now that it's finally warm."

Our parents owned a beach house on North Topsail beach. It was East Coast beach heaven there. Growing up, Shana and I loved going to the beach with our parents. Dad grew up going to the beach every summer and carried on the tradition with us. The love of the ocean ran deep in all of us. It was the one place we could all relax, take in the beauty, close our eyes, and with no demands we could truly unwind.

Our parents had rented a place for one week each summer until two summers ago when they surprised us by buying a house there. Now, we got to go as a family whenever there was a renter-free weekend, and especially when there was upkeep to be done. The next weekend, the whole family, including Beau, was headed there to get the house ready for the onslaught of summer rentals. It was always fun to have a sister date before heading to the coast. Shana and I were experts at finding updated relaxation clothes, in other words, yoga pants and bikinis.

"I like this coverup dress for myself, and I think I'm going to get this vest for Miss Corrie. She said she needs layers, and her birthday is in a couple weeks. She won't let me get her an official gift, so if I pick this up for her and just show up with it, she'll be more likely to accept it." I juggled the clothes piled over my arm as I decided what to keep.

"Sneaky. Want to stop by there today? I'd love to see her again. Is she, by chance, having yard work done today?" She waggled her eyebrows at me over the clothes rack.

"Nice try, but no. He doesn't work today." I smacked her ponytail on the way to check out.

"Stop! You'll mess up my hair, Stinky." She always did get the last word.

When we arrived at Miss Corrie's house, Joshua's truck was sitting in the driveway. *Aw man.* I hung my head. Meanwhile, Shana was practically convulsing with excitement next to me.

"Isn't that Joshua's truck? It has to be his truck. Where is he? Do you see him? You're going to get to talk to him. I'm so glad we stopped by here today." You would have thought it was Christmas morning the way she carried on next to me.

I desperately tried to conjure up a reason to turn around or a way to make myself invisible. Much to my horror, neither happened. Shana hopped out of the car like a firework, exploding out the door then slamming it shut before I could give her any instruction. She stood next to her door like a tourist at a long-awaited monument. I, on the other hand, emerged from the truck like a turtle, slow and deliberate.

I had not actually laid eyes on Joshua, so there was still a shred of hope we would miss him. I wasn't ready to face him, even a tiny bit, so I held tightly to Miss Corrie's present, hugging it to as I made a beeline for the house.

"Come on, Shana. I know what you're doing. Stop looking for him! He's here, but clearly not nearby so please, let's just go to the door." I clutched the vest in my arms with an unbreakable grip.

"Okay Naomi!" Shana over enunciated like she had a megaphone attached to her face. *"I'm right behind you!"*

"You are so ridiculous. Come *on.*" I had a sudden burst of courage and marched confidently through the yard up to the side door. I didn't even have to knock before Miss Corrie opened the door for us. She looked terrible. Her eyes were sunken in like big round marbles covered in a purple halo. She moved sluggishly and was slightly hunched over as though she was halfway down to pick something up off the floor. Her breathing was quick, and she strained as she pushed the door closed behind us, as if it took all her strength.

"Miss Corrie, are you alright?" I grabbed her by the elbow in an attempt to steady her.

"Oh, yes, yes, I'm fine my dearest dear heart." Miss Corrie had begun to call me that, pretty much exclusively. Whenever she used that term of endearment, I felt a burst of warmth in my soul.

"You look...no offense, but awful." Shana peered out the window looking for Joshua. I rolled my eyes at her overacted antics.

"Naomi, I didn't see him out there, but I'll keep watch here," she said stealthily like we were talking through a door. "Operation Find Joshua is underway."

"Would you knock it off? Miss Corrie is sick!" I scolded her while ushering Miss Corrie to take a seat in the kitchen.

"Oh, I'm not sick. I just didn't sleep well last night." She spoke in a pained whisper.

"Why? You weren't feeling well? Did you eat something that didn't sit well with you?"

"Oh no. Occasionally I have nights where I have bad dreams, vivid flashbacks of times gone by. Last evening, I happened upon some letters George wrote me during his travels. They made me miss his face. I have this recurring dream where I can see him walking away from the young man who shot him, and I'm right there watching. But no matter how loudly I scream, he doesn't hear me. I watch him die right in front of me and feel completely helpless. I usually wake up abruptly, like someone is robbing the house. I can hear the gunfire as though it's right next to my ear. So real. So real," she mumbled. "Then, I just can't get back to sleep, which then, turns me into a human rotisserie."

"Want some tea or something?" I asked gingerly.

"No, I'm okay, really. Nothing a good nap this afternoon won't fix." She laughed as she patted my hand.

"What did I do to deserve such a kind visit? And why is your lovely sister staring out my window so intensely?" Corrie looked in Shana's direction by the kitchen window.

"Give it up, Shana! I don't even want to see him anyways. I guarantee he doesn't want to see me either. I'm sure he's out there hiding in the bushes to avoid me."

"Why are you hiding from Joshua? Because of your date? That is ridiculous! You should be ashamed of yourself. Did you not hear anything I said to you the other day?" She shook her finger at me with feigned exasperation.

"Listen, I just feel like…"

"You need to stop that jabbering and listen to *my* story," Miss Corrie began. "Shana, you sit down. You're stressing me out with your carrying on there by the window."

Shana looked like a puppy who had just been scolded and quickly took a seat next to me at the modest dinner table. If only this table could talk. It had served many a person over the decades and had heard an avalanche of tales. Miss Corrie's table was an informative place to be.

"When George and I were first married, I always dressed in the closet. I loved our intimacy, but the idea of changing my clothes in front of him just sent me into an emotional tizzy. I couldn't bear the thought of him seeing me with the lights on, the flaws he'd undoubtedly notice."

I couldn't believe Miss Corrie was talking about this and felt a sudden need to stop her before she started. She was obviously delirious from lack of sleep. It was up to me to save her from sharing too much.

"Miss Corrie, don't you think—"

"I said to listen up, missy. I don't need to be censored. As I was saying," she drew out, "I was a modest bride, one too proper for her own good. It used to drive George mad that I would go as far from him as possible to use the bathroom or even floss my teeth! I had become far too calculated. We lived in France at the time, and I was working with a tutor once a week to help me learn the language. My tutor, Margot, would bring me delicious food, often some French delicacy. One day, she brought aged cheese and crackers. It smelled like a foot but tasted like heaven. I still have no idea what kind it was, but I will never forget the way it coated my tongue with intense flavor. Anyways, I ate more of that cheese than I care to admit. I gorged myself, put myself into a cheese coma, and laid on our outdated flame-stitched sofa."

She raised her eyebrows and threw a grin in my direction. "George came home from a long day at work to discover me curled up, taking a cheese induced siesta — a rare occurrence for me. He came over and kissed my forehead to wake me, but as I rose from the couch, a sound left my body like a foghorn off the coast of Maine. All that cheese performed a rock concert in my intestines!"

"Miss Corrie!" I clapped my hand over my mouth.

"It's true, dear! Nothing shameful in the truth. The deep baritone sound bellowed. It echoed. It rattled the couch cushion it was so loud. I stopped dead in my tracks and could not bring myself to turn around to see George's face." She hid her eyes as she relived the embarrassing experience.

"That's when the smell hit, the rotten egg air wave that permeated all the particles in the room. I could feel myself turning red, magenta even, with embarrassment. George didn't say a word. Well, I didn't give him a chance to. I ran from the room screaming,

'I'm a terrible wife!' and locked myself in our bedroom for the rest of the night. I sounded like the horn section of an orchestra all evening long, and despite George's best efforts, I stayed locked in our room alone all night and refused to even speak to him, poor fella. It wasn't until the next day at breakfast, when I knew my tummy was finally silent, that I crawled out of my hole of stink."

She hugged herself, "George sat at this very table, seriously, almost sternly, waiting for me to come down. I'll never forget how he kept his eyes glued to his newspaper as I entered, yet I felt him acknowledging me without looking up. He uttered calmly, 'You're going to need to figure out how to be human in front of me, dear. If passing gas is a sign that someone is a bad person, then I'm in a lot of trouble. If that's the worst thing you ever do as a wife, I'll be a lucky man.' He kissed me on the cheek and said, 'I love all of you, Corrie, even the parts that are imperfect. Well, I especially love those parts. They're what make you, you.'

She rubbed her eyes gently. "Girls, let Joshua and Beau see all of you. Don't be ashamed of your shortcomings. Embrace them. So, you had an odd end to the date? That shouldn't cancel out all the great times you did have that day. Does that make sense to you?"

We both sat in intense silence.

Miss Corrie's soliloquies were becoming commonplace for me these days, but Shana had never experienced one before. I looked over to see her eyes brimming with tears, like she was a dam about to burst. It tickled and touched me to see her so deeply affected by her humorous, but wise, advice. Only Miss Corrie could use the topic of flatulence to make people feel encouraged or bring them to tears.

"Yes ma'am. Message received. The only catch is, Joshua isn't my husband, not even close. But I will take note of your advice in the future, if I ever meet someone else." I stood up to get the gift I brought her, the original reason for the visit that had been quickly forgotten in all the discussion.

"Oh, Miss Corrie," Shana erupted the words loudly, "I have absolutely no issue passing gas in front of Beau, but I do struggle to show my humanity to him and admit it more authentically. Thank you for telling us this story!" She threw her arms around Miss Corrie.

I laughed to myself and shook my head at Shana speaking so freely of her farting habits with Miss Corrie. I was visiting with two open books. I sniggered as I sat back down, amused by their interchange, which was ironic since I was usually the queen of emotional antics.

"Miss Corrie? I hate to interrupt your bonding moment, but we did stop here to give you something."

She whipped her head around, her eyes looked stern and prepared to snap at me for getting her a gift.

"It's nothing big, so you can relax." I handed her the gift, still in the bag from the store so she wouldn't get upset about me wrapping it.

She pulled out the hot pink vest. Miss Corrie loved color and she especially loved pink.

"Oh, my dearest dear heart, I love it! Thank you." She began to try it on but stopped herself when she couldn't comfortably twist to get her arm through the vest. "I think I'll try it on later. I'm feeling, well, a little warm right now."

I didn't know what she was attempting to hide, but I could tell she was stretching the truth. I had begun to realize after all these months that Miss Corrie was a chasm of feelings and emotions, just like I was. I knew there were times when prying wasn't wise, and right now I didn't want to put her on the spot in front of Shana. I would wait for another time.

"Well, we better get going. Our family is headed to the beach this weekend, so we have to go pack. I'll see you next week though. You mentioned needing help going through your clothes, right?"

"That would be wonderful, dear. Thanks for remembering." She stood shakily and insisted she walk us to the door.

We had almost made it down to my truck when Joshua stepped out from behind the bed and waved. "Hey there, stranger."

"Hi yourself, Joshua!" Shana answered back.

I glared at her from the other side of the truck with an evil eye, desperate to telepathically tell her to stop talking!

"How are you?" He lightly kicked the dirt in front of us while looking at his feet.

"I'm doing fine. I hope you're well," I also gazed down at his feet.

Don't say anything wrong. Keep quiet.

"Could y'all just quit acting stubborn?" Shana piped in.

Joshua's head bolted up from staring at his feet with a shocked expression on his face.

"Let's all be adults here. Joshua, our family is headed to the beach this weekend. Would you care to join us? I'm sure Naomi would love to have your company. Wouldn't you, sis?" Shana gave an exaggerated head turn in my direction with a sly smile and silent stare.

"Would you, Naomi? I mean…like me to come with y'all?" He ran a shaky hand through his sandy brown locks.

I'd been put on the spot and immediately began to sweat. Of course, I'd love for him to come, but I suspected he didn't really want to, even if he was acting semi-interested.

"Um, well, I mean, sure? You're welcome to come with us. That is, only if you want to. Don't feel any pressure." I wanted to dig a deep hole, stick my head in it, and hide there until everyone had left the premises.

"Great! That settles it. Joshua, we'll see you at around eight tomorrow. Get to my parents' house early because in our family we leave about fifteen minutes earlier than when we say we're going to, so do the math. Bye now!" She waved cheerfully as she got in the truck and slammed the door.

I stood there wide eyed, waiting for him to fill the dead air, but he just stared back at me. His eyes were so genuine. I could see he felt just as uncomfortable as I did and began to feel sorry for being the reason he felt out of place. I didn't know what to do, so I quickly said, "See you then," gave a mild wave, got in, and drove off.

"I *cannot* believe you invited him to the beach with us! What were you thinking? I just...I'm so mad at you, Shana! You had *no* right to interfere like that!" I shouted.

She sat next to me, completely unfazed by my anger. One might say I was "the yeller" of the family. Not feeling heard often led to frustration, which usually resulted in me increasing my volume, sometimes until my throat hurt. It wasn't pretty, but my family members were, sadly, quite used to it.

"You weren't getting anywhere with him. He obviously wanted to talk to you, but for whatever reason couldn't, so I took care of it. You guys will get a chance to hang out and chat, put your feet up together, for a couple days. You know deep down you're thrilled I did this for you," she sang as she leaned toward me and put her head on my shoulder, pushing out her lower lip pathetically.

"Maybe...like, deep, deep, deep, *deep* down," I said flatly, followed by a sisterly poke in the armpit.

I was still fuming, but the flames had waned into a slight smoke. The truth was, I was stricken with an emotion I could only call blind optimism or hope. Hope that having Joshua come would not just be a good thing but a great thing.

My mind began to race with thoughts of our upcoming trip. *How should I dress? Will he try to be alone with me? Will he want to kiss me? Will my mind have mercy on me?*

Truth was, the beach and I had a love-hate relationship. It was a destination I delighted in going to but also the one place I had the hardest time not worrying. The constant peace, quiet, and lack of distraction caused my brain to speed out of control without warning. I didn't want Joshua catching me in a thought storm like I was on our last date, so I'd have to try extra hard to hide it.

I usually got invading thoughts when we were on the beach. I found myself fidgeting and tense when I should be laid back, soaking up the warmth of the sun. I felt self-imposed pressure to make my time on the beach perfect but often left "vacation" feeling exhausted.

Ironically, the beach was also where I had some of my sweetest memories—looking for sea glass, playing horseshoes and paddle ball, or just reading in my colorful beach chair. The weekend with Joshua was uncharted territory and, oddly enough, I had a thrilling suspicion I was going to have an experience of a lifetime.

The island was moist with drizzle as we crossed the bridge onto Topsail Island. The bridge was the part of the trip that got my heart racing for more than one reason. It was a sign that we were almost to our beach house and the ocean was within our grasp, but it was also a ridiculously high bridge that could plunge us to our deaths. If we made one wrong turn or another car veered into our lane from oncoming traffic, we could be toast. My brain on a bridge became saturated with visions of people and cars careening to the bottom of the ocean, causing me to drive my nails into the back of my hand while muttering words of comfort under my breath. What a relief I wasn't driving.

Once, I was the one driving us over, and my knuckles were as white as snow, gripping onto the steering wheel with the strength of twenty men. The image of me flinging the wheel toward the guard rail and causing us to plummet over the edge flickered like a candle in my mind. Of course, I didn't want to crash the car, but feeling the impulse somehow convinced me I wanted to go through with it.

Joshua, myself, Shana, and Beau were all in Beau's red SUV, while my folks drove behind us in their minivan packed with enough food to feed an army. You would have thought they were preparing for the apocalypse with the amount of food they brought. Never mind there were grocery stores at the beach. No, everything we were going to eat had to make the entire trip with us.

My folks were beyond excited to have Joshua come with us for the weekend. My dad packed up all the beach games in a hurry, ecstatic to have two young men to compete with. He was a loving and gentle father to his two daughters, always willing to try and think like a female if seeing from our perspective meant he could love and understand us better. But deep down, he waited patiently for a guy to join the family so there would be more than just his own testosterone to balance out all the estrogen in the house. Son-in-laws were a glimmer of hope on the horizon. Shana and I both knew Dad would make whoever we married feel like one of his own because he loved richly and with intense authenticity. I knew he was keen on Joshua. This had to be an answer to prayer for him. And Shana was brimming with pride as her plan came to fruition. Her invitation was abrupt and impulsive, yet I could tell by her excitement she must have been percolating on how to help us get together for some time.

Beau was a confident driver, so as we began to ascend the bridge, he also started to accelerate. I put my head down slightly into my lap and cleared the phlegm rising in my throat.

"Okay back there NayJay?" he said with a twang, looking back in his rearview mirror. He was the king of creative nicknames, and NayJay was mine. My full name was Naomi Joy, so he put them together to come up with NayJay.

"I'm fine. Just ignore me while I choose to stare at the floor instead of the beautiful view," I whimpered.

"Well, if you're okay, then I guess I'll go a little faster." He revved the engine into the next gear while I proceeded to tighten my death grip on the door handle.

"Oh, leave her alone, Beau. You're speeding as it is. I don't like it when you barrel down this road. Come on, slow down." Shana gently hit his forearm. Thankfully she had my back on this one.

We drove down the main two-way street on North Topsail that advertised majestic blue ocean on one side and the serenely green sound on the other. The houses were lined up neatly in two rows.

Some of them looked worn, like old shoes, peeling paint from the wind and severe coastal weather. I always loved seeing wet beach towels hanging from decks, flapping in the ocean breeze after a fun day full of sun, sand, and saltwater.

The first breath of sea air filled my lungs with a richness only moist beachy air can give. The family farm stand we often visited on the way to the beach was brimming with spring fruits and vegetables. Soon, it would be strawberry season, and we would indulge in strawberry shortcake topped with whipped cream as often as we could get it. Tall ocean grasses blew in the breeze, and every so often, we would pass a planted palm tree at the end of someone's driveway, oddly out of place among more native species. Pelicans flew in a smooth formation over the rows of houses, gliding unapologetically low in the air, so close at times it felt like I could reach up and touch them. Their shadows followed behind them, gracefully passing over roof after roof, until the delightful birds reached the other end of the island. There were people running on the side of the road, exercising whatever plagued them away, undoubtedly hoping to consume vacation treats as a reward for their discipline.

As we got out of the car, I gazed up at our rectangular house with turquoise shutters and white siding that had yellowed over time. I noticed Joshua taking in all the same things. It was easy to hear the ocean, even from the driveway, crashing with an intense but comforting explosion as waves met the sand, leaving white foam sliding down the shore in its wake. We all just stood there taking it all in until Beau patted the roof of his car like he had come to a conclusion.

"We can't stand here all day, y'all. These cars ain't gonna unload themselves." The rest of us moaned in unison.

My mom cooked simple dinners at the beach house, and we all preferred to eat early so we could spend more time walking on the beach before the sun went down. After dinner, the six of us made our way down the long wooden boardwalk that ran parallel to all the other boardwalks. The rows of houses and boardwalks fit together like a game of Tetris. The dunes, the great protectors of the houses and the beach itself, rested at the top of the walkway. They looked like clouds on earth — pure white, except for sporadic grasses that would shoot up at random. The nails on the boardwalk were warped, some standing too tall, crooked from years of abuse holding the manmade path together.

"Watch out for those nails. They'll take the skin right off your big toe something fierce," I warned as I dodged one with an exaggerated step.

We climbed one at a time up the stairs that crested at the top of the dunes. There we each stopped for a moment to take in the vastness of creation. The view of the ocean never grew old or went unappreciated in the Lang family. The ocean was one place I could feel God, hear God, and smell God. Standing here, things made sense.

The ocean, in its massiveness, had God's name written all over it. I felt the sand sinking in between my toes, soft and cold, massaging my heels with each step. We were all silent for a little bit, enjoying the rumble of the waves. The tide was going out, so the beach was wide, with plenty of shells to investigate. Our family loved to hunt for sea glass to collect. Sea glass wasn't much more than glorified trash: broken glass lost at sea or abandoned on the beach and rolled and smoothed by the turbulence of the water over years and years. But each piece told a unique story or hid a mystery. It took time for the sharp, dangerous edges to become rounded and for the shiny outer shell to feel soft as velvet. There was nothing more satisfying than to catch a splash of green, brown, or white hiding amongst the shells and discover a piece of misshapen sea glass resting there after its tumultuous journey. Those unwanted pieces found a forever home in our family.

Joshua was trying his best to figure out how to look for sea glass because not only had he not grown up looking for it, he didn't even know what it was.

"East coast beaches are so different than the ones back home." He stopped to pick up a seashell, looked at it then chucked it back into the ocean.

"Really? Better or worse ya think?"

"Not better or worse, just different. Kind of makes me miss home a little bit, which feels sad."

I tried to conjure a sympathetic response but couldn't think of something that wasn't dismissive. *I wonder what he's even thinking. Is he even having a good time? Should I ask?*

"Are you having a good time?" I bumped my shoulder against his arm as we wandered together, the sun beginning to set behind clouds bursting with blue and pink.

"Yeah. Why? Do I not seem like I'm having a good time?" Joshua had been quiet at dinner, but my family tended to keep conversations moving at warp speed and after the missing home comment I really didn't know how to interpret him. He seemed to enjoy just taking the experience of being with all of us in, instead of fighting for the floor to say something. I hoped that was more the reason for his silence.

"Oh, I didn't mean that. You've just been kind of quiet. That's all." I dragged my big toe in the sand with each step, leaving a row of lines one after the other trailing behind us.

He's so quiet because he doesn't know what to think of me. He's annoyed with how much I talk about useless stuff. He can tell I'm worrying about nonsensical things.

"I hate being called quiet," he said softly. "I know you didn't mean anything by it, but all my life people have focused so much on how quiet I am. Or they say I'm shy, which I'm really not at all. I enjoy just listening to people or spending time with someone one on one." The back of his hand brushed mine. "Since we're talking about communication, I also wanted to apologize for not calling you after our last date. I know you must've been nervous about that, and I'm sorry. I honestly wasn't sure if you'd really want me to call you, so I figured I'd give you space to call me. Then you didn't." His head hung down a little bit as he spoke.

"I'm the one who is sorry, Joshua. I should've called or texted too. I didn't know what you thought of how I behaved the last time we were together. I'm sure you thought I was…who knows what… like I said, I'm sorry."

"Don't do that, Naomi." He turned toward me as we walked. "Don't label yourself like that. We're all messed up, trust me. Let's *both* try to start fresh this weekend. Give up our insecurities."

His hand started on the back of my arm and slowly slid down until his fingers intertwined with mine and rolled around a second before he held on for good. I didn't know what to do with myself in that moment. He was holding my hand, and I was lost in his acceptance of me. As much as I wanted to believe it was possible for him to like me, I still wondered if he would feel the same way if he *really* knew the thoughts I had or the feelings and fears I experienced. He might feel this way in this moment, but if I ever said those things to him out loud, he'd surely walk away. I didn't want to keep things from him, but strangely I trusted his reassurance that he truly was okay with me as I was.

The smell of coffee permeated the upstairs of the beach house, slowly reaching each of us in our beds like a floating cloud of deliciousness. My dad was an early bird who liked to have his coffee and quiet time before everyone woke up. As I came up the stairs to the living room, I saw the back of a ruffled head of hair sitting on the couch in front of me. Joshua sat at the end of the sofa with his coffee in hand and his Bible open.

I suddenly felt self-conscious about my appearance and veered into the half bath next to me so I could take a peek in the mirror at my own wild hair. I tried my best to tame my messy bun, but it definitely looked more like a mess than like a bun. Joshua had told me to just be myself, so I figured that's what I was going to do.

"Mornin', Glory," Dad said cheerfully. He was by far the happiest morning person I'd ever met. He saw the start of the day as an opportunity for fun, excitement, and learning. His cheerful morning attitude used to annoy me, but nowadays, I found it refreshing. Even when my own life felt out of sorts, his joy in the morning was a security I could count on.

"Morning, Dad. Good morning, Joshua. How'd y'all sleep last night?" I inquired tentatively.

"I slept like a rock, all the way to five a.m. It felt good to get in a solid night of sleep in my most favorite place." Dad slid a pan of bacon into the oven.

"I slept okay," Joshua answered. "I never sleep well in a new place on the first night."

I felt myself starting to feel responsible for his bad night of sleep, but I stopped the thought before I could start obsessing over it.

"I'm sorry to hear you didn't sleep well. Maybe a day on the beach will fix it for you," I suggested.

"No doubt a day on the beach can fix anything. I can't wait to get into the water and body surf." Joshua sipped his coffee and closed his eyes as though he was envisioning his version of relaxation on the beach.

"You do realize the water is only like, sixty degrees? Did you bring a wetsuit, or are you just that tough?" I gave him a smirk.

"I guess that's true. Looks like the sand activities will have to do. Can I at least get my feet wet?" He looked at me like a little boy begging his mother to play catch for five more minutes.

"If you're a good boy, then yes, you can," I teased.

After breakfast, we all mobilized to the beach, carrying umbrellas, chairs, and beach games like pack mules down the boardwalk. The air was crisp and cool, but the sun served as the nutritious warmth we needed to make the breeze tolerable. We took beach relaxation seriously, no matter the weather, and needed every possible beach tool or toy at hand to take full advantage of it.

"So, who's ready to lose playing horseshoes? Any takers?" Dad said as he hung one of the heavy horseshoes on his pointer finger, swishing it ever so slightly.

"I dunno if you can handle my beast mode, sir. Are you ready to get beat so early in the day?" Beau picked up another horseshoe and rolled his arm doing a bicep curl. "What kind of heat you bring with you Joshua?"

Joshua looked at Beau, eyes big like saucers. "Um, oh yeah, I totally brought all kinds of heat. I'm about as good at horseshoes as I am at putt-putt." Dad beamed at the bantering. His dreams were coming true and the all-boy horseshoe competition began with gusto.

"I think Joshua is a sweet young man, Naomi. How do you feel your time is going with him?" Mom asked as we watched the guys hurl horseshoes down the beach. Mom was respectful of my privacy, but she knew I would offer up details to her and my sister. They were safe places.

"He's a gem. That's for sure. Such a gentleman. He's hardworking, truly loves his family, and his faith is strong. It makes me wonder why he likes me so much," I told them as Joshua shot me a faint but coy smile from where he stood.

"Wow, girl. He's got it bad for you! Look at the way he was just kissing you with is eyes." Shana threw her head back and laughed.

"*Stop!* He'll hear you!" I hissed through clenched teeth.

"It wouldn't matter if you wore an octopus on your head, Naomi. That boy has got it bad for you. Has he kissed you yet?" She rolled over onto her tummy to sun her back.

Her towel was one we had since childhood and worn to threads on the ends. Shana was guilty of laying out all day until her skin was a nice crispy red color. She would end up in a great deal of pain the day after, which resulted in her spending the rest of our vacation convincing Mom she was going to stay under the umbrella. Then she would secretly sneak in more sunbathing to darken any white parts she had left when Mom went up to the house for one reason or another.

"No, he hasn't kissed me yet, but we've gotten close, I think anyway. I seem to mess things up during any kissable moment. I have a habit of killing romance, it seems." I pulled my chair back into a reclined position to appear as if I were enjoying the sun when I was really just admiring the boys playing their game.

Joshua had on a blue athletic shirt, shorts, and an NC State ball cap, which was shoved on his head backwards. I couldn't stop thinking about how his ears stuck out slightly and adorably. I knew he was competitive, but during this game, I witnessed his desire to win on a whole different level.

Dad was obviously having a great time, egging Joshua on whenever he scored a point or got a ringer, taunting him flagrantly. I was elated to see them enjoying one another so much.

"Well, let's make that kiss happen here at the beach, then," Shana pronounced with authority. "There's no need to keep him waiting any longer. Go get him girl!!"

"Stop bossing your sister, Shana. It'll happen when it's supposed to. You won't have to force it. The good ones will wait a long time for that first kiss because they know moving too fast can be dangerous."

The game ended with Dad throwing a horseshoe into the sand with a giant thud. The three men walked up to the tent where we sat, Dad bringing up the rear.

"This kid has a lucky arm and clearly likes to win." Beau pointed at Joshua with his thumb.

Dad gave Joshua a gentle shove on the shoulder as they walked together.

"Sorry sir, I can't seem to make myself hold back when it comes to sports and games. I sure hope you won't hold it against me." He offered up a soft smile.

"Son, it's a pleasure playing with such a strong competitor. I'm used to 'Miss Just Keep Your Eyes on the Ball' over there, who never seemed to learn how to catch despite my best coaching efforts." Dad lifted his chin and gestured toward me.

Everyone knew gross motor skills were not my strong suit. I stuck out my tongue at him, not bothering to lift up from the chair.

"Okay Beau, let's get some practice in before our next round with Mr. Horseshoes. Are you up for it?" Dad took a big swig of water, then rubbed my mom softly on her head.

"You got it, Mr. Lang." Beau hopped off his towel again with enthusiasm. "Do you wanna join us, Joshua?"

"No thanks. I was actually hoping Naomi would run back to the house to get some snacks with me. That game made me hungry. Interested?"

"Sure. I could go for a snack. Anybody need anything?" I got up from my chair excitedly. I was pretty hungry too, and time alone with Joshua was a bonus.

"I'd love some Hershey's *Kisses* to snack on if we have them." Shana rolled over waggling her eyebrows.

"I don't believe we do, Silsta," I said through clenched teeth.

"Okay, then I guess some M&M's will have to do. Thanks guys." She plopped her head dramatically back onto her towel.

Joshua walked ahead of me, and I could feel myself beginning to perspire. I lifted my arms up to let the ocean breeze blow away the nervous sweat but quickly flung them back down when Joshua turned back to see if I was behind him. I wasn't really sure why I was jumpy, but all of Shana's kissing talk didn't help.

I had spent plenty of time with Joshua and had no reason to be apprehensive about going on a food run with him —but I did. When we got inside, we started gathering up pretzels and Twizzlers to bring back to the beach, so our conversation was light and down to business. We joked about how he slaughtered my dad in horseshoes and how nice the weather was. Suddenly, as I was reaching into the pantry for the Goldfish, I noticed he was right beside me. I turned to find him standing with his arms crossed and a purposeful look in his eyes.

"Do you...you... need something in here?" I stammered.

"Yes, I guess you could say that." He lifted the hat off of his head and scratched his forehead before putting his hat back in place.

"What do you need? There's peanuts, Oreos, Pop Tarts, Cheerios," I blubbered. My guard was going down with each step he took in my direction.

"Do you know that I was convinced I liked you from the moment I first spoke to you?" He took a step closer to me, this time taking the Goldfish from my hands and placing them on the counter next to us.

"No, actually, I did not know that, but I appreciate that little tidbit of information," I replied in a staccato rhythm.

"It's true, Naomi, whether you believe it or not. You have me totally mystified. Could I, maybe, kiss you, please?" he asked with a boyish innocence.

"Can you kiss me?" I parroted back, not really sure how to answer.

"You heard me. Can...I...please...kiss...you?" he repeated again, but this time with a little shakiness in his voice.

"Um...I guess so—"

He planted his lips softly on mine. I could smell the sunscreen on his face and could taste the one M&M he snuck before he worked up the courage to come over to me. His hands were on my back, and he was bending his knees to reach me, lifting me slightly as we embraced.

The kiss started with one easy peck but slowly grew into a far more passionate meeting of the lips. I was delighted to feel completely at ease in his arms. I felt no rushing fears or panic, as though I was being swept up in a tornado of calm as we held each other. He pulled away as quickly as he began but continued to hold me in a close and tender hug.

"I've been wanting to do that for a really long time, but I would always lose my nerve." he said affectionately.

"I'm a little speechless," I managed to squeak out.

He kissed me on the cheek as he grabbed the Goldfish from the counter. I felt like I was standing on a rocking boat, my knees unable to find my balance. I'd never experienced anything like that before.

"Come on gorgeous. Let's get these snacks to the family. They're going to wonder where we are here pretty soon." I heard him sigh to himself.

I followed behind him with an immovable grin plastered on my face.

As we rounded the dune, Shana rolled over to look back at me and could immediately tell something more than just grabbing snacks occurred while we were gone. She grinned to herself, nodded her head like she was agreeing with someone, then shot me a wink.

"Okay, NayJay. That's what Beau calls you, right? Let's play some paddle ball. I hear it's your favorite beach game." Joshua set his armload of snacks down on the same ratty old beach towel Shana crisped herself on, then tossed me a paddle.

"Are you sure you can handle *me*? I'm even better at this than Putt-putt," I teased.

"You don't scare me, Naomi, even if you are a piece of work." He hit the ball to me to begin our first rally. Something had been discovered when we kissed, as if a red carpet rolled out to guide us into a new and thrilling partnership.

Our time on the beach as a family was precious and memorable with Joshua there. He got along great with everyone and, despite being quieter than the rest of us, still participated in a very genuine way. We played paddle ball, walked on the beach, collected sea glass, and laughed at story after story. Mercifully, my fears stayed away for the most part. There were a few moments I felt a temptation to obsess about a fleeting fear, but I was so distracted by my newfound interest in Joshua that my brain stayed occupied.

During dinner, as Dad was telling a particularly compelling story, my phone rang faintly from the other room. I didn't want to interrupt his creative flow, so I ignored it. Not even a minute later, it rang again. Who could be calling? Everyone important to me was with me. Everyone, but Miss Corrie. I suddenly felt frantic thinking it could be her needing me, and I jumped up from the table, knocking over my water as I went.

"What on earth are you doing, dear?" Mom threw down a napkin to mop up the water spilling all over the floor. I grabbed my phone, only to realize the number was one I didn't even recognize. They had called twice, and I'd missed both calls.

"Sorry Mom. It's a wrong number, I think. I heard my phone and was worried Miss Corrie might need me. But it wasn't her, so it's probably a mistake. Sorry for spilling the water! I didn't mean to lose my cool so suddenly."

I would have loved to be known as one who stayed calm in emergencies, but my whole family knew I wasn't ever calm, especially in crises. Here my phone was just ringing, and I caused a tsunami of ice water on the table in response. I put my phone down next to me and no sooner had I picked up my fork to begin eating, it rang again. I looked over at Joshua, who had an inquisitive look on his face.

I answered the phone hesitantly. "Hello?"

"Miss Lang?" a stern voice asked.

"Yes? I'm Miss Lang. What can I help you with?" I got up from the table with everyone watching me.

"Miss Lang, I have you listed as Mrs. Corrie Dean's emergency contact. Is that correct?"

"Um, yes ma'am," I lied. I had no idea I was listed as Miss Corrie's emergency contact but didn't mind that she hadn't told me.

"Miss Dean was transported to the hospital by ambulance earlier this evening, and we are required to let her emergency contact know of her condition." I felt a lump growing in my throat.

What had happened to her? Why wasn't I there to help her? Why did I have to leave her when I knew she wasn't doing as well as usual the last time I saw her? My gut told me she didn't look good.

"What...what happened to her? Is she okay?" I looked over at Joshua, who had gotten up to pace behind me.

"We're not at liberty to discuss her condition with you over the phone, but we can tell you that she is currently stable. She is at Rex Hospital if you would like to come see her. She will be moved into a room within the next couple hours." The woman on the phone sounded as though she was ordering Chinese food, not giving a loved one bad news.

"Okay, well, I'm out of town, but I'll do my best to get there. Thank you for calling, and please let me know if anything changes," I said roughly before hanging up.

"What happened? Is it Miss Corrie?" Joshua started to rest his hand on the small of my back, then pulled away.

"Yeah. She was transported to the hospital for something, but they wouldn't tell me what. Why call me and not tell me what is wrong with her? I mean, what am I supposed to do with this information?" I held the phone in my hand like I was expecting it to ring again.

"With HIPA regulations they likely can't tell you over the phone, especially since you aren't family. Did they say whether she was stable or not?" Mom asked calmly. She was the person to have by your side during a crisis. She always knew the right questions to ask and how to attack problems wisely.

"They said she was stable, but I mean, what do I do? Do I go there now or wait? I feel so bad. She wasn't feeling well when Shana and I went to visit her. Didn't she look bad, Shana? This is all my fault." I was talking so fast the words were slurred together.

"Calm down, sis. You don't even know what's wrong. She might have just called 911 because it's the weekend, and she couldn't get herself to urgent care. She might simply have a virus, like the flu. You just don't know." Shana continued to eat her dinner as though nothing was wrong. She chomped on her salad seeming entirely indifferent, yet she ordered me around at the same time. My hands balled up by my sides in fury, feeling like a rocket about to blast off.

"Don't tell me to calm down! I need to figure out what I need to do here! I should've been there for her! You could afford to care a little more, Shana! I mean, come on!"

"Okay, listen Naomi, what do you want to do? Do you want to go back to Raleigh now? I'm more than happy to take you back so we can check on her. Take a deep breath and relax. We can get you there if you want to go." Joshua was clearly as concerned for her as I was but using his energy to find a solution, not panic.

As soon as I got frantic about something, my ability to make good decisions flew out the window.

"I don't know. I could go, but we'll get there late, and who knows what we'll be walking into. I should've asked her if she was okay the last time I was with her. Does she really not have anyone else to call but me? What can I even do for her? This is just too much." I wasn't able to offer any helpful suggestions because I was now hyper focused on my own insecurities and fears. I made it about myself, even though I *thought* I was caring about Miss Corrie. I was sinking deep into my thoughts, reliving my last moments with her. I was beating myself up over questions I should have asked her that day and conjuring images of the awful things that most likely happened to her in my absence.

It's my fault she's there. I knew she was sick and didn't get her help. What if I was secretly hoping something would happen to her, and now I've caused it to happen. I will have to face her and apologize. How awful of me.

"Naomi, we should go." Joshua jumped in. "I'll be happy to drive you. Mr. Lang, would you mind if Naomi and I drove back to Raleigh tonight in your van? I think it would be best if we both went to check on Miss Corrie."

"Absolutely, son. I think that's a great idea. You guys won't be missing anything here anyways. We're just going to pack up in the morning and head home. You two go and check on your friend. Make sure she's okay." He turned to Beau. "Are you okay with driving us home tomorrow?"

"Yessiree. Y'all just can't critique my elite driving abilities. There's only one Dale Earnhardt Jr., but people say I'm a close second." Beau could always be counted on for comic relief in tense situations.

Joshua took me by my shoulders and ducked down to meet my eyes. "Go pack your stuff, and I'll meet you back here in a few."

"Okay, okay. I'll meet you back here," I muttered distractedly.

"Don't you two want to finish eating? You don't want to leave and get hungry on the way. Who knows how long you'll be up tonight?" Mom shoved a pack of peanut butter crackers in my hand before I could object.

"Thanks Mom." I hugged her tightly, not wanting to let her go.

She was my secure place in times of chaos, which was largely why I didn't want to leave home. She helped me sort through whatever changes I was facing, and in that moment, I secretly wished she would come with me.

We hit the road with Joshua driving, taco in hand. I pressed my forehead to the window and gazed out, choking down a peanut butter cracker as it passed the knot in my throat. I was mad that I let myself get into such a frenzy, but I also felt justified to be so preoccupied with how I had failed Miss Corrie. My stomach felt like I was hosting a bowling tournament in my gut. The smell of his taco made me want to barf.

After about forty-five minutes of silence, I finally mustered up the nerve to speak to him. "Thanks for being so sweet to me tonight. I was paralyzed and couldn't make a good decision about what to do. Your decisiveness is greatly appreciated."

"It's okay. I get it. What do you think is wrong with her?"

"I don't know. I just don't. Sometimes she seems tired or more worn out, but I just figured it was because she was older. She likes to joke she has the spirit of a turtle. What if there's something terribly wrong with her, and I never knew? I've spent so much time with her and just kept excusing her off days, attributing them to old age… even though she's not *really* that old." I stared up at the giant moon as I chattered on.

The moon followed us all the way back to Raleigh. Joshua listened to my jibber jabber the whole ride. My oral diarrhea was flowing as I attempted to work through all the unfounded guilt I had for leaving town in the first place. Once I got to a good stopping point and took a breath, Joshua placed his hand lightly on my arm which brought me back to earth.

"I think we should pray for Miss Corrie right now. May I?" He took hold of the steering wheel with both hands gripping it hard.

I felt unnerved by his request but also a stirring to go along with his petition. "Well, sure. I think that would be a good thing for all of us." He put his hand on top of mine once again as he composed himself.

He smoothly transitioned into a conversation with the Almighty God as though he had done it a million times. "Dear Heavenly Father, please help us as we go to see Miss Corrie. May we be an encouragement to her and show her Your love in our visit. We don't know what's wrong with her, Lord, but we do know You are ultimately in control of everything, so we trust You with her. We're scared, but we ask that You send your comfort in this time of worry. We love You and thank You for our newfound relationship. In Jesus' name we pray, Amen." He put his hand back over mine.

"Amen," I whispered.

Joshua's faith was compelling and extremely attractive. His love for the Lord was obvious in the way he effortlessly communicated with Him. I envied his faith. He spoke to me as though my faith was just as deep as his, which forced me to investigate my heart.

Could I possibly believe in God more than I ever thought I did? Joshua left his hand on top of mine well after the prayer was over. I suddenly became self-conscious of the scars and scratches I had given myself, so I curled my hand into a fist under his. I was overwhelmed with emotion for this man I had just begun to get to know.

It was about ten o'clock by the time we made it to Raleigh. Neither of us were tired. The dramatic events following the phone call and intense ride home had us jacked up on adrenaline. I needed to lay my eyes on Miss Corrie and see that she was still breathing before I could calm down.

"I'm heading straight to the hospital, right?" Joshua double checked.

"Yes sir."

He pulled into a parking spot at the hospital, simultaneously giving me a fist bump that made me smile. "Let's do this."

Eight

"I'M LOOKING FOR a patient who was admitted earlier this evening. Corrie Dean?" I inquired at the front desk of the hospital.

The attendant sent us to the patient tower where the smell of sickness, illness, bleach, and fecal matter hit my nose like a sledgehammer. I wanted to abort the mission, but my devotion to Miss Corrie pulled me to see her.

I'm going to catch a stomach virus or Ebola in this place. I can't touch anything. Don't touch anything. Is that vomit on the floor? It looks like puke. Did I just step in it? They wouldn't let vomit be on the floor without cleaning it up. But what if I just stepped in it, and it's on my shoes. I'll throw up. I should go back and check to see if it really was vomit. But I don't want Joshua thinking something is completely wrong with me, so I'll just have to assume it wasn't throw up...but if it was, I should wash my shoes.

When we found her room, I stopped dead in my tracks right outside the door. I could hear another patient coughing in the room next to her and a television blasting from the room next to that. My feet were glued in place, and I didn't want to go inside, afraid of what I would find.

"What's the matter?" Joshua asked.

"I...I...I just can't go in." My skin felt like it was crawling with germs, my shoes were forever contaminated by the disgusting hospital floor, and I was terrified that whatever was wrong with Miss Corrie was somehow my fault.

"You can go in, Naomi. I'm here with you. We can do this together." He grabbed my hand and began to pull me.

I could feel the warm tension start in my core and spread to my extremities. Joshua pulled me behind him gently, yet forcefully, until we were all the way in the room. The curtain was drawn in front of Miss Corrie's hospital bed, so we couldn't see her even after we entered the room.

"Just say something," Joshua said softly.

"Knock knock, Miss Corrie. Two of your favorite people are here to see you."

Joshua's expression changed rapidly from a light smile to a grim fake one.

I felt my own face fall as it registered, she looked really bad. She was propped up on pillows with her eyes closed and her complexion as pale as the sheets. Her eyes looked dark in their sockets, and her skin was ashen. The hot pink nail polish she wore on her fingernails was chipped on one hand, and her left eye had a light purple bruise just below it. A bandage covered her cheek on the same side. Her lips were chapped, crusty, and made her look like a corpse.

I stopped cold. "She needs some water. She's parched. Nurse! Nurse!"

Joshua grabbed my arm and put his finger over his lips.

I couldn't stand seeing her look so frail. What could have caused this? Why was she so sick all of the sudden? I started digging my nails into the back of my hand. It wasn't working. My heart was clambering for rationality and justification for why my friend, my mentor, was sick in a hospital bed, looking on the verge of death. And it was my fault for leaving her.

Joshua and I stood next to each other for about a half hour before the nurse came in to check on Miss Corrie. She checked her vitals and gently moved her pillow to straighten her head. "Are you Ms. Dean's daughter?"

"No, no I'm just a friend. Her emergency contact though, so I think I'm allowed to be here," I answered timidly.

Miss Corrie finally opened her eyes as the nurse was talking to me but didn't notice we were there at first. She gave a tentative smile to the nurse, then suddenly noticed Joshua in front of her. "Joshua!" she said weakly. "When did you get here?"

"Hi, Miss Corrie. How are you doin'? I brought a special gift for you. I thought she might cheer you up." He gestured in my direction by the curtain. I had yet to be able to fully enter the room.

Miss Corrie's expression lit up immediately. "Oh, my dearest dear heart!" She held out her hand for me to take it.

I felt pulled to move closer, and I carefully took her hand. I didn't want to hurt her. I didn't know what to say, so I just started crying. I put my head on her chest and ugly cried as she rubbed my head with her good hand.

"What's all this about?" she asked.

"I...I...I'm just so sorry I left you and that you're hurt. I don't even know what happened to you, but I can tell it was bad by looking at you. This is all my fault. Please forgive me for leaving you like I did," I blubbered.

"Well, thanks a lot there, dear. I guess that means I must look pretty...pretty terrible, that is. I suspected that was the case, but now it's confirmed seeing the way you're looking at me. Nothing is your fault either. I'm just an uncoordinated old coot."

"Oh, I didn't mean you look bad... I'm sorry I said that." I sniffed loudly, wiping my nose.

"I look terrible, I'm sure. Just look at my hair! I've got it in a rat's nest behind my head on this rock of a pillow."

"Oh, please, you look great. The natural look is totally back in." I said, pulling myself back together slightly.

"You think so, dear?" She fluffed her bangs with her good hand.

"I hate to break up this hair stylist conference, but is there anyone else here who would like to know what happened? Miss

Corrie are you planning to inform us, or do we need to call the doctor in here?" He crossed his arms over his chest.

I composed myself during our hair discussion and was now standing at the end of the bed with Joshua.

"Yes, yes, I know. I should tell you what happened. It's no big deal, really. I was just trying to move one of my flowerpots and tripped on the top step."

"We see you have a bruise, but did you hurt anything else?" Joshua's voice cracked again, like it had when he'd asked me out.

"I seem to have fractured my left ankle, but mildly. My hip is also going to turn many shades of purple, so I've been told. But I should be okay once I get out of here."

"Miss Corrie, how are you going to get around? You'll have to be on crutches, right? Will you need me to work more?"

"Dearest, you don't need to worry about that. I can figure it out." She waved her hand as if she was swatting a fly, dismissing me.

"I think we should figure it out right now. We need to all sit down and discuss with the doctor what your needs will be, come up with a plan," Joshua declared.

I was impressed by how direct he was being and how confident he was to get her set up with the right care.

"No need to talk to my doctor, dear boy. I'll make sure we have a good plan. Naomi, of course I'd love it if you could come to work a few more hours a week, when you're able, to help me recover. I'll make sure to compensate you."

"There's nowhere I'd rather be, Miss Corrie." I was relieved she asked me to be the one to help her once she got home.

Joshua and I decided to get going in order to let her rest, since it was almost midnight, and we were all exhausted. As we drove back to my place, Joshua was quiet, which I assumed was from exhaustion. My apartment was especially dark since my folks weren't there, so like a gentleman, he escorted me to my door. We climbed to the top of my stairs, and he stayed a couple steps below me and reached out for a hug. He was considerably taller than me, but when I was two steps higher, our faces met perfectly. I hugged his neck and took in his manly smell. I liked the way his arms wrapped comfortably around my waist and his ears brushed mine as we embraced.

As we stood there, I could feel him begin to tremble slightly, and his breathing became more rapid. I pulled my head back and looked at him inquisitively. He stayed silent but just rested his chin on my shoulder while pulling me into a stronger hold.

"Are you okay?" I breathed into his ear.

He didn't answer me, but I could feel his heart pounding in his chest as it rested up against me. *What is wrong? Why is he acting so strangely?* I knew what a panic attack felt like, and it seemed like he might be having one. I was beginning to fear he figured out I was too much for him and was mustering up the courage to break it off with me.

My ridiculous behavior with Miss Corrie, crying and carrying on, it was uncalled for, and he wants out. I was about to ask him when he cleared his throat to say something. I could hear his voice box trying to engage, faint growls coming from him as though he was trying to get the words started but couldn't. In an unlikely moment of bravery, I swept my lips comfortingly over the side of his neck.

"I..." he finally uttered quickly.

"You what?" I whispered into the crook where my lips rested.

"I think I..."

"What? You think what?"

"I think I...I love you," he blurted out so fast I almost didn't hear him.

When I realized what he'd said, I pulled my head back and stared into his gorgeous hazel eyes that were full of anticipation. We lingered there for what was only a few moments but felt like an eternity. My response to him came abruptly and suddenly.

"No, you don't," I stated matter-of-factly.

"I don't?"

"No! You absolutely do *not*...love me that is. You don't love me. You can't possibly! I mean, you barely even know me...that much... yet. You care about me, I know, but there's no way you could go as far as to say you love me! It's just too soon, right?" I stared into his eyes, trying to make sense of his confession.

"Okay. I guess I must be wrong then. I will look forward to seeing you tomorrow. Do you want me to pick you up in the morning so we can go visit Miss Corrie? I'll have to get your parents' van back to them too." He went on like nothing happened. He never appeared to be disappointed or upset at all, by any of it.

"Sure. Yeah," I said. It was all I could get out considering I was still stunned.

"Great." He kissed me long on my mouth, then ended with another kiss on my cheek, almost to prove he wasn't upset about my "I love you" rebuttal. "Get some rest. It's late. See you in the morning around ten." He let me go and sauntered down the steps with a light and airy rhythm. I stood there until he drove away, dumbfounded.

Joshua picked me up the next morning, right on time, and even though I had slept soundly, I still managed to relive the events from the day in my dreams. I couldn't figure out what possessed Joshua to think he loved me. I was blown away by his bravery, but I was convinced he couldn't possibly be sure about his feelings for me, not yet anyway. As I looked at myself in the mirror before he arrived, I let myself daydream about what a life with Joshua could look like. I shook my head, trying to shake out the desire for the daydream to come true.

In my ever-changing world of anxiety, I didn't feel like marriage or wife material. I guess dating Joshua was futile since I wasn't marriable, but I enjoyed his company so much. I couldn't bring myself to stop going out with him. Plus, with Miss Corrie's situation, we were about to be spending even more time together, so I decided it was better not to muddy the waters with discussion of all my insecurities just yet.

Joshua pulled up, and as I climbed in his truck, he greeted me with a smirk. "Good morning! Man, I love you...in that outfit!"

"Ha. Ha." I laughed as I leaned over and kissed him on his cheek. "Good morning to you too."

Joshua had a way of disarming me and making me feel safe, no matter what the circumstances were.

When we arrived at the hospital, we both realized it was Sunday. We were so tired from the night before, neither of us remembered to go to church that morning.

"Miss Corrie is *not* going to be happy with us," Joshua warned as we neared her room.

Miss Corrie was sitting with her bad ankle propped up on a pillow under a tissue thin hospital blanket. She looked much improved from the night before but still had tired circles under her eyes. The bump on her forehead had turned a deeper purple overnight.

"Hi, you two!" she cheerfully called out as we peered around the corner to be sure she was awake.

"Good morning to you! How'd you sleep last night?" I went over to give her a hug.

"Oh, this annoying bed just kept moving on me, and I think it ran out of air in the middle of the night. I felt like I was sleeping on an inflatable cracker!"

"Any word on when you can break out of here?" Joshua settled into the recliner in the corner. It was obvious he was still worn out from the night before.

"The doctor came and checked on me this morning and told me I should be good to go home by tomorrow. I think he wants to be sure they have my cast set correctly."

She was still hooked up to an IV, which was odd, considering she had only broken her ankle. But I didn't ask about it because I figured I didn't know what I was talking about when it came to medical matters. We played a couple games of Rummy, and she beat both of us.

"Joshua, are you hungry?" My stomach growled loud enough for him to hear.

"I guess, but by the sound of your stomach, you *definitely* are."

"I will warn you both, the food in this hospital is mediocre at best. I could really go for a biscuit. Would either one of you feel like running out to get one for your broken-down friend?" Miss Corrie made a pathetic attempt at pouty lips.

"I'm happy to go get one for you and for all of us." Joshua took our orders and headed out to save us from starvation.

Soon after he left, I caught Miss Corrie staring at me from the bed with a vague grin on her face.

"What's that look for?"

"So..." She drew out the word and let it hang between us. "How are you two doing? How was your weekend, before I ruined it?"

I pulled my chair closer to her bed, unable to hold back my girlish grin. "Miss Corrie, I can't even tell you how wonderful he is. Truly. He has a way about him that's so comforting and calming, and—"

"Which you need, dearest."

"I know, I know. I do need that. Anyways, last night...he... Well, he...he told me he loved me! Can you believe that? After only knowing me this short time, he tells me something like that."

"So, my dearest, how do you feel? How did you respond?" Her eyes twinkled in anticipation.

"I told him there was no way that was true. Miss Corrie, he doesn't know me that well. He knows me a little, but there's a lot going on that he may not want to handle once he figures out what's inside. I have to give him an out, and if I indulge him, it will only make things more difficult in the long run." I tapped my head as I explained my reasons for being unlovable.

"Stringing him along is a better solution then?" she asked seriously.

"I'm not stringing him along! I'm just…giving it some time. I don't want him saying something like that until he really means it. He doesn't have all the information yet to make that kind of decision." I sat back in my chair with my arms wrapped around myself in a defensive hold.

"Who are you to decide that for him? He was saying what he felt, and let me tell you, he is not the type to go blurting things out on a whim. He is a calculated young man who makes decisions carefully. If you're not interested in him, the kindest thing to do is to let him go. You date for a husband, my dear, not just for the attention. Tell me, do you love him, or do you think you *could* love him one day?"

I sat up and put my hand on her wrist as it lay next to her leg in the bed. I thought for a minute and listened to hear what my inner voice had to say. All I heard was, *I'm not wife material. I am broken. I am faulty.*

"I think… yes. I care deeply for him, but that's not the issue. The issue is that the real Naomi may not be what he wants for his future. Maybe right now he thinks so, but that may not last once he gets to know me better. I'm just trying to prepare myself and be realistic."

"Do you want to know what I think?"

"I know you'll tell me no matter how I answer, so go ahead." I huffed.

"I think you're terrified this might actually work out. I think you're looking for him to find something wrong with you because at the end of the day, you don't feel worth loving. Until you rest in the love Jesus has for you, you will never feel good enough for anyone. Joshua is a man who will love you and take care of you, no doubt about it. You just have to be willing to accept you have a Savior who died for you because He loves you, and it appears He sent a man who will love you here on earth as well." Her eyes looked misted, as she rested her hand on the top of mine for a moment.

I sat there absorbing her words and wisdom like I had many times before. When she finished, a middle aged, but wrinkled looking doctor in a white lab coat entered the room, catching her off guard.

"Hi, Dr. Madden! How are you this fine day? Naomi, be a dear heart, and find me a Dr. Pepper to go with my biscuit. I could really use the caffeine today."

I nodded politely and left the room. I walked the halls, staring at the floor and trying hard not to imagine all the germs lurking there. I'd have to wash my shoes when I got home to remove the vomit and excrement I was undoubtedly picking up with every step. I found a vending machine at the end of the hall and got us each a Dr. Pepper with change from my purse. I stood in front of the machine staring at it while replaying Miss Corrie's words in my head.

Maybe she was right. Maybe I *was* afraid of Joshua's acceptance and how my future could look with him in it. The lies began to creep in.

But I won't make a good wife. I'll end up messing things up somehow. Who wants to marry someone who can't use a hammer, thinks there's vomit on every surface, and obsesses about what people think about them all the time? What if he wants kids? I'd be a terrible mother. What if I hurt one of our children or mess them up with all my fears about germs?

I shook my head, balanced the sodas in my arms, and slowly walked the hall. I made my way past the nurse station back to Miss Corrie's room as Dr. Madden glanced at her medical chart. His eyes met mine, and he looked back toward Miss Corrie.

"Have you told your friend here about your diagnosis?" he asked bluntly.

"I was planning to but haven't found a good moment to tell her." Miss Corrie looked suddenly ash colored.

"What diagnosis? She fell. Did the fall do more damage than I'm aware of?" I stared at the doctor, gripping one of the cold cans tighter.

"Miss, Ms. Dean has Multiple Sclerosis. She will be severely impaired in a matter of a year or so. She appears to have a more aggressive version of the disease, so her prognosis isn't great. She fell because her muscles are weakening, and she was likely overworking herself. She's getting to the point where being alone is unwise. She assured me she's made appropriate plans for her care, so I'm surprised she hasn't told you anything. I'm so sorry I had to be the one to tell you. Will you be able to care for her at home in a few weeks, after she completes her short-term recovery in a rehabilitation center?" His words were beginning to sound like useless noise instead of helpful information.

Before I could answer him, Joshua came in with the bag of biscuits. He must've been able to tell I was upset because he made a beeline for me and the babbling doctor. "Is everything okay in here?"

"Everything is fine, I assure you. She's just digesting some news is all." Miss Corrie blinked rapidly and crossed her arms across her chest.

"Um...well...no...things are *not* fine. She has...what disease is it again?" The Dr. Pepper can shook in my hand.

"She has an aggressive form of Multiple Sclerosis. Her muscles will soon begin to malfunction. She will lose her ability to speak and will likely need full time care in the near future." The doctor spoke like Miss Corrie wasn't in the room, which was annoying.

"When did you learn about this Miss Corrie?" Joshua's face was stiff and serious, and I could tell he was as upset as I was to learn she kept her illness from us.

"I've actually known for about two years, give or take." Her voice was muffled behind a pillow that was pressed to her chest.

"Her decline has been slow so far, but about six months ago it began to speed up. She promised me she had made arrangements for herself. I assumed you two were part of those arrangements." Dr. Madden was speaking to us like we should've known Miss Corrie was hiding things from us.

"Thank you for getting us in the loop, Dr. Madden. We will be sure and work with her to get her the care she needs as best we can," Joshua said as he placed the bag of biscuits on Miss Corrie's lap.

Dr. Madden nodded then left the room slowly, reading her chart as he walked out. He was unfazed by the heaviness of the conversation and appeared unscathed by the severity of his words to us.

"I can't believe this! I guess it makes sense, though. Your overall health has definitely gone downhill since I started working for you last year, but you never told me anything, so I assumed you were fine." Joshua flopped into the recliner next to her bed.

"What he said isn't good, Miss Corrie. It isn't good at all," I said, my voice quivering.

"I know, it's not good, but I have a plan, so no worries." She kept talking as she started eating her biscuit as though we were discussing what clothes she would wear next week, not how she planned to manage the rest of her life with a debilitating disease.

"This *is* a big deal. What are you going to do? How are you going to take care of yourself?" I asked abruptly and slightly agitated.

"What Naomi means is, what can we do to help you? We're honored to be in your life and want to help you as best we can, but it sounds like you're going to need quite a bit of care." Joshua cut his eyes at me.

He asked all the right questions when all I could focus on was the betrayal of her not telling us she was sick. She felt free to speak into my messy life whenever she saw fit but wouldn't extend the same level of intimacy in our friendship by sharing about her mess in return.

"Dearests, there is no rush to make a decision here. I'll go to rehabilitation like the good doctor ordered. Then I'll head home. I'll take it from there. It's not your job to solve my problems for me. I can call in nurses as I need to, and it'll all be fine. Okay guys? Everything will be fine," she said with one heavy nod.

Obviously, she already had time to deal with her diagnosis, but I felt like the rug had been pulled out from under me. The three of us ate our biscuits in silence. Before we left, Joshua and I made a plan to go visit her in rehab. It would likely be a few weeks before she could return home, so I wouldn't be working for a while. I hugged her when I left but felt empty as I did. My perfect mentor wasn't so perfect after all. She was human and broken, just like me. Could I still trust her words of wisdom?

After parking the van Joshua stayed at my apartment for the afternoon so we could watch television and unwind after our stressful couple of days. It was nice to relax together without anyone else around. We hadn't had much time alone. Joshua introduced me to *The Office* — his favorite show. We sat together and indulged in the mindless drama, ate pizza, and tried to forget the serious topics of the day.

Over the next couple of weeks, he made a habit of coming over after work to have dinner with me and my family, or we would meet up and watch television at his house. We didn't go on extravagant dates or talk about deep things. Our time together was relaxed and simple. Even so, I woke up each morning excited, anticipating what we would do that evening.

Joshua was good about checking in with me in the morning, and we would banter sarcastically back and forth throughout the day via text messages. He was still sometimes hard for me to read. There were times he was very intentional about the conversation topics he chose and other times he simply wanted to sit peacefully in my company. He could be affectionate, but when he was focused on work or sports, or had something on his mind, he treated me more like a friend. Those moments left me feeling uncertain about us because he didn't need reassurance from me about my feelings for him. I knew he cared about me, but after having rejected his profession of love, I wasn't sure he would be brave enough to try telling me again. I cared deeply for him, but I didn't know when to start characterizing those feelings as love.

We often visited Miss Corrie together or took turns checking on her. Nothing more was mentioned about what was discussed in the hospital. I was in denial, hoping that somehow the diagnosis was wrong, and she'd be healthy for longer than the doctor predicted. Our main focus was helping her get well enough to be sent home as soon as possible.

She was becoming an ornery patient who made it obvious to anyone who cared for her that she did not want to be there anymore. The nurses drew straws to determine who would have to handle her, and therapists hated working with her because she claimed she already knew what to do. I brought in cookies, donuts, and coffee for the staff in appreciation of their hard work as they cared for our dear-yet-difficult friend.

The Saturday before Miss Corrie was scheduled to be sent home, Joshua invited me to a concert at a local bar downtown. A heavy metal band he liked was playing there that night, and he wanted to see them perform. It was getting warmer outside, and flowers were finally beginning to peek out. The days were getting longer, and the sky was more often than not a deep but bright blue, a welcome contrast to the drab grays of winter. He also invited Beau and Shana to the concert. Beau and Joshua had different interests, but they liked the Lang girls and loved the Lord. With those important things in common, they had an easy time together.

"This place is, I'd say, interesting. What's with all the rusty, old license plates on the wall?" Beau looked the place over with a critical eye.

He was looking dapper in a pair of blue jeans and white collared shirt. The left pocket of the back of his pants was stretched out and worn from his wallet. I noticed it the first time I met him and told Shana it made him look like a bona fide man, not a boy. My sister wore her curly, brown hair down her back with a few wisps pulled up at the top of her head held with a single bobby pin. She wore cowgirl boots and an adorable red with orange striped flannel shirt. They were the perfect couple together, alike in how they valued productivity and truth, while living generously for others. Her beautiful oval diamond glistened in the neon lights as she hung her arm over Beau's shoulders. They'd be married in a month, and it was obvious they were counting down the days.

"I certainly don't come here for the aesthetics, that's for sure. The band we came to see is called The Derby Boys. I was friends with all the members in college and went to most of their gigs back then. I even stood in as a bass player a few times when they needed someone to fill in. The guys still play a random show at dives like this because they love music so much. Most of them are married now, but I don't think their wives come to these late night shows anymore."

Joshua crinkled his nose as he gave the room a slow once over. "This place does seem a little raggedy doesn't it? I don't remember it feeling quite so disgusting when I was in college."

"I like it. It smells like an armpit mixed with dirty gym socks. What could be better?" I jabbed him with my elbow.

Truth was, I was going to have to take an extra hot shower later to get the grimy stink out of my hair and scrub doubly hard to wash away the contaminated funk of this place.

The band started to play, and the sound made the walls shake. The vibrations shot through the floor and up to our feet.

"Hey, let's get up closer!" Joshua grabbed my hand to bring me up to the front with him. His thumb brushed over the crusty scabs and bumpy scars on the tops of my hands, and he brought his gaze up to meet mine.

During warmer weather, I wasn't able to hide them by covering them with the ends of my long sleeves anymore. I stopped cold and returned his gaze while doing my best to hide my intense embarrassment. I knew he was aware of the deeper struggles I had, yet he still kept choosing to take my hand and spend his quality time with me. Maybe he really did care for me as deeply as he claimed so early in our relationship.

He hadn't mentioned the "I love you" incident again and seemed to have moved on like it never happened. He didn't appear upset or hurt by my response either. His patience with me was astounding.

"This music is...loud!" Shana shouted at me as she danced. She could be counted on to dance with me any time, and we enjoyed cutting loose on the dance floor whenever the opportunity presented itself.

"I can't believe he likes this kind of music!" I hollered back as the guitars shrilled and the drums pounded away.

Joshua was bouncing in place while bobbing his head up and down with the rhythm of the music. I could tell he knew the song because he was faintly mouthing the words. I wasn't sure what the words were, because they sounded like a bunch of screams and screeches to me. More and more people began to gather on the dance floor, and what had started as a small crowd had now grown into a multitude of grimy, smelly, intoxicated college students.

I kept close to Joshua and Beau because the magnitude of bodies was beginning to squish us. During the fourth song, a mosh pit broke out. A couple of young college boys began pushing one another back and forth in what looked to be the beginning of a fight. People began running purposefully into each other, then forcefully pushing each other away. It was a swarm of chaos all around us, and suddenly I was drowning in a sea of out-of-control people.

I could no longer see Beau, Shana, or Joshua, so I started calling out their names as I was being jostled about in the savage blob of humanity. A young man came hurtling toward me with his hands out ready to give me a swift thrust in my chest when, out of nowhere, Joshua flew in front of him with his body locked in place to absorb the impact. He pushed the boy away from me first then began clearing a path for me to escape by continuing to shove away anyone who was even remotely close to me.

I made my way to the side of the dance floor and spun around to see Joshua with his arms up ready to take out any other threats in my direction. The floor still rumbled with the writhing mosh pit, and the crowd had begun to lift crazed fans over their heads while the band raged on unfazed.

"I'm so sorry, Naomi! I don't know what happened there. Are you okay?" Joshua put his arms on my shoulders and rubbed them slightly while we both panted and caught our breath.

I stood there and gazed at him, taking in his masculinity and strength. He had just protected me from harm once again. It seemed he was consistently finding ways to love me well. And no matter what part of my brokenness showed, he still accepted me. I knew in that moment that I did, in fact, love him.

"I love you, Joshua," I said at normal volume.

"What? Did you say something? I can't hear you in all this racket," he shouted back.

"I said, *I love you!*" I shouted as the band ended the song, and the room went almost completely silent.

Joshua stood in front of me while the crowd gave a quick "aww," before the band began to jam again.

He looked deeply in my eyes and smirked a nervous smile. "What? I'm sorry. Can you say that, like, one more time? I don't think I got that."

"I know you heard me that time. I said, I love you. I really do. And no, it's not too soon to say it. I hope I didn't blow my chances with you after my reaction when you shared your feelings with me the first time." I stared at the floor.

"Oh, don't worry. I knew you were wrong, so I just kept right on loving you and simply didn't fill you in on it anymore. I knew you felt the same way I did but hadn't put all the pieces together. I figured I could wait. You're worth it." He hugged me, then kissed my neck tenderly. I felt like it was Christmas morning, a bundle of anticipation.

"Are you guys okay? We got stuck in that corner over there and couldn't find our way back to y'all. This place is full of people!" Shana practically ran into us.

"I had to give a couple kids a decent kick in the pants to get them out of our way. Phew!" Beau shook his head. "And congrats on the love thing. We were close enough to hear the announcement," he said with a grin.

"Thanks. I definitely didn't mean for that to go as public as it did." I buried my face in Joshua's side.

"I guess that means you're more than just her plus one for our wedding now, wouldn't you say Joshua?" Shana patted Joshua on the shoulder.

"Your wedding will be a lot of fun. I'm sure I'll have the best-looking date in the place," Joshua slung his arm over my shoulder.

"I'm going to have to disagree with you on that one. I'm pretty positive I'll be the guy leaving with the best broad in town that night," Beau argued with a hefty nod toward Shana.

She blushed and put her arm in his, melting into him. She was beaming.

It looked as though the Lang girls had pretty great taste in men, and I was flabbergasted that I was standing next to a man who fit so seamlessly into my disorderly existence.

Miss Corrie got word to me that it was time for her to go home from the rehabilitation center, and even though she was still compromised, her ankle had healed enough that she could walk with crutches around her house. She had gained some strength back, and her bruises were now a faint green instead of the eggplant purple they had been for some time.

She had hired physical and occupational therapists to come a couple of times a week to check on her and help her recovery. I knew I would have to discuss her future with her at some point, but I held back because I didn't want to have to tell her "no" if she asked me to help in a way I wasn't capable of or comfortable with. It didn't take any time or effort before Miss Corrie and I got back into a rhythm again.

She moved even more carefully and more at a snail's pace than she ever had before. She would hold onto the furniture around her as she stepped, cautiously weaving her way from one part of the house to another. I felt tempted to keep my hand under her elbow, but if I ever started assisting her, she would immediately shrug off my hand and give me a feisty little jab with her fist.

She asked me to start selling some of her hoarded items on Craigslist to help clear out her home and make it less cluttered. She would give me one of the countless little knickknacks she'd collected over the years, and I would either keep it, give it away, or throw it out. Once, she bequeathed to me a giant clown doll with a bright orange afro and unsightly grin. It was handmade by someone she knew in France. That doll should never serve as decoration and promptly met the bottom of my garbage can.

Beau generously came with his construction talents and built a ramp up to her front door so she wouldn't have to navigate steps. It would also come in handy if she began to need a wheelchair, for easy access. Miss Corrie didn't like that ramp one bit, but I think deep down she knew it was necessary.

"You are so kind to help me get settled back here after all this craziness. You and Joshua have been more than gracious to me. I really appreciate it," Miss Corrie shared one afternoon over tea.

"We love you, Miss Corrie, and we want you to be safe and well cared for. I know you'd do the same for me. You've loved me pretty well, I guess I can return the favor if I have to," I teased.

"Would you mind helping me pack up some clothes, dearest? I need to get rid of a lot of the clothes I saved over the years. Most will likely never go back in style. They are up in the attic and need sorting."

"Absolutely. Maybe you've got something I could start a new trend with!" I joked as I pulled down the cord for the attic overhead.

We spent the afternoon organizing and sorting clothes from all the decades Miss Corrie had lived. Bell-bottom pants, hats with feathers, disco sparkle tops, and more plaid than I could stomach. Miss Corrie would defend every tacky item with a vengeance while I would do my best to stifle my giggles.

I had just run into the kitchen to grab another garbage bag when I saw a framed picture of Miss Corrie and George hanging on the wall in a spot I had never noticed. It must have been hiding behind stacks of paper before now. In the crisp black and white photo, Miss Corrie had her bouquet of flowers in one hand, waving them up over her head as though she was cheering. George had a broad smile as he jumped in the air, feet tucked up behind him. Their expressions were priceless. It was beyond question that Miss Corrie and George had loved each other, and the authenticity of their love was captured in this candid photo. I took it off the wall and was studying it when Miss Corrie came shuffling into the room.

"Whatcha got there?" She slid by me on her way to sit down.

"This wedding picture of you and George. It's so sweet. Your dress is gorgeous too. Vintage."

"Everything from my time is vintage. Even I'm vintage now." She frowned. This recent fall had taken a bit of Miss Corrie's spunk away, and I was having a difficult time drawing her out of herself.

"Well, I think you look gorgeous. I will totally wear a dress like that someday…if I ever get the chance." I hung the frame back gently back in its prized place. "You seem so happy and free. I mean, you both look full of love."

"Oh yes, I did love him. I'm glad he doesn't have to watch me deteriorate though. It would have been torture for the both of us. I guess God knew what He was doing when He took George from me earlier than I wanted." She spoke to the floor instead of to me, with a seriousness I'd never heard from her before.

I set my hand on top of hers feeling courage surge up to my mouth. It was time for me to ask the question I'd been patiently waiting to ask. "Miss Corrie, why didn't you tell me about your diagnosis?"

"Oh dearest, I guess there was a portion of me that didn't want to believe I was actually going to begin declining. I prayed for God to heal me, and He is choosing not to. I don't have to like what He's choosing to do, ya know? He lets me speak to Him freely, so that's exactly what I do. I've done my fair share of shouting at the stars over all this. I trust He will provide help for me...and for you too, my dear. Never hesitate to ask for help when you need it, ever. He gave me you. And He gave me Joshua. He gave you Joshua too, didn't He?"

I blushed as she mentioned his name. "Yes, he has been a precious friend to both of us."

"I don't recall Joshua ever telling me he loved me like he told you, dearest. I'd have to argue the two of you are more than just friends." She gave me the first full smile I'd seen from her all day.

We ended our day having tea and talking about her wedding day. George was late for the ceremony because he had gotten lost on his way to the church. Miss Corrie was so mad at him for not planning ahead that she gave him a love punch on the shoulder when she finally reached him at the altar. Miss Corrie always knew how to captivate me with her stories, and on this particular afternoon, I felt the need to soak them in even more than usual.

Nine

SHANA'S WEDDING SHOWER had finally arrived, and as the Maid of Honor, I was responsible for planning and executing the whole event. Despite all the struggles with Miss Corrie and the chaos she brought to my life, the shower was precisely what I needed to keep my busy brain on pause. I had started to attend church more steadily and could tell that God was speaking into my life.

Like Miss Corrie, He wasn't removing the thorn from my side, but He was graciously giving me times of reprieve and new ways to cope. There were even times when Joshua and I were together that I would physically twitch at an awful image or feeling as it flashed through my mind or appeared on television, but Joshua never called me out or acted uncomfortable. His grace and patience with my quirks seemed unreal to me.

Shana's shower was a hit. After the last guest left, she and I were busily loading all her loot into Beau's truck when Joshua pulled up. He was coming to help me clean up the massacre of heart-shaped paper plates, wrapping paper, and garbage left strewn all over my mother's living room. As we were putting the living room back together, he was noticeably more quiet than usual. There were days he wasn't in the mood to talk as much, and I figured today was one of those days, so I left him to his thoughts as we worked. Out of the blue, he asked me a question I was not in any way prepared for.

"Naomi, what are all the scratches on your hands from?" The question hung in the air like a hot-air balloon. "I don't mean to pry, and I'm certainly not trying to call you out on something that will make you uncomfortable, but I do wonder what you're doing to yourself. I'm sorry for putting you on the spot like this." He sat down on the couch and rubbed his fingers through his hair.

I made my way next to him and sat down carefully. "Joshua...I feel so...embarrassed. I thought you might have noticed them. I don't know if I'll be able to fully explain why I scratch myself because I don't really mean to or want to do it."

I can't believe I'm saying this out loud. The words sound awful coming out of my mouth.

"Sometimes, I get these, I dunno, unwanted thoughts, I guess you could call them. I don't really know what to do when I have them, and in the moment I just want to stop them. So, scratching my hand is kind of my way of distracting myself until the thought passes. I'm afraid of what will happen if I don't do it...if I don't stop the thought. I'm not even sure if that makes any sense...like, at all..."

"Yes, that's helpful. I'll confess I can't say I fully understand what you're talking about, but I definitely care a lot. Is there anything I can do to help you?" He studied my face earnestly.

"I wish I knew what could help. Thanks for at least attempting to understand... I'm so embarrassed. I hate having to say it out loud. I'm sorry you have to deal with me like this. I'm sure it's all very confusing for you. I'm sorry." The shame was beginning to take hold of me, and I already knew I would spend hours picking apart the details of my answer as soon as he left.

"You don't need to be sorry. Thanks for trusting me with this. I promise it doesn't change how I feel about you."

I wanted to believe him, but I couldn't help wondering if what he said was true. After we finished cleaning up, I went straight

127

back to my apartment and spent the next three hours pacing the floor, replaying, word for word, all I told Joshua and conjuring up thoughts he likely was having about me. It was self-inflicted torture, but sadly, I was used to it.

The next couple of weeks went by in a hurry. I was finishing up my final semester of school with determination. I studied hard, worked harder, and tried to help Miss Corrie as often as I could. The constant running around was a great distraction, but deep down I knew there were serious issues I was trying to avoid.

Joshua was also working especially long hours since it was flower season, and he had acquired quite a few new accounts. Since he was physically exhausted at the end of every workday, hanging out with me wasn't usually in his plans. We spent time together sporadically, but I couldn't gauge if or how our relationship was progressing. Verbalizing my worries had been challenging for both of us, and Joshua wasn't all that good at reassuring me with his words, so Shana was my sounding board. She'd stay on the phone and listen to me dissect his texts and daydream about comments I wish he'd make.

"Silsta, you have to remember this is a difficult season for both of you. I'm sure whatever you told him is just taking some time for him to digest. I don't like knowing you struggle the way you do either. It's not an easy thing to watch," Shana said one night as we Facetimed to help pick out her clothes for the honeymoon.

She came across confidently in every situation but was continually self-reflecting, looking for how God was changing her. I knew she would help me decipher where I'd gone wrong in this situation but was mostly relying on her to give me the reassurance Joshua wasn't.

My need for reassurance came from the same place as the need to wash my hands a certain amount of times or saying something using just the right words so my world wouldn't fall apart. They were all pathetic and desperate attempts to relieve my fears. These strategies only worked to relieve the anxiety for hours at a time. Then I'd be back to the mental rat race once again. Deep down, I knew I abused Shana with all my over-analysis and oral processing, but she was a willing victim, so I took advantage.

"I know, I know. It's all my fault like it always is. I make life harder for everybody who knows me. The way I operate is hard for people to watch. I get it. Say no more," I threw my hands in the air and rolled off my bed away from the camera.

"You know that's not what I mean. It's not *all* your fault. Everyone in your life cares about you, and we feel like you're working too hard to cope. I don't know what the solution is, but whatever it is, I'm here for you. You know that. Can you come back so I can see you?" Shana was used to my explosions when I felt attacked or felt like I was letting others down.

The truth was, I knew I was a challenge for people and stressed out my family, but hearing it only made me feel more awful about myself. I knew Joshua would feel the strain too, which was why I was apprehensive to date him in the first place.

"I gotta go. I just can't talk about this anymore. I'll see you tomorrow for your dress fitting. If you still want me to come that is. I don't want to ruin your special time with my 'difficult nature.'"

"Don't do that, Naomi. Don't fuss at me then cut me off. I'm not out to get you. Quite the opposite. You ask me for reassurance all the time about things, and I want to give it to you, but then I wonder if I'm just making it worse by indulging your thoughts. Of course, I want you with me tomorrow when I try on my dress. You're my sister! And you're my best friend!"

I knew I was hurting her with my cutting words, but the filter was off, and I was raging.

"I'm obviously not the best kind of friend, the way you make it sound. Like I said, I gotta go." I hung up the phone with a harrumph before she could reply and threw it to the floor.

I hated myself when I acted this way and hated how negatively I affected those I loved, but I felt justified for my nasty attitude, nonetheless. She didn't know what it was like to live with my brain, so how could she possibly have a clue what was good for me? Deep down, I knew what she said was at least somewhat true, but I believed the lies I told myself enough to feel I had a right to act the way I did.

I may have gone to bed fuming, but I woke up feeling lower than a snake's belly knowing how horribly I treated my sister — last night and on countless other occasions. I was well aware that I was not a considerate sister most of the time.

I am a terrible sister. I can't believe she puts up with me like she does. I'm sure she hates me right now.

I had created drama and made it all about myself at a time when I should have been focused on Shana. I didn't want to face her this morning, but I owed it to her to ask for forgiveness. I couldn't eat breakfast because my stomach ached, and I had a cotton ball in my throat. I left my uneaten breakfast in the sink and drove to meet her and my mom at the dress shop.

The two of them were standing in front of the doors waiting for me when I drove up. My heart started to beat faster in my chest. Shana greeted me with her usual warm grin, and I smiled an awkward toothless smile in return. I was sorry for my words, but my heart wanted to still be angry with her for her perfect life. Even though I was well aware of her imperfections, I put Shana on a pedestal despite the fact that she desperately wished to be let down.

"Hey...um...so, I'm really sorry about last night." I wasn't very eloquent, but I could tell she accepted my apology before I even finished.

"I forgive you, Naomi! I'm so sorry too. I didn't mean to make you feel bad about yourself. It's just hard to know what to do sometimes, and you can get so mad at me."

I began to soften as she spoke, realizing again how deeply she cared for me amidst all my quirks. I could count on her, forever. I turned my head away, not wanting her to see my eyes brimming with tears.

"Do you hear me? I love you!" She brought her face close to mine. "You're stuck with me!" She grabbed me in a bear hug.

"I'm just really sorry...really sorry." I sobbed into her shoulder finally letting it all go, and she let me.

"Now, you listen. It's done. She's forgiven you, and we all love you, so let's go get this gorgeous dress, ladies! We've got a wedding coming up in just a matter of weeks and lots of work to do!" Mom clapped her hands and ushered us into the store.

Shana and I let go of one another and dissolved into laughter as she wiped the tears off her shoulder.

"My shirt is soaked! There better *not* be any snot on there! I am the bride after all." She put her nose in the air sarcastically.

We were all still laughing with our arms around each other as the bridal shop attendant came over to greet us.

"Hi, I'm Shana Lang and we're here to try on my dress for the final fitting at 9:30! I promise to be your best customer. But my Maid of Honor here, you have to watch out for her. Hit it Silsta!"

Without skipping a beat, I started humming my pathetic version of a rap beat and dancing. Shana excitedly joined me, hip to hip. We ended in immature laughter as the owners of the bridal shop gave us an unapproving stink eye.

Mom and I sat on an old flame stitch upholstered couch while we waited for Shana to try on her wedding dress. The shop owners hadn't quite forgiven the three of us yet for the initial disruption, but we didn't care because, as Mom would say, we were "making a memory." We chatted over glasses of sparkling grape juice while she changed behind a red velvet curtain in the fancy dressing room. It wasn't a super expensive dress compared to some, but for Shana, this was her dream dress.

She called out from the dressing room, "Y'all ready?"

Mom and I looked at each other, and I could see the anticipation and teary mist building in her eyes. Before we could answer, Shana emerged from behind the curtain in a gorgeous white strapless dress with small flowers embroidered on the bust. The bottom of the satin dress was soft, mildly poufy, with the same flowers embroidered in a perfect circle on the hem. Shana wore a silky veil that barely reached her bustle with a small pearled comb attached to it. The veil lay on the back of the dress like a pillow. Mom pulled a tissue from her purse and dabbed her eyes.

"Mom, are you okay? Why are you crying?" Shana came over to my mom and put her hands on her knees.

"I'm fine, I'm fine! You look so beautiful! I can't believe you're actually getting married! Seems like just yesterday you were born. Take a look at yourself! You're stunning!" Mom sniffled as she pulled herself together from the burst of happy tears.

"I guess you look...*okay*," I exaggerated.

"Ha. Ha." Shana turned around to look at herself in one of the giant mirrors lined up in rows behind her. She gazed at her reflection, perplexed.

"Now I'm going to have to ask *you*, are *you* okay?" Mom walked up behind Shana and put her hands on her shoulders.

"I'm okay. I think I'm in shock that the time is finally here to marry him. We've dated for such a long time, and now we finally get to become husband and wife. We survived our breakup, and God used it to make our relationship stronger, so I think I'm feeling overwhelmed with gratitude." Shana began to tear up, which had Mom grabbing for her tissues again.

Shana and Beau had broken up for a while about a year before they got engaged, and it was heartbreaking, but essential for both of them. Her joy in finally getting to marry Beau came with wounds still freshly healed.

As I stood listening to them gush about her dress and the big day, I felt a heavy thud in my chest. I was overcome with mixed emotions—pure joy for Shana and sadness, fearing I may never get a turn in a white dress. I didn't want to take away from Shana's big moment, so I swallowed the lump and did my best to be present during our time together.

When they were busy fiddling with Shana's hair, trying to figure out how she should wear it, I heard my phone ding from my bag. I was suspicious it could be Joshua, so I rushed over to check.

It *was* a text from Joshua.

Hey you, was all it said.

Hey yourself. I responded with a smiley emoji.

What are you doing tonight? Want to hang out?

Sure. What'd you have in mind?

Basketball, of course.

I was not surprised that watching basketball was his activity of choice for the evening considering the NBA tournament was going on, and he never missed a game. I wasn't a huge sports fan, but I enjoyed watching games with Joshua because he got pretty into them and often shouted at the television, which I found hilarious. It wasn't typical Joshua behavior, but it entertained me to no end.

I was excited to see him, but I also wanted to gauge how he and I were doing on a relational level. I assumed he was either getting comfortable with me or falling out of love with me…

Sounds perfect. See you at 7, your place.

When I pulled up to Joshua's house that night, I could see the television through the window already tuned to the game. Joshua was sitting on the couch with his long arm draped over the back side of the cushion next to him. I felt the urge to have a conversation with him, to make sure he and I were okay, but didn't want to conjure up problems where in reality, there probably were none. My constant need for reassurance about his feelings for me was unhealthy and I didn't want to abuse him like I did Shana or my mom.

I sat in the car for a minute obsessing until Joshua turned and looked out the window. My headlights were shining directly into his living room. *How long have I been sitting here?*

I scrambled for the keys and turned off the car only to look up and see he had already opened the front door and was waiting for me. I fumbled for the door handle, took a deep breath, and got out of the car so clumsily that I got my purse strap stuck in the locked car door. I was rushing to get it back open when Joshua came out to meet me with his hands in his pockets and nothing but socks on his feet.

"Everything okay out here? I was beginning to think you weren't going to come in...or maybe you wanted to watch the game from the car." He hugged me after I finally finished wrestling my purse from the jaws of the evil door.

"I'm totally cool, dude," I said, out of breath.

"Totally cool dude? What are we, like fifteen again?" He gently tickled me under my arm before putting his arm around me. So far, he seemed more engaged in the last two minutes than he had in the past two weeks.

He served us some popcorn, and we settled in to watch the prime games on that night. I did my best to participate, but I spent the majority of the time listening to him yell at the refs or cheer for well executed plays. It was getting late, and I finally mustered the courage to ask about how his life was going in an effort to pry about our relationship's current status.

"How has work been these last few weeks? I haven't heard much from you, and I was beginning to think you'd gotten a new girlfriend." I knew the moment the words came out they were unnecessarily accusatory. I put my hand on my forehead and rubbed it, frustrated with my own lack of discernment.

"Why would I get a new girlfriend? Did you get a new boyfriend?" Joshua asked defensively. *Great, now he's mad.*

"No, I mean, it's just been a little hard to read you is all. I wasn't sure if I'd done something wrong or if you were just busy." I was gasping as I spoke even though there weren't many words.

"Naomi, why would you ask me if I got a new girlfriend? And what exactly do you mean by the statement you can't 'read' me?"

I had never seen Joshua get mad before, but it was obvious that I had struck a nerve. My insecure accusation had successfully instigated what appeared to be our first fight.

"Give me a break, would you? You were working constantly and not all that chatty, like ever. What am I supposed to do with that?" I shot back.

"I don't like to talk on the phone! Sue me! Why does that get interpreted as not wanting to talk to you at all?" His answers were becoming robotic and curt.

"Would it kill you to fill me in on your day every so often? I need a little something from you, especially when we don't have quality time. I'm sorry I said anything." I sat back on the couch with an over dramatic sigh.

We sat quietly for the rest of the game. Joshua was in no rush to talk about our fight, and I sat in the same defensive position with my knees drawn up to my chest. My head was whirling with contradicting thoughts and emotions. I craved his reassurance like a drug. I needed it to survive this relationship, any relationship, and I had no idea how to relate to anyone without it. Finally, I broke the silence because I couldn't take the tension any longer.

"I'm really sorry for my comments. I'm sorry for everything, actually. I shouldn't have said anything. It's all my fault. Sorry I ruined our date." I let the words soak into the air before finally getting up to get a glass of water. I stood at the kitchen window and looked out to the backyard, fighting back the thoughts reeling in my mind.

I'm not good for him. I'm not worth being with because of the wild way I think.

His toolbox sat on the floor next to me. I immediately tensed up. Interrupting thoughts and images of a hammer came blasting in with a fury that made all the muscles in my back tense up like a wall of bricks. I felt a panic attack coming on but attempted to take some deep breaths, hoping to keep the wave from overtaking me.

What if you want to do it? You want to.

No! I don't! That's a lie. Make it stop. Make it stop.

When I got back to the living room, Joshua had turned the television off and was sitting quietly waiting for me. His arm was up over the back of the cushion, serving as an invitation for me to come sit next to him. Suddenly another unwanted thought made its way through my defenses, and before I could stop myself, a compulsive, "please God, no" came whispering off my lips. I sat down silently, paralyzed in the strait jacket of fear.

"You don't need to be sorry for everything. It is *not* all your fault. I could have been more communicative. But when you joked about me getting a new girlfriend, it stung. To me, that's low. You're questioning my character and my loyalty to you. When I said I loved you, Naomi, I meant it. You have to trust me," Joshua spoke gently.

I was hearing his words with my ears but was so overwrought with rapid thoughts, his love wasn't registering. He was giving me the reassurance I craved, yet it wasn't removing my anxiety about his feelings for me like I'd hoped it would. In the same way uttering "please God, no," washing my hands repeatedly, or spending hours replaying conversations in my head only gave me momentary peace, asking Joshua to profess his love for me again and again couldn't permanently relieve my anxiety either.

I believed God was powerful enough to sweep these thoughts away, but He didn't, and I couldn't understand why he let them continue. Miss Corrie always said, "God works in our lives for His glory and our good." How was my constant self-torture glorifying God or good for me? I felt my chest seizing up as Joshua spoke, because as much as I wanted to hear him, all I could focus on were my fears about the dreaded hammer in the kitchen.

"I'm sorry, Joshua. I'm going to let you get back to your game watching. I hope we're okay." I said, half present.

"Yep. We're all good," he replied defeatedly as he took the remote to turn the television back on.

We sat together for a little while longer as my mind raced through hundreds of awful fears about the person I was while Joshua sat dead silent watching basketball. He had done everything I'd asked of him that night. He spoke his feelings to me directly, reassured my self-doubt. I had no need to be insecure, yet his words still weren't enough. His words were in no way filling the holes or calming the storms. Maybe Miss Corrie was right. Maybe Jesus really was the only way to find rest in my weary world. But how was I supposed to rest on Him when so much of this war felt like my fault?

Miss Corrie asked me to drive her to physical therapy the week after that awkward date. Since returning home, she had been settling in well, and even though she was moving more slowly, overall, she made progress. On the ride to therapy, she and I did our usual debrief of our weekends, sharing every detail of our time apart.

Miss Corrie had become a true friend. I never minded spending time with her or listening to her talk. I recently took some of her wise advice and was attempting to pray more regularly, with more authenticity. I told her some of what had gone on between Joshua and me, but to her, the problems were simple and easily corrected. She saw nothing in our relationship for me to be concerned or insecure about, but even her immense confidence left me wanting.

Miss Corrie was walking gingerly still. Even though her ankle had healed, she used a walker in public. I helped her out of the car and got her comfortable with her walker as we made our way into the medical center.

"I don't like my physical therapist. She's fake. Her hair is dyed so blonde and brittle, it would likely set on fire with nothing but a small spark. Would you try to get me that other therapist?" Miss Corrie shuffled her walker inside.

"Which new therapist?" I had escorted Miss Corrie a couple of times to therapy but never went back with her for the appointment, so I didn't know who she was talking about.

"Oh, you know the one. The cute guy with the big blue eyes? You're probably not paying attention since you already have your Prince Charming. If you'd just go ahead and let him sweep you off your feet, you'd be set. But I digress, could you ask at the front desk to see if I can get him to help me instead of the young blondie?" she begged.

"I'll see what I can do. You never cease to amaze me, Miss Corrie, honestly. A hunky male therapist is who you want? You're something else, lady."

I tried to get her the good-looking therapist of her dreams like she asked me to, but the woman at the front desk kindly informed me Miss Corrie had already been told several times he was booked solid and to please stop asking. When I heard this, I turned my head slowly toward Miss Corrie with one eyebrow up. She smirked at me then averted her eyes like a guilty teen, caught but not sorry. I shook my head as I sat down next to her grabbing a *People* magazine.

"I thought maybe you could change their minds with your pretty face, dearest. That's all," she said.

"Yeah right, you goof." I gave her a gentle jab with my elbow.

I tried hard to never be too rough with Miss Corrie after learning of her diagnosis. I didn't want to accidentally cause her more harm or pain. I spent many an evening after my times with her concerned that I'd injured her on the job. I would only get relief from the images in my brain of me harming her when I would see her again.

"I'm going to go see if there's a vending machine. I could use an energy boost. I'll be right back," I said.

"I'll be here, and if I'm not, I'm back in the pit of despair trying to get away with doing as little actual work as possible." She shrugged.

I began my search for a sugary pick-me-up on the first floor of the medical building and got so lost that I ended up on the fourth floor, still with no soda. The hallways all started to look the same, and I was about to give up entirely when a small, but shiny, sign caught my eye. It was placed outside a door to what looked like a regular doctor's office, but when I read the words, they rocked me to my core.

"Stevenson and Stevenson Psychiatric Practice: Helping people find solutions to mental and emotional struggles since 1990."

Find solutions to mental and emotional struggles? Are there really doctors who can do that? I was dumbfounded by this new, yet simple, piece of information. I felt like I had been struck by lightning. It was as if God had pointed a neon arrow directly toward this small silver plaque on the wall, as though this office was the final stop on a treasure map.

I had never contemplated therapy as a source of help for my struggles before that moment, and the sense of possibility filled me with hope. But therapy was for people who were off their rockers, and if I went inside, it would be as though I was admitting to my own abnormal nature. As I stood there like an immovable statue, I realized God was answering my recent emergency prayers for help in an unexpected way.

I had spent my life feeling like a hopeless oddity when all along there were people trained to successfully assist folks just like me, battling similar giants. I wanted desperately to go inside but needed to inspect the types of patients in their waiting room before I pulled the trigger on becoming one of them. There were stigmas that haunt people who sought therapy, and I was fighting the cultural stereotypes.

I peeked through the glass window next to the door and saw an older man looking at his phone casually and a woman in her thirties reading a magazine next to him. They looked relatively normal at first glance, but then again, so did I…on the outside. I felt that if I opened the door, it would be like releasing the seal on a jar closed too tightly. On one hand, there would be a welcome release of the unwanted pressure in my soul. But on the other, did I really want to tackle the fears that held me captive and say them out loud?

I was sure these professionals had likely never seen anyone with fears like mine, but maybe it was worth a try, for the sake of my relationships and my future. I needed to be brave for Joshua's sake too. I took an intentional swelling breath and grabbed the door handle before I lost my nerve. I pulled the door three times before noticing it was, in fact, a push door.

The two patrons in the waiting room looked at me sideways as I walked up to the counter having just made quite a racket with my failed attempts at entry. The woman behind the counter was in her late forties and sported a bouffant hairstyle soaked in sticky hairspray that glistened in the artificial office light. She had a giant mole on her chin, just below her bottom lip sprouting a few stiff hairs.

"May I help you?" she said with a deep New York accent.

"Um…well…maybe," I stammered as I rocked back and forth in rhythm like a child trying to decide what flavor to get at an ice cream shop.

"Are you going to stand there all day?" she asked with growing impatience. Not quite the friendly face I had expected in such an establishment. I was beginning to think this was a bad idea.

I squared my shoulders and took a deep breath. "Yes. You can help me. Is there a doctor or counselor, I guess either one would do, I could make an appointment with?"

"Do you have a referral from your regular doctor?"

"Well, no. I was actually looking for some Pepsi and saw the sign outside your door. I thought I could benefit from the services you provide. Who knew soda could lead to a psychiatrist?" I laughed nervously.

She began to click away on her computer as though she hadn't even heard what I'd said. I could tell she was doing something for me, but since she wasn't saying anything, I was left to stand there uncomfortably, baring my soul to the silent woman behind the counter.

Finally, after what felt like an eternity, she handed me a clipboard containing detailed paperwork and told me to fill it out immediately. The questionnaire was extensive. I had to write about my current physical health, if I was feeling suicidal, how long I'd been experiencing my struggles, and many more specific questions. I didn't want to write any of my fears down, so I chose to acknowledge only the bare minimum. Still, I wrote until my hand started to hurt. Then, I returned to the counter to turn in my clipboard of embarrassment.

"Okay, so you have been scheduled to see Dr. Mary Jo Stevenson tomorrow at nine a.m. Does that time work for you ma'am?" the ornery lady behind the counter asked.

I had to work for Miss Corrie in the morning, but I was sure she would let me come in a little later so I could go to the appointment.

"That should work fine. Thank you for your time," I said with an edge of disbelief that I was actually committing to seeing a therapist.

I wandered my way at a slow and calculated pace back to where Miss Corrie was having therapy. I rehearsed all the ways I would reword my fears to the doctor so I wouldn't sound completely loony or insane. I didn't want to dump every odd thought I'd ever had on this poor woman during our first visit, or to be honest, ever. I knew I would have to be candid with her for therapy to work but hoped simply showing up would be enough to take the edge off. It was Dr. Stevenson's job to fix me, after all, so I'd leave that to her.

Miss Corrie came tottering back to the waiting area with the hot specimen of a therapist on her arm. She had done it again, that tricky broad.

"They finally got some sense and put me with the right man for the job to assist this broken maiden. Thank you, Stuart. I appreciate you being willing to trade patients with your coworkers. You and I are definitely a better fit. See you next time, handsome." She unlatched from his arm and gave him a subtle wave.

"Miss Corrie, how on earth did you get them to let *him* work with you? They told you no so many times!" I whispered as I took her arm tenderly.

"When you got it, honey, you got it!" She laughed softly.

Her physical deterioration couldn't steal away her spunk, but when she was tired, it became more taxing to maintain her energetic glow. As we rode home, I told her all about my accidental discovery on my quest for caffeine. Miss Corrie was elated to hear I decided to follow the leading of the Holy Spirit and actually see the therapist.

"Dearest dear heart, you are going to be so thankful you decided to try this. God is visibly getting your attention. I'll be praying for you in this new endeavor and cannot wait to hear about all you gain from your first appointment." She looked out the window at the trees zipping by.

The shadows from the sun were moving across her face, causing uniquely shaped lights to dance on her forehead. I could tell her strength was minimal because her eyes and lips were twitching as she spoke. She looked like her face was plugged into an electrical outlet. She was aging more by the week, but I refused to accept her spiral into illness was spinning as quickly as it appeared to be.

"I doubt this lady will be able to fix me that easily. She might be good, but she's probably not *that* good of a doctor. You rest, Miss Corrie. You've had a busy morning. We don't have to talk. The silence doesn't bother me." I looked over at her only to realize she had fallen asleep with her head resting gracefully on her seatbelt.

Ten

WE SAT IN dead silence for five whole minutes after our initial cordial introductions. Calming background music filled the room with sounds of instruments and soft singing birds. There was a couch in Dr. Stevenson's room, just as I'd suspected from all the cartoon versions of a therapy office I'd seen.

Dr. Stevenson insisted I call her Mary Jo because she wanted me to feel like I was interacting with a peer, not a stuffy professional. She was one of two psychiatrists in the practice. The other was her cousin, also Dr. Stevenson. Mary Jo was well-trained at sitting unfazed in the lingering silence of the first appointment standoff between patient and doctor. I didn't really know where to begin my story, and although I felt led to initiate the appointment, I was uncertain how many personal details to divulge as I sat there vulnerable.

She had a clipboard on her lap and lightly tapped it with her pen to the rhythm of the music. No doubt she had heard that particular song playing hundreds of times while sitting with various patients. I bounced my legs up and down like I was waiting to get a shot. I felt like a dam, building destructive pressure from the force of the heavy water behind it, desperate to burst open and rush out into freedom. I didn't know what my words would do to the world, how my fears would behave if they made it into the air, out of their locked prison within me. I looked at the clock and realized time was ticking with nothing being accomplished, so I bit the bullet and decided to speak up.

"I guess I should get started on what I'm doing here…wouldn't you say?" I clenched my teeth together, hearing the crunch deep in my ears.

"Of course. I was waiting for you to feel comfortable and to begin when you were ready. I don't like to rush new patients to start talking right away. It can be intimidating to come to a place like this when you haven't had any prior experience with a therapist. You can start with just an overview of what you're struggling with. And don't worry. I've heard it all, so nothing fazes me anymore." She sat back and took a relaxed sip of her coffee like we were old friends.

My mind raced with what to say first, because as much as I wanted to believe she'd heard it all, I had a hard time believing she'd dealt with anyone who had fears as unique as mine.

"I guess I'd say my struggles have to do with being worried all the time. I tend to feel anxious more than I'd like to, or more than my family would like me to. I was hoping you could help me figure out how to stop it." When I got anxious, I spoke very fast, and that morning I was talking a mile a minute.

"What are some of the things you're afraid of?" Mary Jo asked nonchalantly.

There it was. The deep-down question I didn't want to answer. Telling her the truth would be like taking the first step to conquer the peak of my Everest, and I was scared to climb. My insides were on the verge of being brought to light.

"Everything," I said flatly.

"What about everything is scary to you? Could you be more specific?"

I felt like the dam had a hole in it, and the water was beginning to leak out. My desire to just let it burst and flood the whole place was swelling. I wanted to be strategic about what I was saying, but

I could taste the truth rising into my throat. Was I actually on the cliff about to jump? Could I really be on the verge of letting all the disgusting mess out and being free, even if only for a moment?

"By everything, I mean, everything I'm capable of being. Who I am and what my thoughts are made of? I worry that I'm really just a murderer, masquerading as someone who doesn't want to be one. I worry that I'll lose a place in heaven if a bad thought about God even breezes through my brain. I can't even pass a hammer without flinching—physically flinching because I'm afraid of what I might think about or do with it! I try to keep my thoughts under control, but the more I try to contain them, the more senseless thoughts and images come into my mind."

I took a deep breath and forced myself to keep going. "I'm terrified of getting sick...like, all the time. Every surface I touch makes me feel dirty, and I don't feel clean until I've washed any part of me that might be contaminated. My mind never stops racing... *ever*. I never feel like my brain is quiet...*ever*...and sometimes I just want to hear nothing at all. What does a person have to do to get some silence?"

I had worked my way from speaking normally to talking like a machine gun, rapid fire. Mary Jo never changed her expression. She was completely at ease. *Hello? Was she hearing me? Wasn't she worried about what I could do?*

I finished my turn talking with a deep cleansing breath. I had almost begun to cry halfway through my rant but was able to resist the urge by slightly raising my volume.

"Would you say these thoughts are wanted or unwanted?" Mary Jo inquired frankly.

"Absolutely 100 percent UNwanted! Well, I think I don't want them. Yes, at my core, I don't want them. But what's scary is sometimes I think maybe I do want to have the thoughts based on the feelings I may have while I'm thinking them. I convince myself that what I'm feeling is true because my thoughts come from me, so they have to be true, right?"

"Why are you here, Naomi?" she asked.

In that moment, I wondered if my words were computing.

"I'm here because I'm miserable! I am currently in a dating relationship, if you can call it that. I think that's what it is, but I've realized I'm totally not marriage material in my current state. And to someday be a mother, forget it. I couldn't possibly handle that."

My thoughts rudely interrupted. *I would probably accidentally drown my baby. Why do I think things like this? Do I want to hurt a baby? What kind of person am I?*

"I don't like myself like this. I find myself lost in my own fears. It happens so often now, I feel like I'm missing out on life, and I don't want to miss out anymore. I just want confirmation that I *am* all the terrible things I think I am. I'd rather just know so I can do whatever it takes to prevent doing any of the awful things I'm afraid I'm capable of." I took a sip of the water she had offered me when I'd first arrived.

I didn't think I'd want it, but she insisted I take it, and now I was glad she did. After all my confessing, my mouth was as dry as the Sahara. Mary Jo sat in the same position the entire time I spoke. When I was finished, she stood up to get a book from her shelf.

"Naomi, what you're experiencing is easy to diagnose. You've given me plenty of information to, I believe, help you understand why you're suffering. I just have one more question for you. Do you do or say anything to relieve the thoughts and fears you have? Like maybe, wash your hands a certain number of times or repeat a certain phrase or have any routines you absolutely must perform to keep the thoughts from taking over?" She sat with the book in her lap, and I tried desperately to see the title, but couldn't.

"I don't think so. I sometimes ask God for help under my breath in a moment of stress or wash my hands a few extra times to make sure they're completely clean, but everybody does that. I sometimes replay conversations in my head multiple times so I can analyze them and think about my part in the interaction." I didn't know what to do with her question or what my answer would reveal about me.

"What are the marks on your left hand? They look like scratches. Are they from you or from a pet?" She pointed at them with her pen.

I thought about lying and saying my cat did them, but at this point, I had nothing to lose. I had already poured out some of the ugly, so I might as well finish strong.

"Yeah, I make those. I don't do it intentionally. Well, yes I do, but I don't *want* to. I just want the thoughts to stop, so it's like a controlled reflex. That probably sounds like an oxymoron." I shook my head, knowing I was about to receive the worst diagnosis since she had to keep probing me for more shameful details.

"Are there any other routines you need to do to feel productive in your worrying? Anything you feel you must do or say to feel peace in your mind, even if just for a moment? Or do you think performing a ritual prevents something bad from happening?" she pushed.

"No. The only thing I can think of is that I like to ask my mom or my sister about some of my fears…so they can tell me not to be worried. But I don't think that's a routine, is it?"

"When you ask them for reassurance, does it work to relieve the fear? In other words, do you believe what they tell you?"

I was annoyed with how she answered my question with more questions.

"Yes and no. Their reassurance typically helps for a few seconds, but I still end up in a state of worry. Either I go back to worrying about what I originally asked them about, or I start worrying about something new."

Mary Jo wrote on her clipboard every time I spoke. It appeared she was documenting what I was describing, but it felt like I was taking an oral exam, and she was writing my answers.

She flipped through the book on her lap briefly before she began to speak again. "Naomi, what you have is more common than you realize. You have Obsessive Compulsive Disorder. What you have is treatable, with medication and therapy. Your brain is wired differently. You don't produce enough of a certain chemical your brain needs to cope with life. Your body is eating up all your serotonin like candy, and it's not leaving you enough to have a balanced brain, capable of working normally. Hear me when I say that you are *not* the things you are afraid you are. Your thoughts are from your brain, not from who you are inside."

She slipped her shoes off and sat cross legged in the chair, entirely relaxed. "You're distressed by the things you think, and it's obvious by the way you discuss them, but also by how you physically react to discussing them. This entire appointment has been a mild panic attack for you. You've been flush, speaking rapidly, and fidgety. You have lived your life afraid of what you are, and what you are is a person who has been desperately trying to cope with an extremely challenging condition."

Mary Jo spoke with conviction in a way she hadn't the rest of our time together. I heard her, but I wasn't sure she understood me completely.

"So, do you *really* understand what I'm telling you about the thoughts I have? You're saying this, and you just met me. I haven't even described in detail all the awful images I've had. I bet once I did, you'd change your opinion and see how bad of a person I am." I sat back against the couch for the first time that morning, needing her to think again.

"Naomi, you can try to convince me that you're all the awful things you say you are, but it won't change my diagnosis. The truth is you are a classic OCD case. I'm happy to tell you that you're wrong. Your brain is lying to you. Your thoughts are lies. You will, however, be able to learn to face the world with strategies that will help you cope with the real hardships of life, no longer the made-up ones of your imagination. We can work together to identify the voice of your OCD and the voice of the real Naomi. You'll have a lot of free time. Call that boyfriend of yours, tell him you'll be able to go on more relaxing dates." Mary Jo put the clipboard on her desk.

"Wait. Are you telling me there's a reasonable explanation for why I think the way I do? Are you certain of this? How do you know that? What if you're still not understanding me?" I asked in disbelief. Surely she was mistaken.

"Naomi, I've been doing this a long time, and I'm quite certain this is what you suffer from. I can see even now you're using me as a compulsion to relieve your anxiety. You're asking, 'but what if,' which is a classic OCD tendency. You feel like you need me to say the facts over and over in order for them to be true, but it's been true this whole time, and it's alright to accept it. I understand your brain, Miss Lang. It's nothing new to me, and I want to help you. Rest in that fact." Her lips curled into a kind smile. "Let's start with some anti-anxiety medication, and then we'll continue with therapy."

I could tell we were about out of time, but I didn't want to go yet. I was oscillating between wanting to stay to ask more questions and staying to convince her she must be wrong.

"What does therapy involve?" I asked as she handed me my prescription.

"In therapy, I'll give you strategies to help when you feel panicked or overcome with rapid thoughts. You'll expose yourself to things you're afraid of and learn to face the anxiety gradually. You and I will be able to discuss those experiences here in counseling, and you will grow to see that your thoughts hold no power over you. We'll talk about the fears you have and why you have them. We'll dig to find the root of them. You'll learn how those fears are, in fact, lies. It'll be a process, but the medication will allow your brain to rest, so you can actually use the strategies. It'll be a team effort." She pointed back and forth at the two of us as she grinned.

"I feel so... I don't know...mixed up. Relieved, hopeful, doubtful, and thrilled all at once. Is that normal?" I got up off the couch and gathered my things to go, realizing the hour we were together had flown by.

"What you're feeling is to be expected. Get those meds, start taking them, and rest in the diagnosis. You are so much more than OCD, Naomi, and you've got a bright life ahead of you. It'll take some work, but anything good does. Right?" She gave me a friendly side hug.

"Thank you so much for your time, Dr. Stevenson," I said with newly planted calm in my voice.

"That's Mary Jo. You're going to be getting relief soon. It'll be a couple weeks before the anti-anxiety medicine takes full effect, so call us if you need us. Make sure you make an appointment for next week for our first counseling session. I'm glad you found us." She walked away down the hall.

I checked out and made my next appointment, still baffled by what I'd been told.

Relief? Had she really said I was going to get relief? That's what she said, right? Maybe I heard her wrong. I should ask her again.

I followed her down the hall. "Are you sure I'll be getting relief? Like, from all my thoughts, or will the bad ones stay because they are who I am?"

"Naomi, by asking me again, you're 'checking,'" She air quoted the word as she explained the behavior. "Checking is when you feel an overwhelming desire and need to hear the truth with the hope it will make you feel less anxious. You aren't able to trust the facts because your mind is trying to convince you that you're wrong about what you think. You heard me the first time, but I'll say again that yes, you will be getting relief from your unwanted thoughts. Checking will be a temptation you'll be learning how to resist," she answered as she headed back to her office.

She listened to what I said for the entire appointment. She'd heard about the thoughts in my head, and she still thought I was savable.

Did I include enough details? Was I honest enough about what I think about? What if she misunderstood? No! There is an actual medical reason for my suffering. I could hardly believe what had transpired in the last forty-five minutes.

I sat at the wheel of my parked car with my hands firmly placed at ten and two, like I was waiting for the checkered flag to wave at the start of a race. As I stared up at the clouds floating above me, I got the same sensation of a blanket being wrapped around my soul like I had the day before wandering the halls of the medical center. God had answered my prayers for aid and even given me a name for what I was experiencing. I trusted He had called me to that office for an appointment, but I didn't really believe Dr. Stevenson would be able to do much for me. Boy, was I wrong! I was blown away by how He provided that day.

Miss Corrie was thrilled with the diagnosis and brewed a celebratory pot of tea for us to enjoy as we made toasts of exaggerated joy by clinking our glasses. She was supportive in a quirky and endearing way that allowed me to fully enjoy the party we were throwing for ourselves. On that particular afternoon, I was content in my own skin for the first time I could remember in a long time, which was as refreshing as the mint tea we were drinking.

I woke up that day with a familiar void tempting me to fill it with worry, but at least now I knew the reason for my fears and the name of the enemy. I also knew God was calling me to rest in more than the diagnosis He had brought to light. God was calling me to rest fully in Him, no matter what the circumstance, and give all of my life to Him.

It was one week before Shana and Beau's wedding, and my parents' house was transformed into wedding central. There were whimsical decorations piling up all over their living room, dresses hanging from doorways, and lists of things to do piling up by my mother's calendar. Shana called me and asked if Joshua and I could get together with Beau and her to play some cards as means to relieve the constant stress brought on by the upcoming wedding.

I had been taking anti-anxiety medication for about ten days and had been to see Mary Jo a couple of times for counseling. Already I could sense the easing of tension in my whole being, even as I began fighting against the OCD. I found myself getting lost in a television show or a book without any interruption of unwanted thoughts. It unnerved me at first to have this newly acquired mental free time, but it didn't take me very long to appreciate the silence in my soul.

Joshua and I were in a settled routine. He was a subdued guy, and even though I couldn't always read him, I felt vaguely confident he still wanted to be with me. I could never be absolutely sure how to interpret him, especially since learning in therapy I had an unhealthy need for reassurance. I had only just begun therapy, but already I was learning that my brain worked sideways a lot of the time.

"Welcome to our future nest!" Shana met us at the door and hugged me tight.

She and I had chatted on the phone about my appointment, and she was elated that I had gotten some answers. She advised me to tell Joshua as soon as I could, but I was hesitant to open up until the right moment presented itself.

The four of us decided to hang out in the bachelor pad apartment that Shana and Beau would live in once they were married. It had been Beau's home as a single man, so there was a need for a feminine touch. A deer head hung in the middle of the living room wall, and a bear skin rug welcomed us. There were a few oddly placed camouflaged pillows on the couch as well. The apartment looked more like a male sanctuary than a home for newlyweds.

"This place cracks me up, Shana. When are you going to get in here and spruce it up a bit?" I ran my fingers along the edge of the tattered American flag that hung by the door.

"You listen here. This place has got a lot of style. I'm sure Shana will add her own special touch, but overall, it's got a natural charm we both like. Right Shana?" Beau handed Joshua a Coke looking for agreement.

Shana just shook her head and shrugged.

"Yeah man, this place is certainly memorable. Any woman would be lucky to land here. Shana, I think you should move that rug into your master suite. It would be quite a piece to sleep under. You'd never get cold." Joshua laughed and popped the cap on his drink.

"I'll make this place beautiful. Trust me. It's going to need just a bit of elbow grease and a whole lot of femininity." Shana cupped her chin with the back of her hands as she batted her eyelashes.

We all sat down at the table to play Rook, our favorite card game. Shana and I partnered up and the guys worked together to beat us every single time. And this time was like any other. Shana and I got way too full of ourselves being silly and immature, while the men sat shaking their heads at our antics, silently creaming us.

It started to get late, and the discussion turned serious when Joshua asked a deeper question than our usual card chatter. "I know you two broke up for a while. What happened—if you don't mind me asking? I've never heard the whole story."

Shana looked at Beau as if to say, "you can handle this one," and took a sip of her root beer.

"Let's just say, she and I needed some time to figure out what it is that made us good together. It was really hard to be apart, but we knew if we were meant to be together, God would bring us back to each other. Wouldn't you say that was it, Boogs?" Beau said with a casual drawl. Instead of calling her sweetheart or sweetie he called her "Boogs," I never knew why.

Shana took a deep breath and thought for a moment. "Sometimes two people need to be on their own to figure their hearts out before they commit to forever as man and wife. I didn't want to break up, but I knew Beau needed time to reflect on his life and what he wanted in a wife. I didn't want to be with someone who wasn't ready to be with me fully, so I knew I had to let go. I learned during that time I needed to change the expectations for our relationship and rely on God for my contentment. We both grew in our faith while we were apart. Much to our surprise and excitement, He restored our relationship after a couple of months. I think we're stronger because of that time apart, even if it was torture." She winked at Beau.

"Right. I agree. I hated to break her heart, even for a short time, but I knew I couldn't be with her unless I was sure I was ready for forever with her." He put his hand on Shana's. "She didn't deserve for me to only love her part way."

Joshua listened intently, as did I. I saw Shana after Beau broke up with her, and she was an emotional heap of tears. She didn't want to break up, not even a little bit, but she did want him to love her completely. God was calling Beau to take some time for himself, and she knew he had to follow what God wanted for his life, even if it hurt her. As it turned out, Shana had just as much to learn as he did during that time when, as Beau often exaggerated to tease Shana, "the world stopped."

I desperately wanted to stop talking about such a serious topic. Breaking up a relationship for good reason was not something I wanted Joshua getting any ideas about. I could think of a million reasons why he'd want time away from me, and I wasn't ready for him to figure them out. I was comfortable with the current state of our relationship because it had plateaued, which was certainly better than breaking up.

"Thanks for having us tonight, guys. Just think. This time next week, you two will be husband and wife, headed to California for your honeymoon! Hard to believe, really," I beamed at them, trying to lighten the serious mood of the room.

"I know it. It's outrageous how fast this engagement has gone. Seems like yesterday you asked me." Shana leaned her head on Beau's shoulder.

"It's going to be a special day with great things to come," Beau said in the manly southern drawl that made Shana swoon.

I envied Beau's verbal affirmations of Shana. I wasn't sure how anyone could fall in love with me, so when Joshua did, I felt like I had tricked him in some way. People like me weren't supposed to be able to find someone who could tolerate them.

I wondered if I was imagining the change in the substance of our relationship, but I was afraid to scratch the surface by discussing it, so I left it pent up inside instead. I did a lousy job of hiding my concerns and found myself making quiet but snarky comments about other relationships that appeared more loving than ours. I knew at my core I was cycling into a damaging pattern, but my insecurities were deeply rooted.

Joshua drove me home and walked me to my door. "I had a good time tonight. Thanks for hanging out." He kissed my cheek softly. "Have you seen Miss Corrie in a while?"

"I've seen her every so often when I work. She's doing okay. Definitely doesn't like that she needs so much help now, but overall, she seems good to me. Have you seen her when you've gone to her house for your rounds?"

"Yeah, I've seen her briefly here and there. She's stubborn and won't let her prognosis change her lifestyle. That's for sure. I think she's still cooking for herself, which worries me. I dunno. I wish she'd talk to us about her finances or plans. She can't stay in that house forever." He said as he jingled his keys.

My shoulders tensed up has he spoke about her plans and what she should do. She was a grown woman and could make her own choices. Selfishly, I didn't want her living anywhere else, because I needed her too much. I needed her to need *me* too much. She was my confidant, my lifeline, so the thought of being without her in my life didn't seem plausible.

"She's fine. She won't need to move. She'll have me to take care of her if she wants, and besides, that's what nurses are for. She can have them come in." I shrugged like it was all no big deal.

"Nurses cost a lot of money, Naomi. I don't know if Miss Corrie would want to pay someone to be there twenty-four hours like that. She may have to move to a skilled facility one day, and that would be okay too. You'd still be able to visit." Joshua pulled some lint off his shirt as he spoke.

My cheeks started heating up at his declarations. Who did he think he was? He wasn't her son. He didn't know what her needs were. She needed to be close to the people who could care for her, her friends, and her church.

"I don't think you're right on this one. She needs to stay in her home. Her home is where her memories are, where George last lived, and taking her away from that could be detrimental to her healing." My hands balled into fists and I shoved them into my pockets. I took a step away from him, leaning against the wall behind me.

"Listen, I don't want her to have to move any more than you do," he said defensively.

"What do you know? Is she moving somewhere?" I was losing my cool quickly.

Even as I spoke, I could tell my words were coming from a place of unraveling perspective. My insecurities were eating up any discerning thoughts by the mouthful. I was instigating a fight with Joshua out of desperation. I wanted him to tell me how he felt about me, fill me with words of affirmation, and make me feel whole with him again. I needed attention, even if it was bad attention. My subconscious was picking a fight with Joshua in a pathetic attempt to get him to reassure me about our relationship. Checking for reassurance was a habit that wouldn't go down without a fight.

"What are you getting so upset about? Of course, I don't know her plans. She hasn't told me what she's going to do with herself any more than she's told you. Chill out," Joshua snapped back.

I had struck a nerve.

"I'm not mad. I just don't understand why you keep talking about her moving. She's fine where she is," I muttered in an attempt to regain peace.

"You're getting all irritated about nothing. I'm just trying to talk to you."

"Ha...talk to me...yeah, like that's what you like to do," I uttered under my breath.

"Excuse me? Yes, I do like to talk to you. But it sounds like you think otherwise." He took his phone from his pocket and glanced at it briefly.

"No, you just haven't really seemed to want to talk to me these last few weeks. You're always working, and you never stay on the phone very long when I try to talk to you about your day. If you have a problem with me, then you should just tell me. I can handle it," I spouted off.

"What are you *talking* about? I've been working my tail off so I can save money! Maybe one day be able to provide for someone other than myself! And I hate talking on the phone. You know that. Sometimes I just want to be silent after a long day, and believe me, I've had some super long days lately. What's your deal?"

"My deal? What's *my* deal? I don't have a deal. I'm just trying to figure out what your problem is!"

"I don't have a problem, Naomi. I don't. What you see is what you get. I'm not fake, but I don't wear my emotions on my sleeve either. I'm not like you. I'm an introvert. If you think you'll love me more if only you could change that about me, then you're wrong. Changing me isn't your job. It's God's. I am who I am right now, and if you can't accept my imperfections and trust I'm a work in progress as much as we all are, then maybe we shouldn't be together. Is that what you want?" He looked at me with uneasiness in his eyes.

I felt myself begin to panic, but not in the way I used to. This panic was legitimate concern about something real. I was poisoning our relationship. My thoughts were flying, and all I wanted was to retract everything I had just said, pretend I'd never opened the gaping hole in my face. This was not just my OCD. This was my own stubborn selfishness.

"Of course not! It's just, I don't know why you had to bring up Miss Corrie in the first place. She's fine right now, so we shouldn't involve ourselves in her situation. Right? I'm sorry I even said anything." I spoke calmly, trying to erase the last few minutes, but it wasn't working.

"Is that really all this is about? You sure seem to have some pent-up frustrations with me."

I thought for a second about telling him about my diagnosis, but I just couldn't bring myself to throw the new label out there as a way to make him forgive me. Maybe my inability to converse like a normal person with Joshua was yet another byproduct of my obsessive nature.

"No, really. I'm fine," I said. That was the catchphrase I used with Joshua when I wanted an uncomfortable moment to pass. I would declare I was fine and try to change topics or, in this case, get out of there. I craved leaving and staying close to him in the same moment.

"Okay, then I guess I'll see you later this week. Big wedding is coming up soon." He reached out and grabbed my hand, only to let it go quickly.

"Yup. It's coming up fast. You still want to be my date or..."

As my question trailed off, he looked over at me with frustration in his eyes. "Naomi, why would you ask me that? Of course, I want to be your date. Why would you think otherwise? Come on. That's a low blow." He muttered something else under his breath.

"I just figured I'd make sure the plans hadn't changed for some reason. Things happen. Don't take it personal." I shrugged, relieved that he would be annoyed by my question.

At this point, no matter how he responded to any of my questions, the hatred I felt for myself was already raging out of control, and I was drowning in my own insecurity. I knew I needed to tell him about my diagnosis but convinced myself it would either give him grounds to leave or guilt him into staying with me. And I didn't want either.

"Okay, fine then. I'll plan to be here on Saturday afternoon to take you to the church."

He didn't mention us talking before then.

I started to tear up as I opened my front door, released, but not relieved from the scene of wreckage caused by my untamed tongue. "Yup. See you then."

Eleven

I TRIED NOT to torment myself by reliving every awkward silence or provoking word I had unwisely spoken on Saturday night. I hurt him. I knew I had. I was chipping away at our relationship with snippy criticisms and overly sensitive accusations. I didn't want Joshua to break up with me, but I also couldn't bring myself to believe he could genuinely choose me.

I went to my therapy appointment that week and shared all of our relationship drama with Mary Jo. She helped show me how my OCD distorts my thinking and causes me to feel like things are out of control when they aren't. I would have to use a strategy and walk away from the situation uncomfortable, knowing that obsessing over deeds done in my past wouldn't help my future. I shared my faith with Mary Jo so she could help me incorporate my faith in God during our time together, but I felt a longing to talk to Miss Corrie and pray with her about it. I felt the Holy Spirit revealing my sin nature to me. I wanted to be able to decipher where my OCD began and where my sinful heart started and where they overlapped.

The extreme fears I was having were definitely out of my control, but I could not use my new diagnosis as a coverup for selfishness. I felt like a newborn deer learning to walk for the first time. As my head cleared from the fog of anxiety, my sins came into view more clearly. I was gathering my things to go visit Miss Corrie when there was a faint knock at my apartment door. I opened it to see Shana standing on my welcome mat with tears streaming down her pale face. Her eyes were puffy and her hair sopping wet as though she had just gotten out of the shower.

"Shana? What on earth! What's the matter?"

"Naomi, I just had to come see you. I'm sorry for barging in like this," she sputtered between sniffs.

"What happened? Is everything okay with Beau?"

"Yeah, yeah. We're fine. I'm just upset because I think I may have made a huge mistake, and I just had to come confess it to you."

"What did you do? I'm sure it's not a big deal." I led her over to the sofa where we sat down, and I handed her a fresh tissue.

"Okay, so, last night Joshua called Beau, which is unusual. They don't typically talk like that on the phone. When they were done, I asked Beau what they had talked about, and he just said Joshua had some questions about relationship stuff. He said he wouldn't give me too much information out of respect for Joshua, so I decided to text Joshua and see if he'd tell me by accident."

"Tell you what by accident? About what he talked to Beau about?"

"Right. Anyways, we were texting back and forth, and I could tell he didn't really want to discuss their conversation with me in detail. Oh man, I feel so bad about this next part. He wasn't giving me anything, so I told him that you were seeing a therapist and had been diagnosed with OCD. I'm so sorry. I know that wasn't information for me to share. I just, I panicked. I don't know, I guess I was worried he was talking to Beau about our breakup and didn't want that to happen to you, so I thought if I told him about what you'd learned, maybe he'd understand where you are coming from a lot of the time."

"You mean, stay with me out of pity. Right?" I could taste fury rising up from my toes.

"No, not like that. I was hoping I could prevent you from having to go through what I went through with Beau. She had started crying again.

"I thought you said you were thankful that happened? The other night, you two were advertising breaking up like it was some kind of great relationship strategy. Like you're the poster children for breaking up. There should be a billboard with your faces on it promoting taking time off in your relationship for a healthier forever," I said mockingly.

"Naomi, we don't act like that. Come on. We just know that our story can be helpful for some people."

"Well, well done. I'm sure you two shared enough of your story to convince Joshua he should get out of being with me while he can, for all the benefits. What did you actually tell him about my OCD?"

"Nothing much. I basically told him that you saw a psychiatrist, and she diagnosed you with Obsessive Compulsive Disorder." She dabbed at her tears dramatically.

"That's all? You're telling me that's all you told him?"

"I guess I told him a little more than that. I encouraged him. I told him that although your diagnosis makes you a little difficult sometimes, it's not anything you two couldn't overcome together."

"You told him I was difficult? That my OCD makes me act awful? That's pretty much what you told him, right? Thanks. Thanks so much. You've been a huge help." I sent my cup smashing into the sink and rested both hands on either side as I gazed down into the drain. I was trying to think of what strategy Mary Jo would tell me to use to deal with the intense frustration I was feeling, but nothing came to mind. I was a volcano on the verge of eruption.

"Naomi, it was a mistake. That wasn't my information to give, and I'm so, so sorry. I should never have contacted him in the first place. I should've just left it between him and Beau." She came up slowly behind me.

"You have *no idea* what it's like to be me, Shana. I can't believe you told him. Wait, if you told him I had been diagnosed, then how much does he know about what it means? Did you say it nonchalantly or seriously?" I was beginning to piece together how the information she shared could have been interpreted depending on how she presented it.

"I didn't say much. I just told him you'd been to a therapist and you'd been diagnosed with OCD. His responses were short. He seemed fine at the end of the conversation. Oh Naomi, I'm so sorry. I really didn't mean to blurt it out like that."

"How could this have happened by accident? Come on, Shana, you must have had some idea how telling him could mess everything up for me. Do you have it out for me? What did I ever do you that you think I deserve this? I know I'm not the easiest person to love, but come on, telling my boyfriend such personal news? I can't believe you did that." I hung my head in my hands and sat down slowly in the chair across from her.

Her face was stricken with grief and remorse, but I couldn't bring myself to let her off so easily. She had totally crossed the line. I wanted her to taste the guilt she was feeling for a while. The Holy Spirit began to nudge me to forgive her, but my hard heart won, and I stayed locked in anger.

"There's not much more I can say but 'I'm sorry.' Please forgive me. I know I was totally wrong. Loving people is hard and that includes you Naomi. You aren't always easy to figure out sis. You're a puzzle. You come across as this funny, kind person, but you're really a tortured soul who takes out your frustrations on the people who love you most. I know I messed up, believe me I do, but at least own up to being a part of all this. You're pushing Joshua away. He wants to be with you! He wants to love you, and you keep giving him the stiff arm, attempting to keep him at a safe distance. You don't think we all see it? You're going to destroy this if you aren't careful, and yes, as your big sister I tried to help in an absolute wrong way. I'm sorry." Shana began to rise like she was going to leave, then sat back down, waiting for me to look up at her.

When I didn't, she stood up again, slowly walking to the front door.

"I love you, Naomi. I really do. You know that. I'm still very sorry...for everything." She left in tears, just as she had arrived.

I sat in the chair with my head hung low until I began to feel lightheaded. I was late to check on Miss Corrie. I needed to get there to make sure she ate breakfast before taking her medications. Still reeling from what Shana had done, I contemplated texting Joshua but figured it wouldn't be wise since texted thoughts could be easily misinterpreted.

So much of what Shana accused me of was true. Her words cut deep because they were accurate. I knew I was mistreating Joshua the way she described. I was likely going to lose him if I didn't trust him. I had heard a lot of truth spoken to me before but hearing it had never done me much good. I could hear all the answers and rationality about something I was anxious about, but those truths were usually distorted or squashed by irrational ways of thinking. But now, my medication was helping with that unhealthy way of thinking, so I could clearly see that what I was dealing with was sin, not anxiety. My OCD may have set me up for this pattern of behavior, but this time I was choosing to distort the truth.

As I pulled into Miss Corrie's driveway, I was shocked to see all her statues were gone. The landscape looked beautiful, with flowers proudly in bloom, excited for the warmth of springtime. I found it odd that she had taken the statues down, but Joshua dropped quite a few hints about how tacky they were, so I figured his suggestions finally convinced her to part with them.

I sat in the car for a moment to gather myself and read Shana's texts. She'd messaged me multiple times asking for forgiveness. I hadn't replied yet because I didn't really know what to say. I was still peeved with her. She'd have to sit on her discomfort for a while longer as punishment.

I walked to the side door, figuring Miss Corrie would have it open for me like she always did. Oddly it was locked this time, forcing me to use the hidden key she once told me about. Joshua had tried to convince her to find a safer, less obvious spot for it, but his efforts were unsuccessful because the key still lay under the damp welcome mat.

I opened the door to a dark kitchen. I smiled to myself as I remembered how intently she bickered with Joshua when he brought up finding a new location for the key. He stayed so patient with her inconsistent reasoning that burglars would never look under a doormat because that's where everybody keeps their extra keys, and she was smarter than that, ergo, they would never look there. She had actually said "ergo" which forced Joshua to concede. He never stood a chance with her. The door creaked open, revealing the only light in the room reflecting from her front kitchen window, the same window I looked out of countless times to watch Joshua working in the yard.

"Hello?" I called out as I switched on the light. The light came on in a flash to reveal a shocking discovery. All of Miss Corrie's kitchen furniture was gone. The room was empty. I stood staring at the blank walls, mesmerized by the site. I started to feel overcome with worry that maybe she had been robbed.

"Miss Corrie?" I yelled out louder.

I tiptoed from the kitchen into the living room that was also completely dark. Miss Corrie loved bright things. She hated gray days and even once confessed to sleeping with a light on. There was no way her whole house would be that dark with her in it. I flipped on the living room light and gasped. There was no more furniture. No more books, candles, coffee table, or pictures on the walls.

"What is going on?" I whispered to myself. I debated venturing into the bedroom because I was afraid of what I would find. I wondered if she had, in fact, been robbed and was hostage in her bedroom. I wasn't sure if I could cope with seeing something like that.

I had my cell phone in my hand ready to dial 911. I slowly made my way down the hall, turning on lights as I went. I finally reached the bedroom when I noticed something shimmering just beyond the door. It was coming from the doorway that led to the master bathroom and appeared to be hanging from the top of the door frame. I lightly brushed the light switch causing the overhead light to send ugly fluorescent light all over the room. I froze with my feet planted like anchors below me as the blinding light consumed the space, revealing a surprise.

Tears formed on my bottom lids as I absorbed what I was seeing. Miss Corrie's wedding dress hung in the doorway like a lonely invisible bride. Below the dress, on the floor, was her favorite picture of her and George on their wedding day. I couldn't bring myself to go to it, so I stood there perplexed. Where was Miss Corrie, and why was her dress hanging alone in her room like a jewel in a dark cave?

I took deliberate steps to the dress, reaching my hand up to brush the fabric with my fingers. The lace had darkened over time and had a yellowish tinge to it. I knelt down to stare at the photo. I studied Miss Corrie's face as I kept another hand on the bottom of her precious dress, desperately trying to be close to my friend. I reached for the ivory hanger that delicately hung the gorgeous dress when I noticed something stiff sticking out of the bust of the dress. It was a note with my name written on the front in the handwriting I had come to know well after all the shredding I did for her. I ripped open the note and read it hesitantly to myself.

"My dearest dear heart, my sweet irreplaceable friend. If you are reading this, I have finally gotten a spot at the care facility called Deer Path Assisted Living, or as I like to call it, an old folks home in the mountains of North Carolina. I didn't tell you anything about the possibility of my

moving to a place where I can get care all the time because I didn't know when or even if I'd be moving away.

You have had plenty on your plate with your own joys and struggles. I couldn't bear the thought of adding one more job to your list or the list of anyone else. You are a hard worker who deserves to graduate and find something to do that you love. I have so enjoyed our times together. You taught me a great deal about myself, my own fears, and how to love others selflessly like you do.

Please know that you are welcome to stop in on me anytime for a visit. I will never tire of your face or smile. There were many days when I couldn't bear the thought of getting out of bed, but knowing you were coming over made me get myself moving. Thank you for all the ways you have cared for me these last few months. George would be as thankful for you as I am. Someday you will get to meet him in heaven!

Now, in the matter of you and Mr. Joshua, he cares deeply for you, Naomi. Absorb that. Let it sink into your heart and accept it. Stop lying to yourself that somehow, he's better than you are or created superiorly.

My dear, he is as much a sinner as the rest of us, including you. We all need the saving work of Jesus. Now, I'm sure you will likely be furious with me for having left without telling you. I can imagine your eyes bugging at the site of my cleaned-out home as I write this. I hope you can forgive this old bird for doing all I could to take care of myself without burdening others. I pray you'll be able to understand why I had no choice but to keep it from you.

In the matter of my vintage wedding dress, I want you to have it. Use it or don't use it in whatever capacity you would like. Don't feel obligated to wear it on your special day, whenever that comes. Feel free to keep it as a memory of me and a reminder that true love does happen because Christ is our one truest love, regardless of whether we are blessed to marry in this life.

You may dispose of the dress if it takes up too much room in your closet as well. I will understand. I could not be the one to throw it away, so I figured you could do that if you saw fit to. I will never ask about it. I trust you will wisely do what you feel is right with it.

Again, my dearest, I am so sorry to leave you without one last hug goodbye. You are the daughter I never had, whom I love immensely. May you realize your full potential and all your precious God given gifts in this life.

All My Love,
Miss Corrie

I sat in a heap on the floor, clutching the letter to my chest as I sobbed giant tears. She had left me. She up and left me here without her guidance, her friendship, and her soft hugs to comfort me. I felt abandoned in a way that cut me to my core. She had intentionally not shared any of her plans with me after I had let her into the most personal depths of my soul.

She must have wanted to get away from all of us, or she wouldn't have left so mysteriously. I started taking deep breaths to compose myself when I realized I wasn't just inhaling the air alone but the smell of her Frankincense lotion as well. I closed my eyes to take it in. I reread the letter again a few more times to try and comprehend her reasoning.

After a few times, I noticed a suspicious line in the letter. She kept apologizing for not telling me about her move, never mentioning keeping the information from anyone else. *How had she moved all this stuff out alone? Who else could have known she was thinking about moving? Had Joshua known all along that this could happen which is why he made those comments about her moving someday?*

My mind became a whirling dervish of theories of how all this went down without me knowing about it. I sat staring at the floor as I began to pray to God for comfort only He could provide. Miss Corrie was the one who taught me how to pray more genuinely in moments of turmoil and in the calm moments as well.

I stood up, took the dress from where it hung so angelically, tucked the picture under my arm, then carefully carried them through the cave that was her house to the side door once again.

I turned around to study the kitchen where we had countless conversations together one last time. I didn't know what was going to happen to her house, but without Miss Corrie living inside, it was just a useless pile of bricks.

"Goodbye, Miss Corrie. Thanks for everything," I said as I hung my head and turned off the lights one last time.

I didn't know what to do or where to go next. I felt stuck in a hole of emotional quicksand, immoveable. Everything in my world was falling apart. Shana was upset with me, and I had come to discover my cherished mentor was gone, forever.

I pulled out my phone to see if Shana had texted me again. She had not. Joshua's text thread was silent also. I threw my phone onto the passenger seat as I turned on the car, staring forward like a soldier in line. My jaw clenched with my muscles locked in place. I needed my mom, and I needed her now. I picked up my phone and called her.

"Hello?" Mom answered cheerfully.

"Mom! I'm a mess. Miss Corrie is gone," I shouted into the phone.

"Honey, honey. What do you mean she's gone? Is she alright?"

"She left to go live somewhere else. To some assisted living place. Mom, I should've given her more of me and taken care of her better. Shana is mad at me, and I think she hates me now too," I blubbered.

"Naomi, it's not your fault. You know that. Miss Corrie needed to go and get more sufficient care. You can't blame yourself for that."

"But Mom, what if I can't get there to see her? What if I really am a terrible sister and Shana stays mad at me? I also saw a stain on the concrete earlier when I got gas, and I think it was throw up. What if I stepped in throw up, and now I'll be sick for Shana's wedding? I guess it won't matter since she's mad at me. Mom am I going to get sick? Please tell me I'm not going to get sick." I pleaded.

"I think this is your way of asking for more reassurance, right? According to what I've been reading, it's helpful for me not to keep telling you what you want to hear and let you rest in knowing the truth yourself. Why don't we talk about all this in a couple of days or so? Put your mind on hold, and then we can discuss it if you're still worried."

"Mom, I can't wait days to talk about this! It's happening, and I'm to blame, right now. I'm also probably going to be sick in the next forty-eight hours, so I'll really be useless for the wedding, and Shana will hate me even more. Thanks a lot for nothing," I spewed.

"That's not fair. I'm doing my best to help you to not be anxious, but I can't give you any more reassurance. All the books say you need to face your fears, not constantly check to make sure they aren't true. I can only point you to Jesus and a strategy. Do you want me to repeat the strategy again?" Her voice was less calm now, definitely verging on irritated.

"No. I do *not* need you to repeat the strategy. What am I? Four years old? Thanks Mom!" I hung up on her.

I sat fuming. The frustration and panic I felt swirled together into an emotional tornado, turning me and my actions into a devastating storm. *I bet Joshua knew about Miss Corrie's plans all along. He probably didn't tell me because he thought I wasn't worth telling. I probably wasn't trustworthy enough. He thought I couldn't handle it. Miss Corrie thought I couldn't handle it. Look at me, I can't handle it.*

My palms poured sweat as I sat in the hot car. I took rapid breaths, working hard to regain control. I pinched the skin on the back of my hand and curled my left pinky finger onto my ring finger, jamming my nail into my knuckle to dull the pain and keep the thoughts away. *I want to go see Joshua and find out the truth. What if I start yelling at him and get too angry?*

The image of slapping Joshua careened into my imagination, and I closed my eyes as tight as I could and shouted, "Please! God no! Please, God no! Please! Make this stop!"

My chest constricted, and my left arm began to tingle. *I'm having a heart attack. I know it. I must be. My left arm hurts. I'm going to pass out. My chest is pounding. I can't do this. I'm a horrible person. This is all my fault. What if I want to hurt people? What if I never really cared about Miss Corrie or Joshua or anyone? I'm going to die right here from this heart attack, and no one will find me for days.*

I leaned my seat back and stared at the ceiling of my truck. I remembered Mary Jo told me to breathe deeply and calmly when panic came, but I had never had a panic quite this bad before. Every panic attack seemed worse than the one before. Most of my life, I didn't even know that what I was experiencing had a name and wasn't something that happened to everyone when they felt stress. Somehow, knowing it was a panic attack still didn't convince me that I was not, in fact, dying and that all the horrible things I was thinking were not true.

After what felt like hours, the extreme worry passed, and my chest started to open back up. The negative thoughts still loomed, but I was able to sit myself up and begin driving. I replayed conversations with Miss Corrie over and over while simultaneously picturing the nasty pile of potential vomit I'd come in contact with earlier in the day. I was overrun with fears but only had so much brain space and couldn't analyze them all at once.

The fears bounced around as I drove aimlessly through town with no sure destination. I glanced at the wedding dress in the back seat and visualized taking a knife to it. *Please God, no.* I pulled the car over into a gas station parking lot and called my mom again.

"Hello?" she answered reluctantly.

"Hi Mom," I uttered tentatively. There was silence for a long moment before I continued. "I'm so sorry about before. I didn't mean to speak so unkindly. I needed to hear you say those things to me, but I shouldn't have pushed so hard. Please forgive me for losing it with you."

I heard her sigh on the other end. "I forgive you. I often don't know what to do for you, Naomi. You've spent years using me as a sounding board and safe place. I can't be your counselor, but I will always be your mother and love you through this. You can't expect me to go easy on you, though. I love you too much to let you suffer anymore, and that may sometimes take some tough love on my end." She sniffed loudly. "Remember those times when you were a kid, and you would look to me for reassurance about a worry? It would come to a point where I would let you ask me if things were okay only one last time, and then you had to let it go. Do you remember how firm I had to get with you?"

"Yes, and I remember deep down feeling relieved that you were so firm. Your frustration convinced me to trust that if it was really something to worry about, you would tell me."

"Exactly. Trust me when I tell you that all the thoughts you're having right now are lying to you. You've had a difficult day. It's normal to experience frustration and doubt. Your brain has gone too far now, and you need to use a strategy. Which one are you going to choose?"

"Well, I felt like I was having a heart attack earlier, so I'm willing to try anything. I mean, it wasn't a heart attack, I don't think. Don't you think I'd know if I had a heart attack?" I rambled.

"If you had a heart attack, we certainly wouldn't be chatting on the phone right now. But I'm not going to reassure you anymore. What strategy are you going to use to move through this?"

"How about, let's talk about all this in a couple days. If all these awful things are true, they will still be true two days from now, and we can discuss them then."

"Great. I'm betting you won't even remember what they are," she answered back. "Where are you headed?"

"I think I'm going to take a walk outside somewhere. Clear my head."

"Be careful. Keep your phone with you. I'll talk to you later. I love you honey," she said with a quiver in her voice.

"Thanks again, Mom...for loving me."

"It's my pleasure. Love you. Bye now," she said softly.

I sat in the parking lot and did my best to keep my mind focused on the most important things. *I've got to talk to someone about Miss Corrie.*

I knew reassurance was bad for me, but the temptation to get even a little was strong. I felt a surge of frustration thinking Joshua must have known about Miss Corrie's plan all along. He must have purposely not shared the inside information with me. He knew all about my new diagnosis from Shana and didn't even contact me with any kind of comfort. Nothing. *What kind of guy was he anyway?*

Miss Corrie accused me in her letter of pushing him away, said it was all my doing. Joshua was the one comfortable with the silence. He was the one who never wanted to rock the boat with hard conversations. I was the one who bore my imperfections every time we were together, whether I wanted to show them or not. He and Shana were just perfect, weren't they?

As my list of grievances and jealousies grew, so did my urge to go see Joshua immediately. He needed to face me, confess that he deceived me and lied to me by omitting what he knew about Miss Corrie. He didn't care about my emotional struggles or my feelings, not one bit. I had never thought so clearly before, and I was going to use it to my advantage when confronting Joshua.

I rehearsed what I wanted to say to him in my mind as I drove, almost missing the turn to his house entirely. I had to strike while I was brave and catch him off guard. I wanted him to see how his lack of compassion affected me, up close and personal. He needed to understand he was wrong in more ways than one. Good thing I was headed there to tell him.

Twelve

AS I ROUNDED the corner toward Joshua's house, I saw something red moving in his driveway. I took the curve slowly, realizing it was Joshua finishing up a hug with a young woman I'd never seen before. She had strawberry blonde hair, was wearing a bright red NC State shirt, and smiling a huge cheesy grin. I slowed down a few driveways away so they wouldn't see me coming. I pulled the car over and sat for a couple minutes, watching the beautiful trespasser as she covered her mouth to laugh flirtatiously. *She must have bad teeth.* I slunk down in my seat, seething.

I almost forgot the frustrations that drove me there as a seed of envious anger began to grow. *Who was she? Was she why he'd been so busy with work recently?* This was just one more deception from him. One more omission of the truth. He looked like his casual calm self, unflappable like usual. He laughed at something she said while kicking the dirt and looking down at the ground. He looked like an innocent schoolboy getting ready to ask a girl out for the first time. Little Miss State Fan finally skipped back down the street.

My eyeballs were burning with rage at the sight of him hugging someone else. *He's going to dump me. He's so perfect, and I am so broken. Who was he kidding with his charade?*

I pulled back onto the road and slowly drove into his driveway just as he reached his front door. He noticed me out of the corner of his eye, almost doing a double take as I made my way into his driveway.

"Hey you," he said calmly as I walked up to meet him halfway up his front stoop.

"Hey yourself," I replied with a sting in my voice.

"What's wrong with *you?*" he asked.

"Ha! Like you don't know," I snapped back.

"I *don't* know. You're going to have to fill me in on this one. I'm clueless."

"You knew all along that Miss Corrie was moving. You knew she was going away, and you never told me! You kept it from me! What else are you keeping from me?" My voice rose an octave with every accusation.

"What do you mean Miss Corrie moved? You don't have to yell. Come inside. Let's talk calmly about things."

"Too bad that little lady you had here earlier didn't leave before I could catch you two. You almost got away with that too." I walked ahead of him and let the door fall, intentionally not holding it for him.

"Dude. Chill out. What's with the nasty tone? What lady are you talking about? Julia?" He pointed toward the driveway where they stood earlier, eyebrows raised in surprise.

"Julia? You mean your *other* girlfriend Julia?" I was dumping all the anger I had for myself all over Joshua. Deep down, I wanted to be more mature, but my insecurities were screaming at me to fight him instead.

"I'll have you know that Julia is my neighbor. She's my friend. We have a neighborhood golf league, and I play with her on it. You're going to have to give me a little break here. Put your frustration away." He put his hands up defensively.

Tackle him.

"What do you mean, put my frustration away? You have misled me more than once. Admit it!" I held my hands in fists in a desperate attempt to argue with him while keeping unwanted thoughts at bay.

"What exactly are you accusing me of? You've mentioned quite a few things, and I'm not really following what you're actually mad about." He sat down on the couch, gesturing for me to sit too.

I was pacing the floor. "Okay, first of all, you lied to me!"

"Lied? To you? When?" Now his voice went hard. It took a lot to get Joshua mad, and I was succeeding this afternoon.

"You didn't tell me about Miss Corrie. I *know* you knew she was planning on moving. You had to have known she was packing up for somewhere. Why didn't you *tell* me?"

"Listen, Miss Corrie only told me she was investigating care facilities. She asked me not to mention it to you because she didn't want you to worry about it. That's all I knew. I promise. What happened today?"

"She's gone. That's what happened today. Her house is empty, and she's gone. Forever," I answered.

"What? Like she moved out already?" He sat up straighter as he leaned forward with surprise.

"*Yes!* Are you not hearing me?" I yelled back as I threw the letter from Miss Corrie at him.

He read it intently before covering his face with his hand, then sat back, deflated. "I should've known. Man, I can't believe I didn't see this coming. I'm so naive."

"What are you talking about? What do you mean you're naive?"

"Just last weekend, she had me take all her cat statues to the dump. I know how much she loves those silly things and was shocked she wanted me to get rid of them. She told me I'd finally worn her down, that they really were ugly, and she wanted them gone. I can't believe I didn't put it together and think to ask her more. Especially since she briefly mentioned moving in a previous conversation. I didn't think she'd do it without telling us."

"See! You did know! You knew more than me, and you purposely didn't tell me about her secrets. You should've Joshua. You should've. You lied!" I finally fell into the seat next to him.

I knew calling Joshua a liar would cut him deeply. He was an extremely loyal, honest, and dependable person. The accusation hurt him, and I wanted it to. I wanted him to feel the pain I felt when I walked through Miss Corrie's empty tomb of a house.

"Excuse me? You are calling me a liar?" He scooted to the edge of his seat.

I had gotten to him. *Success.*

"That's right. You also haven't even mentioned what my sister told you about me. You can't even text me and let me know that you know there's a reason why I act like I do sometimes? Were you just going to pretend you didn't know anything? Were you going to keep acting like you had *no* idea why I struggle all the time? Or that you think I'm unlovable and want to leave me for someone who isn't?"

"What? You mean about you having Obsessive something or other. Why would I text about that? That would be so insensitive. I figured it would be better for us to talk about it in person, face to face. You've really got it out for me, don't you?" He dragged his fingers through his hair. "Anything else you want to add to my rap sheet, or are you done tearing me apart?"

"No. No I don't. I mean, I'm sure your gorgeous neighbor would be insulted if I kept bringing up your flaws. We wouldn't want to upset her, right?" I breathed the sarcasm like fire.

Joshua shook his head with disappointment and stared at the floor. "Naomi, I don't even know what to say. You're seriously angry at me, like, furious even, and I have no words to respond to you when you're like this."

We sat in silence for a good while as he studied the floor, no doubt pondering my irrational charges. I was beginning to feel remorseful, but as we sat in silence, my frustration continued to grow. *How is it that he has nothing to say?* Deep down, I wanted to get him riled up in hopes we could make up and have a real discussion where he would reassure me.

If he really loves me, then he'll tell me, even if I'm acting out of control. I'm out of control. Look, he knows I am, and he just sits there quietly. How can he be so silent?

Clearly, my plan was backfiring. He wasn't reassuring me at all, not even a little bit. That was the moment I realized...Joshua wasn't the enemy. I was. My anger transformed in an instant, reversing its direction toward myself. I had to fix what I so badly damaged with my invasive and demeaning rebukes. *I have to get his attention. How can I get him to see me and understand?*

I looked next to me and noticed a pair of slippers lying by the chair. Impulsively, I picked one up and slung it nonchalantly at Joshua on the couch. As someone with horrific aim and poor coordination, the slipper didn't softly land in his lap like I planned but instead hit him straight in the face. What I had envisioned as a flirtatious way to get his attention became yet another assault, only this time, a physically painful one.

"Ouch! What on earth are you doing? Are you throwing shoes at my face now?" He stood up, holding the slipper in one hand while the other was in a tight fist. "Are you trying to make me even madder? That's what you're doing here, right? You're trying to make me mad and push me away again."

He took the slipper and hurled it with all his strength at the wall across from us. The slipper hit so hard all the pictures rattled. He turned back in my direction, allowing me to see the deep pain behind his eyes. I was the reason for his pain, but I had no clue how to recover and make things right.

"I...I," I stuttered, not knowing where to begin.

I hurt him when I threw that! What if I wanted to hurt him? How could I do that?

"You know what, Naomi? If you're trying to make me out to be the bad guy here, then job well done. I've completely lost my cool. If you want us to be over, fine, it's over. I'm tired of playing games and feeling bad that I don't always operate in a way that makes you feel completely comfortable. I'm quiet sometimes, I don't like to share my feelings about every little detail of my life, and I can't be perfect for you, Naomi. I can't. Please just go. This thing we had, it may have been everything I thought I was looking for, but clearly, I was wrong. You have no idea how much I want to love you, no matter what your struggles are. I was hoping you'd be the one to help me with my own stuff too. But you can't seem to accept the fact that you aren't the only one who has demons and unlikable characteristics." He started to walk out of the room with big steps.

"I'm so sorry. It's all my fault." I choked back my tears.

"You think *everything* is your fault. I'm sorry too, Naomi, believe me, I'm sorry too. You can see yourself out." He walked down the hall and left me alone, sitting in the emotional devastation I had caused.

I ran out the door, clutching my purse to my chest, holding in the massive sobs that were starting to escape. It fittingly began to rain, drenching me to the bone by the time I got into my seat. I looked up toward his house through my tears and saw him moving around upstairs. I had just unintentionally ended a precious relationship because I was too proud and selfish. I knew I couldn't blame it all on my OCD this time. I couldn't use the diagnosis to justify myself or my terrible actions. I drove through the rain until it stopped, finding myself at the dam of a local lake we all loved to visit. The dam looked over the lake, which was rippling from the recent rainfall. Before I got out of the truck, I shot Shana a text.

I messed it all up with you and now with Joshua. He and I are over. I'm so sorry for how I hurt you today. Please forgive me. Tell Mom and Dad I'm at our spot…gotta sit and think about some things.

Shana and I often went to the dam when we needed to talk or to have some quiet time away from the rest of the world. We would sit on the giant concrete ledge with our feet slung over, feeling like we were on top of a mountain, looking down on the vast lake below us, guarded by tall, yet from here, tiny looking trees.

I knew she would know that's where I was when I texted, but deep down I hoped she wouldn't take my telling her as an invitation to show up. I needed to process, think clearly, by myself. Joshua liked to process alone, and maybe I could stand to be more like him. My mind was always racing, but it never felt like I yielded anything productive. After all the drama of the day, I wanted to attempt to process in a healthy way.

As I gazed down at the lake, I noticed that despite all the sadness I was feeling, I wasn't plagued by unwanted thoughts trying to claw their way in like usual. I battled against them earlier in the day, but that night, all was quiet. I was able to think through my interaction with Joshua accurately and recall my own actions without imaginary occurrences thrown in. My brain was still running feverishly, but it felt different, better somehow.

I noticed some geese flying in unison over the lake like a team on a journey together. In one day, I had lost three of my most valuable teammates. I threw Shana under the bus when she came to confess her error to me. I had given her no grace, no mercy, no understanding in the slightest. I wanted her to grovel in her repentance and basically humiliated her.

Losing Miss Corrie hadn't been my choice, but her decision not to share her housing options with me was indeed, my doing. I had given her no safe place to bring her thoughts because I was so suffocated by my own. I smiled through my tears as I thought about the wedding dress in the back of my car. I'd be shocked if I ever got to wear the thing. After treating Joshua in the embarrassing way, I had, I was convinced I annihilated our relationship for good.

What am I doing? Did I really believe provoking Joshua would make him feel safe to share how he feels? Or tell me he loves me again? I pulled my knees up to my chest and hugged my legs as I wiped my tears on my jeans. It started to sprinkle again lightly, but I barely even noticed as I wallowed in my disappointment. Mary Jo had been teaching me that I wouldn't ever be perfect. I couldn't make bullseyes every time, so I didn't need to despair or be shocked when I fell short. I just had to accept the reality that I would fail others, and I needed to be open to receiving forgiveness when I did.

I had no idea how I was going to undo what I had done, but I knew I had to try to make it right. I decided to start by asking forgiveness from the most important One, God. I closed my eyes and quietly prayed, asking God to forgive me. I asked Him to rebuild my heart, help me lean on Him and desire Him more than anyone or anything else in this world. He could use my OCD for His glory and my own good. I believed that now. I opened my eyes, feeling cleansed and redeemed with newfound hope that God could use my brokenness.

OCD was the thorn that brought me to my knees, the cry of my heart, leading me straight into my Redeemer's arms. Maybe God would keep using these struggles for my good. They had already brought me closer to Him. Repenting brought fresh calm to my soul, and I basked in it.

Next on my list was Shana. I knew she would forgive me, because she always did. She'd had plenty of practice at giving me second chances. I was contemplating getting up when car lights shined past me. It looked like another car was parking next to mine. I turned around to see who it was but couldn't make out the car. It was getting dark, and the headlights were blinding me. I spun my legs around to prepare myself for whoever it was while trying to keep from panicking that I was about to be murdered by this mysterious stranger.

Then I heard a familiar sound bellowing from the parking lot. The car mooed. Beau had installed the novelty horn on his truck and often pulled it to announce his arrival at our house. It sounded just like a cow, and it never failed to make me laugh, even in that sad moment.

"Hey there, NayJay. Has life got you down?" Beau's boots crunched on the gravel as he emerged from the truck.

"Hey Beau. How'd ya know I was here?" I yelled back.

He came towards me, hands in his pockets as he sauntered to where I sat.

"You Lang girls are pretty predictable. I knew this was your spot to come and sort things out. Shana was a heap of sadness when she stopped by my place. You must've really given it to her," he said with a smirk. "Yeah...I really messed everything up today, big time," I replied.

"I would have to agree with you on that. You had a way with words that left some marks."

"Shana told you what happened, I guess." I flinched before he even answered.

"Yes, I talked with Shana...and Joshua too."

"What? You talked to Joshua? Why? Did he call you? I mean, how did you talk to him?"

"Let's just say he wanted to say goodbye," he said.

"Ah, I see. Goodbye, huh? That's too bad. I guess that makes it official then." I felt the tears begin to slip out again, and I turned my face so he wouldn't see.

"Hey, hey, now no need to turn on the sprinklers. You're going to get dehydrated with all that water coming out. Take it easy. He spoke nothing bad about you. He made it sound like it was what you wanted." Beau put his hand on my shoulder and squeezed.

He had become like a big brother to me. I knew I could count on him for protection and emotional support. He had never sought me out to comfort me quite like this before, but at this moment, I was glad he did.

"I didn't want that, not at all. I think I just don't know how to accept love from people. I think I'm too out of sorts to be with someone like him. It was inevitable we'd break up. I would've ended up being too much for him anyway. Don't you think?" I scrubbed at my tears with my already damp shirt sleeve.

"Hmm...I'd have to disagree with you on that one. I came here with a specific purpose, Naomi. Shana told me she had informed you that Joshua and I spoke recently. She thought she knew what we were discussing, but she was mistaken."

"What do you mean?"

"When Joshua called me, he had one main question for me based on something I'd briefly mentioned about myself when we were together."

I rolled my eyes. "I bet he wanted to know all about when you broke up with Shana."

"Are you listening? I just said Shana was wrong, and you are too. A few months ago, we were hanging out when I casually mentioned my struggles with anxiety. Joshua called the other night to ask about my experience with it. He wanted to find out how Shana was a support to me. He was calling to see if I could help him understand you better. He wanted to find out how he could love you better, especially when you were worried. He never brought up, let alone discussed, our break-up, and neither did I. He also wasn't calling to contemplate the pros and cons of breaking up with you."

"Are you kidding me? You're telling me he wasn't planning to break up with me?"

"You got it." He nodded as he broke a stick in two and threw it.

We sat together in silence as the moon rose and began to shine above us. The clouds had cleared, as had my perspective.

"I feel so ridiculous. I let myself get so out of control. Nothing made sense even though my thoughts at the time felt so clear. I'm used to filtering out the extreme stuff so much, I've forgotten how to handle real relationships wisely. I sabotaged the whole thing, just like Miss Corrie warned I could. That probably doesn't make any sense to you." I waved my hand, almost to dismiss my comments.

"I get you more than you realize, Naomi. Since you brought it up, anxiety isn't just a thorn in *your* side." He spoke softer this time.

"What do you mean? What do you know about my anxiety?" I knew Shana had likely told him things, but I was unsure how much.

"I know from my *own* experience. I've lived with quite a bit of anxiety for a lot of my adult life. My mind runs constantly. I don't sleep well most of the time because I can't shut off my brain. You're not alone in your battle. We share that in common." His words were full of compassion.

"You? But, but you're so together all the time. I don't see you losing your cool." I furrowed my brow in skepticism.

"Just because you can't see my fear doesn't mean it's not there. I may hide it well, but like you, I've had to learn how to function amidst the battle. I use strategies to face my giants. We may not share the exact same diagnosis, but anxiety is no stranger to either of us."

"Wow. I'm shocked, and believe me, I didn't think that could happen again today," I said.

"Listen, I know you think you're unlovable, but aren't we all? Shana loves me in spite of my struggles, and she's been a huge support for me, not just with my anxiety. You are worth loving that much too, NayJay. I want to encourage you to know you're not a lost cause. God has someone for you who will support and point you back to Jesus. And if you never meet someone to be your human partner in this life, it's not because you're more damaged than anyone else. God has a plan and purpose for your life, so spouse or not, you'll never be alone because *He* is your true love."

I soaked in his words. "Do you really think so? It'll take some time to get over Joshua—that's for sure—but I appreciate the encouragement."

"I know so. Now, can we please go talk to your sister? I had to force her out of my truck when I was on my way here. She's wanting to make things right with you. We *are* getting married the day after tomorrow. She'd like to be on speaking terms with her maid of honor. She's currently pacing at your house." He elbowed me.

"Yeah, I guess I can't run from her forever. Thanks for following me here, Beau, my bro." I stood up and wiped the dirt and rocks from my pants.

We started walking up the hill to our cars when I heard Beau laughing to himself.

"What's funny?" I called out as he started to get his keys ready.

"A shoe? You threw a shoe at him? And at his face! What were you thinking that would accomplish?" He chuckled.

"Oh no way! He told you about *that*? Man, I wasn't thinking. I was trying to be cute or funny or... something. And to be clear, it wasn't a shoe. It was a super soft slipper. No seriously, I felt like I was having an out of body experience, just hovering over a wild person who was trying all the wrong things to fix a problem."

"But a slipper even? At his face? When did throwing anything ever become a good strategy to calm an argument?" He shook his head, still laughing.

I couldn't help but let out a slight snicker myself. The whole scene had been horrifyingly comical. I still couldn't believe any of it really happened.

"This too shall pass, NayJay! Now go make things right with your Silsta. She's not so patiently awaiting your arrival," he yelled out the window as he drove off.

I got a sudden pang of sadness as he spoke, remembering the same words I saw on the back of Miss Corrie's car the day I met her. I sighed deeply, remembering that God works in strange ways and maybe He was, in fact, trying to work His ways in me.

I pulled up to my parents' house, and even though it was getting late, all the lights were still on. Beau's truck was in the driveway. Of course, he beat me home. I had successfully stirred everyone up because of my actions that day.

I walked through the door to have Shana come flying at me. She dropped the cup of tea she was sipping on its saucer and jumped up to grab me in a bear hug and wouldn't let go. At first, I felt too foolish to hug her back, but as she tightened her embrace, I melted into her acceptance. She wasn't saying anything to me, no frustrated words or anger.

"I'm so sorry, Shana. So, so sorry. I hope you can forgive me. I didn't mean to treat you like I did. Okay, maybe I did mean to, but I regret it," I said into her collarbone.

"I forgive you! I hate fighting with you!" Shana replied instantly.

"I'm sorry I ruined it all. I've messed up your wedding weekend." The temptation to start self-loathing returned. I wanted to keep apologizing until things felt right like it used to, but Mary Jo was in my head telling me to let it go.

"Oh stop. You didn't ruin my wedding weekend. We're all good now. I'm sorry I tried to "help." You weren't the only one who had bad judgement." She let me go and looked at my folks, who were standing in the doorway with Beau.

"All is right in the world. The Lang sisters are back together again. I can sleep tonight," Beau gave us a crooked smile.

"Some things never change. You girls have fought and made up like this your whole lives. I'm just thankful you know how to make things right and choose to forgive." Mom came over and pulled me into her arms next.

I felt myself relax into her like I did when I was young. I was a good two inches taller than her, but in that moment, I was nine again, safe in her motherly comfort.

"I'm just glad we didn't have to witness the fighting firsthand. We got to see the good part." Dad patted me on the shoulder as I hugged Mom.

"We're so sorry to hear about Joshua. Your dad and I sure did like him," Mom brushed my hair behind my ear as she let go of me.

"It's okay. I did it to myself. I guess I'll be dateless this weekend. I'm not sure what I'm sadder about—Joshua and I breaking up or Miss Corrie moving away."

"Miss Corrie moved away! When?" His eyes widened with shock.

"Yeah, I went to work today to find her house completely cleaned out. She went to live in a retirement home in the mountains."

"I'm so surprised. She didn't tell you anything about it? Not even any hints?" Shana asked skeptically.

"Nope. Joshua had a little information, but he chose not to share it or didn't think it was important enough to tell me. I wasn't all that forgiving when he told me he suspected she could be moving. Hence, the breakup. But enough of that. Let's all get to bed. We've got lots of things to look forward to!" I squeezed Shana's arm.

"It's hard to believe the rehearsal is tomorrow! I'll be giving my little girl away in no time." Dad weaved his arm around Shana's leading her to take calculated steps as if they were headed down the aisle.

"It's going to be one memorable weekend," I said half-heartedly.

I was thrilled for Shana and Beau but also extremely sad I would have to attend her wedding alone. I had looked forward to having Joshua there with me, dancing and celebrating. As the family ate ice cream together that night, excitedly preparing the final details for the upcoming celebration, I wore a mask of happiness that hid my underlying defeat and regret from that terrible day.

Thirteen

THE SUN WAS extra shiny the morning of Shana and Beau's wedding day. Shana and I spent the night before going through pictures with Mom, remembering all the fun we'd had together over the years as a family. Shana was more than ready to marry Beau. It was obvious in the way she beamed from ear to ear as she ate breakfast. I felt a well of emotions ranging from elated to downright depressed.

My brain was quiet enough that I could actually experience a normal range of emotions, including regret. I looked back on the recent days and saw my sin splattered all over my interactions. OCD had no doubt influenced me, but I knew I needed to ask for forgiveness for my poor behavior, actions I knew were within my control, then forgive myself.

Knowing I was responsible for losing Joshua forced me to rest on Christ. I didn't know what Joshua was thinking about me or my actions, but I had to trust that what he thought didn't matter. God's opinion was most important. I had to rest in my true identity—daughter of the King. I had received Christ's perfect record in exchange for my sin. I was forgiven. There was no room for obsessing or worrying anymore. I had a life to live. Miss Corrie may have been gone from her house, but her words were in my heart.

"Whatcha thinkin' about?" Shana asked with pink curlers in her hair. She looked like a beauty queen preparing for a pageant as she sat in the softest leather chair at the salon. Her cheeks were rosy, even without blush, because she was bursting with adrenaline.

I sat sitting drinking a cup of coffee, swirling the stir stick around and around while I let the hair blower dry my hair. We booked our hairdresser's entire studio to get primped, waxed, combed, and beautified.

"I'm just thinking about how exciting this day is going to be. I can't wait to tear up the dance floor later."

"You're a bad liar, Naomi. You're thinking about Joshua," she stated as a fact.

"Yeah, he's in there somewhere, but more toward the back of my thoughts today. You and Beau are front and center," I unintentionally shouted.

The blow dryer was so loud, I could barely hear myself. As I spoke, the whole room turned to look at me.

"I'm not in Florida! I'm right here! You don't have to shout." Shana said, cracking up.

I couldn't help but laugh at myself. It was in that moment I realized it was my choice whether or not to be present in the experiences God was giving me. Before medication and therapy, I had very little control over how I spent my mental energy. But this day was about Shana, Beau, and the love they had for one another in Christ. I was determined to be present, and I was going to enjoy myself. I pushed the dryer off my head and began dancing around the room.

The other bridesmaids started laughing, then jumped up to join in. Shana turned on some music from her phone before taking her spot in the middle of the dance circle. We jumped, sang, squealed, and did all the girly things women do when they get together for a celebration. Even Mom and Grandma joined in the immature romp. The hairdresser began to get irritated as our curlers fell to the floor, smooth hair began to tangle, and their workload doubled as we ruined what progress they had made with our locks.

"It's nice to have you back, Naomi... I've missed you," Shana said in my ear as we dispersed back to our seats.

I smiled at her and squeezed her hand, knowing exactly what she meant. The confident girl who'd once dressed up in a toilet paper toga to make people laugh was starting to come back!

As I walked down the aisle, I couldn't help but think of Miss Corrie wearing her lacy wedding dress when she married George. He must've been thrilled to see her youthful, freckled face coming toward him in such a gorgeous gown. I waved to familiar faces in the congregation before finding my spot on the duct taped X on the floor. I took a moment to look at all the other bridesmaids standing tall in our matching strapless red dresses at the front of the church.

The door at the back of the church closed, and the trumpet sounded, announcing that Shana, the beautiful bride, was coming. I saw my dad for a brief moment through the doors before they closed them, overcome with emotion. The "Wedding March" began, and everyone stood for her grand entrance.

Beau looked dashing. His hands were frozen in front of him as he anticipated his long-awaited bride. I thought about how much he loved my sister and how grateful I was he was promising to take care of her for the rest of his life. The wedding coordinators pulled back the two church doors as Shana and Dad began their steps together in rhythm down the aisle.

Shana looked ecstatic. She grinned from ear to ear, waiting for her groom to come into view. Her bouquet of pure white Gerbera daisies shook ever so slightly in her hand, her other arm linked tightly with Dad's as they made their way down the aisle.

Suddenly, her eyes met Beau's, and it was as if fireworks went off. They gazed at one another with intensity, both with grins so big their cheeks looked red and tight. My eyes moved rapidly between the two of them until Shana finally reached her prince charming.

"Dearly beloved, we are gathered here today to join this man and this woman in holy matrimony," Pastor Don began.

With those words, these two people I cared deeply for began the ceremony to officially become one. The whole experience was thrilling. Each phase of the ceremony was calm but full of zeal. God was glorified in their union. It was obvious to all who were witnesses. When it came time to exchange the rings, Shana handed me her bouquet and gave me a sly smile. I could tell she was having the time of her life.

I was adjusting the bouquets to keep from dropping them when I eyed something peculiar on my hand. I realized I had healing scabs, no longer the fresh self-inflicted wounds I normally found there. I hadn't been self-harming to keep intrusive thoughts out anymore. My wounds were healing. There would be scars there, but they would serve as the reminder I needed to never let it get that bad again. I would continue to fight against the nemesis that taunted me for far too long.

I let my thumb run over the unfamiliar patch of hard healed flesh over and over as I watched the rest of the service. These scabs would become scars, tattoos that would tell the story of my life, and I couldn't help but feel proud of them.

"With the power vested in me, I now pronounce you husband and wife. What God puts together, let no one tear apart. You may kiss your bride." Pastor Don opened his arms wide with enthusiasm, tears in his eyes.

Beau grabbed Shana's face with both hands and kissed her. He pulled back to look her in the eyes one more time, only to quickly plant another kiss on her. I watched with tears in my own eyes as they embraced, thinking of all the ways our family had been blessed.

They turned to walk out of the church when I felt my left knee tighten, so much I couldn't bend it. I was so enthralled with the ceremony, I forgot to follow the golden rule of being a bridesmaid— keep moving to keep the blood flowing. As I recalled the wedding coordinators words, "don't let your knees buckle," I felt my right knee lock into place with a snap.

Suddenly, I was surrounded by beautiful stars flashing before my eyes. I didn't know Shana was planning such spectacular special effects. Before I could process what was happening, I flopped onto the floor like a puppet, my bouquet covering my face.

"Naomi? Naomi?" Dad repeated as he lightly hit my face with the back of his hand. He was uncomfortably close to my face, breathing coffee breath directly into my ear.

"What...what happened?" I whispered.

"You fainted. You must've forgotten to—"

"Not lock my knees...I know." I cautiously sat up.

"Take your time, now."

I sat up to see a hundred pairs of eyes watching, a hundred smiles grinning, and one camera rolling...all in my direction. I took my dad's arm, and he escorted me out, alone. All the other bridesmaids and groomsmen had proceeded with the recessional since it was taking a moment to revive me. I waved as I walked like an injured football player leaving the field, gathering my sea legs. The audience answered with amused applause.

"Ya know, kiddo, the funniest thing was as you went down, you muttered 'yaaayyyy.' It was like you were cheering on the happy couple even as you were about to take a whole different kind of plunge." He tried, and failed, to stifle his laughter.

"Just go ahead and laugh, Dad. It was funny, I'm one hundred percent sure."

"You are more right than you know. It was hilarious! Best maid of honor ever! You just started sinking down onto the ground. You looked like you were made of Jell-O." Shana squealed as she came flying around the corner. I'd never seen her look happier.

"Congratulations, Shana. Beau, you take care of her." I hugged them both together.

"I still can't believe you fainted. All you had to do was stay upright," Beau muttered under his breath, chuckling.

I gave him a pretend punch on the shoulder.

"You better leave my sister alone. You've gotta live with me from now on, and she's mine to protect," Shana said proudly.

We signed the marriage license and took some photos of the bridal party before finally my mom yelled out, "let's get to the party!"

The limousine took our overly zealous group to the reception hall where the newlyweds were announced for the second time as man and wife. I paid close attention to how Beau gently held Shana's waist as they moved together across the dance floor.

Joshua used to touch me like that. He would put his hand gently on the small of my back as he guided me through a doorway. I loved when he did that. My heart shot a twang of self-pity through my core as I drank the sweet sparkling white grape juice in front of me. When Dad and Shana met on the dance floor for the Father-Daughter dance, I felt a hand on my shoulder.

"Are you doing okay, dear? I feel like I haven't seen you all day!" Mom sat next to me. She looked lovely in a dress that matched the sparkling punch I was drinking. It was floor length, and her hair had tiny white flowers swept into her updo.

"You know something, Mom? I'm more okay than I've been in a very, very long time. Even if I am feeling a little sad."

"I understand. I'm sure you really miss Miss Corrie. She has been your go-to person here lately," she said with a shaky tone.

It hadn't occurred to me until that moment that my mom might have felt threatened by my relationship with Miss Corrie as it grew deeper. Mom was not a jealous person, but she had once been my sole confidant. The time I spent with Miss Corrie definitely affected how much time I spent with my mom. Over the last few months, I hadn't relied on mom like I used to. Of course, she'd feel hurt.

"Mom...I... I know...I just feel so bad. I can be insensitive. I never thought about how my friendship with Miss Corrie might make you feel. I hope you know you're still my number one lady." I leaned my head on her shoulder the same way I did when I was little.

She reached her hand up and rubbed my cheek in the loving way only a mother can do. "You're stuck with me, whether you like it or not. But thanks for saying that. You know, you should go dance with your dad. He's been practicing all his dance moves for the last three weeks gearing up for today."

I didn't have to say much to reassure her, and I was relieved. It was nice to be reminded that I wasn't the only one who benefitted from reassurance at times. My dad finished his dance with Shana and gestured for me to come to him, his giant pointer fingers waving in my direction.

"Uh-oh. Here he comes." I stood and slowly backed away from him like I was pretending to escape.

He put his arm around me as he bounced up and down to the swing song playing. He flung me around the dance floor like he used to when I was little. We found a good rhythm, and he hummed along with the song.

"Naomi, I have to tell you that you were not the easiest child to raise," he said against my temple.

"Well, thanks a lot Dad. What a thing to tell your daughter on a day like today." I rolled my eyes and threw my forehead down on his shoulder.

"Come on, let me finish. Someday you'll understand when you're a parent. Watching your children suffer is no picnic, but watching *you* suffer was torture. You have always been a bright personality. You light up a room. You also never ceased to blow out your own flame. I have to admit, seeing you blossom these last few months has been refreshing for your mother and me. Prayers answered." He pressed his cheek to my head and gave my hair a peck.

"Thanks Dad. That really means a lot." I melted into him like warm wax.

"Give Joshua some time too, honey. I think he'll see you're blossoming into the beautiful flower we've all known you to be all along."

"I love you, Dad. Your words mean a lot. But, even if Joshua doesn't see that, I'm okay. I have Jesus. I have His eternal love. Whether Joshua comes to understand me or not, it doesn't matter. I have what identifies me...what makes me whole...I have God's love."

As I spoke, I could feel my dad sighing with relief. He may not have intended to test me while we danced that evening, but he had, and in that moment, I knew I'd passed.

The dancing went on for hours that night, and every guest received a warm and personal greeting from the bride and groom before the party was over. I knew it was getting close to their departure, so I snuck out of the reception hall to do a little dirty work. I'd concocted a plan to make this day extra memorable for Shana, but I needed to be sneaky about it.

I tiptoed to the bathroom at the reception hall, which on another day would've made me cringe, but not this day. This day, I saw the bigger picture. I saw more than ever my need to overcome those uncomfortable fears of contamination I carried with me like luggage for too many years. I took a deep breath, like Mary Jo taught me, pulled the handle to the restroom, and confidently walked inside.

I pulled the toilet paper from the holder, carefully breaking it into long pieces as I wrapped them strategically all over my body. I worked my way down by first covering my head, then finished with the crinoline at the bottom of my dress. I looked in the mirror and smiled at the image reflecting back at me. *Shana won't see this coming in a million years.*

For once, I was not obsessed with germs, worried about what a person thought, or concerned God hated me for being frustrated with Him. I thought about Shana only. I grabbed the door handle, using a paper towel to protect my hand from yucky bathroom germs. I still couldn't bring myself to touch it, even though Mary Jo told me that was next on my to-do list in exposure therapy. *Not today. After all, Rome wasn't built in a day!*

I crept around the corner to hear the DJ announce that the bride and groom were getting ready to leave, and all the guests would need to proceed to the hallway to see them off. I heard Shana calling out my name from inside the dance hall. I figured she wanted to say goodbye to me before they hit the road in Beau's hideously decorated truck that was covered in balloons and streamers.

I rounded the corner and tried to blend in with the other guests by crouching down as I found my way to the end of the lines that formed. Everyone had a bottle of bubbles and had been instructed to blow them as the happy couple came running down the aisle we'd created. Shana was nervously looking around for me as they began to run toward the truck, holding hands with Beau as they were showered with bubbles.

When they finally reached the end of the line, I jumped out in front of them, dressed in my toilet paper toga. "Ta-Da!" I hollered.

The toilet paper was shredded in spots, and I was certain some of the more elderly guests believed I was a criminal who had come to take their money. Shana stopped in her tracks and jumped up and down like she'd won the lottery.

"Toga Girl! There you are! You're back!" She hugged me with purpose, arms wrapped tightly around my neck.

"I love you, sis. You two have a great trip. Thanks for loving me, no matter what," I whispered in her ear as the crowd began to clap in unison.

"You'll never get rid of me, Silsta," she whispered back.

"Okay ladies, that's enough. Let's get the real party started." Beau eagerly grabbed Shana's hand and opened the truck door for her with a Cheshire grin in her direction.

Everyone cheered as they drove off. Shana waved and blew kisses from the passenger side window as they disappeared down the road.

"Am I missing something here?" Dad asked in my ear as I waved back to the departing couple.

"You mean, what's up with the toga?" I laughed.

"Is that what that is? I didn't know what to think when you jumped out like that. You'd better be glad nobody took you out." He wrapped his hand around my elbow and escorted me back inside.

"Dad, I'm an onion. So many delightful and pungent layers. Aren't you thrilled to find out what else is in here?"

"You know, you do kinda look like an onion dressed like that now that you mention it." He threw his head back and laughed as the door closed behind us.

Fourteen

THE WEATHER WARMED up, and my schedule buzzed with activities. I finished all my college classes, labored extensively over exams, and excitedly walked across the stage with my diploma in hand as my parents cheered from the cheap seats. I interviewed for a job at a local private school and began working there as a human resources assistant shortly after graduation. It was mostly clerical work, but it paid the bills, and I made a lot of new friends. I finally got to meet people as myself.

The anxious parts of me were taking a back seat to the true Naomi. I was no longer clothed in my fears. Mary Jo was teaching me new strategies each week in therapy. I felt like I joined a behavioral therapy sorority, and her homework for me felt like hazing for initiation. Each week, she gave me a task to accomplish that forced me to face one of my fears. One week I had to eat with my hands in public, despite being convinced I could catch a stomach bug. Another week I had to leave an uncomfortable conversation I had with someone at work without texting for extra reassurance afterwards. And during yet another challenge, I had to wait to wash my hands after touching something I considered contaminated like a dirty shoe or my cell phone. And when I finally swung a hammer at a board with my eyes tightly shut, my mind was unafraid of what I might do for the very first time.

Treatment wasn't easy or pleasurable, but what I discovered through it was progress. I felt successful and accomplished. I developed endurance and grit. The strategies worked, and I finally had tools I could call upon when I needed them. I learned the world didn't crumble around me when I experienced some of the worst scenarios I had once imagined, and I had a newfound wisdom about the world by purposefully facing so many of the demons my OCD brain convinced me to create over the years.

Miss Corrie and I began to write back and forth every so often. I decided not to confront her about leaving without telling me. I didn't need her to explain herself to me, even if I did disagree with her decision. She believed she was doing what was best, and the most generous explanation was she wanted to take care of me. Miss Corrie always wanted to take care of me, and I loved her for it. I didn't have the courage to go see her because I couldn't bear the thought of witnessing her living in a facility filled with sick and elderly people.

Joshua and I had not spoken or seen each other since we called it quits. I saw his truck once on my way to work when it was parked at a client's house. I felt my heart begin to race at the idea of seeing him again, but the light was green, so I booked it through the intersection without threat of that idea becoming a reality. God had changed me since Joshua and I last interacted. He was molding me into the kind of person I once only dreamt of being, but it was too late for Joshua and me as a couple. It was too late for me to convince him I was anything other than a terrified ostrich with my head in the ground while the world passed me by. Someday, I would find someone as my newly reformed self who would know me a little less broken.

One afternoon, I was filing some paperwork at work when my cell phone rang. The area code showed the call was coming from Boone, North Carolina. I did a double take, wondering if it could be Miss Corrie calling. When I answered the phone, all I could hear was static on the other end, then a man's voice saying my name over and over.

"Hello?" I kept repeating back.

"Hello? Miss Lang? Can you hear me now?" he finally asked with clear reception.

"I'm here! Who am I speaking with?" I replied.

"Sorry. The reception here isn't always the best. My name is Dr. Thomas Bjorn, and I'm Miss Corrie Dean's primary care physician. Miss Dean suffered a fall and fractured her femur. This happened quite a few weeks ago, but Miss Dean insisted we not inform her family until now. We tried on many occasions to convince her otherwise, but she's one stubborn lady," he said.

I was reeling from the information and silent for a moment after he stopped talking.

"Hello? Miss Lang? Are you still hearing me okay, or have I gone out again?"

"I'm here. Yes, she certainly *is* one very stubborn lady. So, how is she? Is she recovering okay? Will she be able to walk again?" I asked, rapid fire.

"Miss Lang, I can assure you she has been in good hands these last few weeks. She spent quite a bit of time at a rehabilitation facility and was just transferred back to her apartment yesterday. She needs a nurse with her or checking on her for much of the day and will likely need to limit her time on her feet once the fracture has healed, but for the most part, she has recovered as well as can be expected with someone in her condition. She wanted me to be sure and include that she doesn't need any special treatment from you. She doesn't expect visits and demanded I hear you promise not to visit, send flowers, or gift her chocolates of any kind. Do I have your word on that?" He semi-chuckled as he spoke the last part.

"That sounds about right. Thanks. Yes, you can tell her I gave my word, but we both know that's not going to happen. Can I ask, have you called anyone else concerning Miss Dean? I want to make sure all necessary family members have been notified." I wanted to be sure I wouldn't have to call Joshua about her situation. I didn't think I would have the nerve to call him if the doctor told me he hadn't already been contacted.

"Um, let me see, okay yes, I see we've also called a Mr. Joshua Michaels. He was notified earlier this morning by my nurse. There is no one else on her list of contacts. Does that sound right to you?" he asked.

"Yes sir. That sounds right. Thank you so much for the information and for your time. I'll be sure to make my way to see Miss Corrie sometime soon and check up on her."

"Well, when you do, please assure her I gave you the direct orders she instructed me to. I don't want to get in any more trouble than I've already been in with that one. You have a nice day, ma'am." I could hear the grin behind his words, but knew he was also quite serious.

That woman meant business, and it was no fun to cross her. It looked like I was going to have to make my way to the mountains to lay eyes on my friend once again to ensure she was recovering well. This would be yet another time I'd have to face my emotions, but this time, instead of facing fear, I'd have to face all my buried sadness about missing Miss Corrie.

I took the Friday of my spring break to drive the four hours it took to reach Miss Corrie and check up on her. I planned to surprise her and stay overnight in a hotel so we could spend a couple of days together. I spent the drive thinking about how I would shock her. I knew if I had called to tell her I was coming, she would insist I not waste my time and make me promise not to come.

Shana offered to come with me, but I wanted my time with Miss Corrie to be just the two of us. There was a lot I wanted to update her on in my life, and those conversations were best when we had tea for just two. I settled into my hotel and made the call I rehearsed the entire trip to Boone.

"Hello?" A familiar voice answered.

"Miss Corrie? It's me, Naomi," I replied.

"Well, hello, my dearest dear heart! How are you?" she asked earnestly.

I felt myself melt when she spoke the nickname she reserved only for me.

"I'm good. I'm good. How are you? Be honest now."

"Well, I'm having an okay day. I can't complain. What brings you to ring me up?" she asked.

"I'm just calling to let you know I'm taking an important trip this weekend to a city you know well, and I may need your help figuring out what I should do while I'm gone." I smirked, pleased with my cleverness.

"Where on earth are you headed? Maybe I can give you some ideas for things to see." She was buying into my plan perfectly.

"So, I'm sort of already at my destination, and it appears to be right around the corner from you, coincidentally. Any ideas what to do in say, Boone, North Carolina?"

There was silence on the other end, then a sudden *click. * *She hung up on me!*

I sat with the phone in my hand, mouth open in disbelief. She actually hung up the phone mid-conversation. I called her back, only this time when she answered, she already knew it was me, and I could hear her muttering to someone in the background before she even said hello. She sounded like she was fussing at someone, accusing them of not doing something she'd asked them to. I guessed it may have been poor Dr. Bjorn.

"Hello again? Miss Corrie? Miss Corrie?" I kept saying while she ranted with the phone in her hand.

"Oh, my dear. You must really not know how to follow directions. I'm here giving Dr. Bjorn a piece of my mind because he was supposed to insist you stay put! He assured me you agreed to my terms, but apparently neither one of you has sense enough to listen to your elders," she complained.

"You don't really have a choice sometimes, lady," I snapped back jokingly. "Are you ready for me to come visit, or do I have to break down your door?"

"Oh please, you don't have to be so dramatic. Sure, come see me. I may not be beautified, but in this joint, no one sees very well, so it doesn't really matter. Come on whenever. Bye." She abruptly hung up again.

I shook my head at her ridiculous antics. Only Miss Corrie could make a doctor feel like she was in charge of him instead of the other way around.

I arrived at Deer Path Assisted Living, Miss Corrie's new home, without really knowing what I was walking into. The air was thick and humid. Even though it was seventy-five degrees outside, it felt like the heat was running inside. I felt a little panicky at the sight of all the aged patients, sickness lingering in the air, and the potential for death in every room. *Mary Jo would be so proud of me walking through here like this. I gotta check this off the list of fears to practice.*

My thoughts were gentler than they had ever been in my life. I made my way past the cafeteria that reeked of fish sticks and found Miss Corrie's room at the end of a long narrow hallway. As I peeked through the door, I saw there was one tiny window in her room and a small outdated television on top of her dresser. There was another bed next to hers that was empty, but I could tell someone must have been living there because there were photos on the wall. The space was small and cramped, but Miss Corrie could make any room feel welcoming.

"Knock, Knock," I said as I made my way in the room completely.

"Oh, my dearest! Come here, come here! Give me a hug!" she called out from her wheelchair parked in the far corner of the room.

I pretended to run in slow motion as I made my way to hug her. She felt frail in my arms, light as a feather. Her hair was in a messy bun like usual, but I could tell she hadn't showered in a few days because it was greasier than I'd ever seen it. I could still faintly smell the frankincense lotion she typically wore, but it wasn't as pungent as the remnant fish stick smell lingering from down the hall.

"I guess you've forgiven me then? How are you doing, Miss Corrie? Like, for real? Do you really like it here?" I wrinkled my nose with doubt.

"It's okay, I must say. I do get lonely sometimes, but who doesn't? I get a new roommate every couple of weeks, which keeps things interesting. The last two were constantly disgruntled, so that was entertaining." She shrugged her shoulders.

"You look like you're way too young to be in here! Everyone else is in their nineties. Was there really not a place you could go to that would be better, somewhere closer to Raleigh?" I asked.

"Dear, I had a choice to make, and I made it. There's no need dissecting what could have been. I'm satisfied with my decision, and I'm living with it. It's an adventure! Now, tell me about *you*. Tell me everything." She grabbed my hands in hers and looked into my eyes like she had the first day I met her.

I spent the next two hours telling her about my daily adventures, describing the new strategies I was using to combat my anxiety, and making her laugh with the silly stories I had bottled up to tell her since we'd last been together. She was an active audience.

"Ahem, excuse me, Miss Dean?" a deep voice called out from her door.

"Oh yes, hello Dr. Bjorn! Come in! Come in!" she said excitedly, then under her breath through her teeth muttered, "Since you came all this way, might as well take advantage of it."

I wasn't sure what was meant by her comment until I saw Dr. Bjorn. He looked older than me, but still young and striking. He was short and stocky but muscular. His hair was jet black and cut with a hard part down the side. He wore a stark white lab coat with a blue collared shirt underneath that caused the white coat to pop. The shirt looked like Tarheel blue, which wasn't a selling point for me, the diehard State fan. Despite the hideous color, I caught myself staring until he spoke. I quickly moved my gaze to the arm of Miss Corrie's wheelchair.

"I'm here to check in on you this afternoon. How's everything healing up? Is your leg still feeling sore, or has the pain improved? And more importantly, have you forgiven me since this morning when you found out your granddaughter was here?" He gave her a tender smile.

"I'm doing okay today, Thomas. No need for any more apologies. It's been quite delightful having Naomi here visiting with me. Have you two met?" she asked innocently.

"Ah, no ma'am. We only spoke on the phone. Nice to finally meet you, Naomi. I've heard wonderful things about you." He reached out to shake my hand.

I was overwhelmed by the butterflies taking flight in my gut. I hadn't felt anything close to that since I'd first met Joshua, but this time without the fog of my anxieties.

"Yes, it's…well…yeah…great to meet you." I raised my hand to shake his. I was no longer terrified to shake someone's hand out of fear of germs or fear they'd discover my wounded hands.

"I'll leave you two to visit. Naomi, feel free to come by my office if you have any questions about your grandmother. I'm sure it's difficult seeing her like this, but we're here to care for her as best we can, and I'm happy to relieve any uncertainties you might have." He walked backwards and accidentally bumped the doorknob with his back before he finally left the room.

"Miss Corrie! He's too cute! And your granddaughter? Why does he think I'm your granddaughter?" I squealed like a middle school girl who recently saw her crush walk down the hallway.

"I know it. He's easy on the eyes…and Catholic too! I said you were my granddaughter because no one would believe I could be your mother. Dear heart, you're my family, so I'm gonna tell people so. Maybe I should invite him to come eat with us tonight in the cafeteria?" She schemed out loud.

As she mentioned the cafeteria, I suddenly got an idea and jumped up to run out of the room, chasing after Dr. Good Looking. "I'll be right back!"

"Excuse me! Dr. Bjorn?" I called out as I caught up to him in the hallway.

"Yes, Naomi. What can I do for you?" His kind smile got my butterflies fluttering again.

"I know this may seem like a strange question, but is there any way I could take Miss Corrie out for dinner tonight? Is there anyone who could help me get her to a restaurant close by? Or is that an impossible request?"

"Hmmmm...let me think. She is definitely capable of doing that, but you'd need someone with you to assist in getting her in and out of the wheelchair. You could take one of our handicap accessible vans to transport her, but you'd need an approved driver. It's getting close to dinner but let me see what I can do. I'll see if I can find someone to help you take her before it gets too late." He patted my shoulder lightly.

"Thank you so much!" I turned and skipped back down the hall to Miss Corrie's room.

"What was that all about?" she asked suspiciously.

"I wanted to see if I could take you out for dinner tonight. Dr. Bjorn said he would find someone to help me take you to eat somewhere other than that disgusting cafeteria." I shuddered.

We spent a bit more time chatting and brushing out Miss Corrie's hair when suddenly there was a knock at the door. It was just about dinner time, and we hoped it was the nurses' aide Dr. Bjorn promised for our outing.

"Come in," Miss Corrie answered.

We both turned to see Dr. Bjorn standing in front of us with car keys in his hand. He was no longer wearing a white coat but was now dressed in jeans and an NC State shirt. A doctor who liked NC State? It seemed almost too good to be true!

"Are we ready to break this little lady out of jail for the evening?" He spun the keys around his finger playfully.

I sat there with my eyes wide in shock. I could not believe I'd be having dinner with him, as well as Miss Corrie. *What is happening?*

"Yes sir! Let's get this show on the road! Giddy-up!" Miss Corrie slapped her knee.

As excited as I was to get to know Dr. Wonderful, I got a strange sense that I was doing something wrong. I felt like I was being unfaithful to someone, even though I wasn't attached to anyone romantically. The thought came and went quickly in the moment I saw Dr. Bjorn, or Thomas as he asked me to call him, help Miss Corrie into the van. His compassion and care were illuminating, and it gave me a strong desire to get to know him better. Maybe Mr. Right would actually be Dr. Right?

I had not dated a lot before or since Joshua, so I was surprised by how relaxed I was on our dinner date with Dr. Bjorn tagging along. Maybe because it wasn't an official date or because I was already used to having three people on a date, but I was shockingly comfortable throughout the entire evening. I found myself astonished by how fantastic the food tasted. Before starting therapy and medication, food was an undesired necessity, but now I found myself craving all kinds of different foods and enjoying them immensely for the first time.

We decided to go to The Olive Garden because it was close to Deer Path, and Miss Corrie said she wanted something naughty to eat. We loaded up on salad and breadsticks while we were chatting about her adventurous life. I had heard many of the stories already, but I didn't mind hearing them again.

"Miss Dean, you have been a remarkable person to get to know. I'm sure your family feels blessed to have you. You must be thankful she's your grandmother," Dr. Bjorn said as I stuffed my face with Pasta di Portobello.

"Well, to be clear, she isn't *actually* my granddaughter. I may have fudged a little on that one. I don't have any children, and Naomi here is the closest thing I'm ever going to get to a daughter or granddaughter." She set her hand on mine lovingly.

"That's so sweet. Your relationship must mean a lot to both of you." His knee jiggled up and down under the table.

We discussed religion and politics. We laughed about our animated waiter who spoke dramatically about the food on the menu with an ironic French accent, not at all Italian, and acted like he was at an acting audition each time he visited our table. It was a relaxing evening, and Miss Corrie was soaking up every moment of freedom. Dr. Bjorn insisted I call him Thomas. I could tell he was interested in me by the way his eyes lingered on my face as I spoke. He also made sure to give me a hug when we dropped Miss Corrie back off at her room late that night. We kept her out later than we should have, but neither one of us regretted it.

"Thank you so much for your help tonight. I know this night meant a lot to her. I'm really glad I got the chance to treat her like that," I whispered to him outside her room after we got her settled in.

"It was my pleasure, really. I was happy to help. May I walk you to your car?" he asked softly.

"Sure, I think I can make it, but I don't really remember where I parked in the giant parking deck this afternoon, so you might be able to help me."

When we found my truck, he fumbled with his keys then reached out and gave me a friendly hug. "I hope to run into you tomorrow, Naomi. Maybe we could grab lunch before you head home?"

"I'd like to run into you too, Dr. Bjorn. And lunch? Sure, Miss Corrie would love that," I twirled the hair in my ponytail, nervous about what he implied.

"Miss Corrie doesn't have to come this time." He smiled flirtatiously. "And, please, call me Thomas."

"Okay...Thomas." I swallowed hard.

"I most certainly enjoyed my evening with you two." He smiled again before kissing my cheek and walking away.

I tossed and turned through the night as the air conditioner in my room blasted and hummed obnoxiously. I felt particularly sluggish when I arrived to see Miss Corrie and can only imagine what I must've looked like after spending the night sleeplessly spinning like a rotisserie chicken.

"You look like you ran here, dearest," Miss Corrie commented dryly as I entered the room.

"Nice to see you too. I didn't sleep well. A/C was making all kinds of racket. You wouldn't have slept either." I threw my purse down on the chair with a thud. "How about we just watch some television after our wild outing last night?"

"Whatever you want, dearest." She turned on the morning news, and we watched for a while, discussing the latest happenings in Hollywood.

Dr. Bjorn came and picked me up for an early lunch, and Miss Corrie insisted she stay behind to rest. Thomas and I ate a mediocre lunch together in the cafeteria with mediocre conversation. He was a kind man who clearly loved many of the same things I did, but something was missing. Maybe I was looking for a spark or chemistry that just wasn't there. Either way, deep down, I somehow knew he wasn't for me. I was comforted in knowing I'd be leaving that afternoon for home. He made it clear at the end of our lunch that he was interested in keeping in touch, but I deflected his request as best I could.

That afternoon while Miss Corrie read, I had all but fallen asleep in the chair next to her. My rich lunch of overcooked and over-gravied Salisbury steak was sitting heavy, and my eyes were fighting to stay open. Suddenly, I became aware of voices whispering next to me. At first, I thought they were from a dream, but as I woke, the voices got louder. I stirred a bit, then sat up abruptly.

"Hey—oh. Sorry I fell asleep. What's going on?" I spun around to see the shock of my life.

Sitting in the chair next to Miss Corrie was Joshua. My heart jammed into my throat, and I began to have full blown palpitations. I was not emotionally prepared for what I had woken up to, and for a few short moments, I still would have sworn I was dreaming.

"Hi there, Naomi." His hazel eyes pierced through me as he gazed at my disheveled face with the same quiet confidence he always possessed.

"Well, what a coincidence! You both came to visit me on the same day after all this time having no visitors! Who would have thought this was gonna happen? I certainly would never have guessed it! I'm so surprised and thrilled to see both of you! I guess it was meant to be!" Miss Corrie beamed at us.

I could tell by her tone she must have had something to do with his sudden appearance. I was confused by why she would ask him to come, especially after practically throwing me at Dr. Bjorn. Did Joshua know I was here and decide to come anyway?

"Good morning...eh...Joshua. How are you?" I was unsuccessfully attempting to hide my desire to shrivel up and hide in a tight ball as my face turned various shades of red.

"How are things going?" He sat back in the recliner, also trying to appear unphased by our sudden meeting.

Miss Corrie must have left him in the dark about my being there when she asked him to come based on his nervous posture. He wasn't easily shaken, but I could tell he was unnerved as his legs shook up and down.

"Yes dear, fill him in on how good things are going for you right now." Miss Corrie jumped in. "The college graduate has a fantastic new job and is loving it! She's making her own money. She's even met a nice doctor whose been wooing her."

"Miss Corrie! I haven't been wooed by any doctor! What are you talking about?" I said, suddenly defensive. I didn't want him thinking I was seeing anyone. I wasn't sure why, but I was certain I didn't want that to be a lasting topic of conversation.

"Ya know? I think it's probably time I get back home. You two need to have some time together without another person intruding." I fumbled to fix my bed head.

"Don't feel like you have to go. I'm happy to have you stay. We haven't had a chance to catch up since I last saw you. I'm sure there's lots for us to talk about."

Did I detect a hint of desperation in his voice?

"Oh Dearest, don't go. I'd love to have the original trio back together, even for an afternoon," Miss Corrie pleaded.

She could obviously see her plans unraveling. Whatever she concocted wasn't going to work. I had broken my own heart where Joshua was concerned, and there was no way I would let myself be with him long enough to feel anything again. I grabbed my bag from the end of the bed, only to have the strap get caught on the bedpost a few times before I could finagle it free. My smooth exit wasn't smooth at all.

"No, I'm going to go. I need to get back home to get ready for work tomorrow. I love you...*Miss Corrie*... I mean, I love you, *Miss Corrie*. I'll talk to you soon." I kissed her on the cheek and scurried out the door.

I heard a faint, "Bye," from Joshua as the door closed behind me.

I don't remember much about the drive home, but I do remember doing a lot of praying, crying, and convincing myself that Joshua and I were an impossibility that was never going to happen.

Fifteen

THE NEXT COUPLE of days after my impromptu trip were a blur. I went to church and work feeling consumed with remorse about running off when I saw Joshua. I'd frustrated myself by being a chicken and for abandoning Miss Corrie. I selfishly tried to run from having to face Joshua, and now I was living with consuming regret. I was spiraling into an obsessive vortex, and old habits were returning.

Mary Jo had warned me not to become complacent in my success with therapy. OCD was a monster lurking to creep back in, and I had to be vigilantly aware of my own tendencies. I hated the idea that Joshua might think I still struggled to live a balanced life.

About a week after the whirlwind weekend, I was headed home from work, distracted by my thoughts and trying desperately to gain back some level of peace of mind like I'd had before. The medication definitely gave me more stability, but I was still unlearning bad habits. My folks had invited Shana, Beau, and myself for dinner to discuss an idea and get our input. None of us had any idea what they wanted to talk about, so we all accepted, curious about the mysterious topic of discussion.

"Come in! Come in!" Mom belted out as she opened the front door to the three of us. She kissed each of us on the cheek as we entered.

"Mom, what smells so good? Are you making lasagna?" Shana asked with excitement.

Lasagna was one of our mom's specialties, but she didn't make it often because the recipe had so many steps and took hours to put together. Shana and I were both salivating at the thought of her masterpiece dinner.

"Yes, you're right. Your mother has been slaving over that all day! I've been tortured by the delicious smells all afternoon. We must reek of garlic and onions." Dad came in patting Beau on the back.

"So, what's this intentional dinner all about?" I asked as we made our way to the dining room.

"Let's at least get started on dinner before we get into all that." Mom placed the piping hot lasagna on a trivet in the middle of the table.

Dinner was served, we prayed, and everyone began devouring the delicious meal when finally, the three of us noticed our parents were mouthing something to each other across the table.

"What in the world is going on? You guys are being so mysterious! What gives?" Shana demanded with a yeast roll shoved in her cheek.

"Okay, well, your mom and I have been considering doing some renovations, and since we would have to use quite a lot of our savings, or your inheritance, we thought we should present the idea to you three first," Dad said.

"What idea? Y'all want to move to Mars or something?" I kidded.

No one laughed, and I could tell my folks were in no mood for jokes.

"We would like to make our home more appropriate for aging people, like your mother here."

"Hey! You watch it." Mom swatted him with her napkin.

"I mean, your mother and I aren't getting any younger, and we'd like to make a bedroom downstairs out of the extra living area. We want to make everything handicap accessible, so when we get old, we won't have to move away until we absolutely must. Now, this will chew up a lot of the savings we have, so you may not receive quite as much money when we pass like we had planned." Dad whistled to himself as he nodded.

"I'm out then. I want my moolah." Shana snorted.

My parents did not appreciate her antics and made sure she knew it with their stoic stares.

"I don't really care about the money, y'all. You two have provided so much for us, and if this is where you guys want to grow old, then you should make it a house where you can easily do that. Don't you agree, Naomi?" Shana said, this time seriously.

"Of course, I agree. You two have to do what's best for you. We're fine with whatever you decide. But you guys are so young. Why now?" I asked.

"Sometimes you just get a prodding from the Lord about what His timing is. Your father and I have been praying about this for a long time and feel we need to investigate how we can make it happen. We aren't getting any younger, you know," Mom answered.

"You two are so funny. Look how official you are about such a small thing. I sure hope you do some redecorating while you're at it. Might as well update the joint during the process." I added.

"Ooooh, Naomi thinks your house is ugly! I bet she thinks the outside is in desperate need of help too!" Shana teased.

"No! No! I never said that! Not at all! Stop that, Shana!! Mom, I didn't mean it like that. I'm sorry!" I tried to keep from over apologizing. Old habits die hard.

Mom looked at me and winked. She wasn't offended at all, and I had to rest in that. Time to walk away uncomfortable again.

"Shana, you make a good point. We should probably call Joshua and have him help us with some new landscaping ideas. If we are going to make the house bigger, maybe we should consider having him help us beautify the outside too," Dad added.

"Um...you're...uh...going to call Joshua?" I blurted out without realizing it.

"Yes, we will if we decide to update the outside. Your mom likes to garden, but we may want a water element or something she can't do by herself. This is going to be the home we grow old in, honey, and we might as well make it what we want. Do you feel uncomfortable with that?"

I pondered his question and sat there moving my food around my plate.

"No. You and Mom should be able to work with whoever you want. I can be grown up about it. If he's around here a lot, I can make myself scarce," I said.

"You shouldn't have to disappear, dear. Joshua cares about you." Dad put his hand on his heart and pointed in my direction.

"Now, that's enough, you two. Let's get dessert." Mom began clearing the table. She gave my dad the look, and everyone knew what it meant.

When Mom looked at Dad like that, he knew it was his turn to be quiet. She clearly didn't want him discussing anything more about Joshua. I started to help her clear the table as an attempt to settle myself down. I was hurt that my parents would want to stay connected to Joshua, but I also felt strangely excited at the thought of having to avoid him. I scraped plates and rinsed them while Mom stacked up the dirty pots next to me.

"I'm sorry your father threw out the idea about Joshua without really considering your feelings. He can be pretty black and white about things. In his mind, you should be ready to move on," she said.

"I know. It would be ideal for me to be around him and not feel strange, but it's still an open wound. I've changed a lot since we were together, but OCD will always be a part of me, and the jury is still out on whether or not I'll be able to hold down a healthy relationship. God may choose to keep that experience from me, and I'm prepared for that."

"I hear you. You also need to prepare yourself that it may very well be what God *does* want for you. I bet that sounds scary to you too, right?" she leaned down to make eye contact with me.

The plates I was rinsing started to blur with tears.

"Yes Mom…it *is* scary. I can't love someone and have kids with them. How can I? I'll probably be afraid to take care of a newborn. Scared I'll hurt him or her intentionally somehow. I can't even imagine what will happen if I don't like my own kid. The scary scenarios are beyond what I can handle when I try to picture myself with someone. Breaking up with Joshua was actually freeing for me, sadly enough. I didn't have to face the potential fears that being with him would force me to face. Dating him was one of the scariest things I've ever done. Trusting that someone could love me in my severely broken state felt impossible." I rambled so long my mom finally turned off the sink that I'd left pouring alongside my tears.

"Let me tell you something, sweetie. I originally agreed with your father that I shouldn't share this, but I think you need to know," she said.

"Tell me what?"

"Joshua has been meeting with your father ever since you two broke up," she answered.

"*What?* Why?" My face felt hot.

"According to your Dad, they get together to pray, read scripture, and just talk."

"Talk about what?"

"I don't know, sweetie. I'm not there, but I'd imagine they talk about life. I think Joshua looks at your dad as a mentor. Your father has an endearing and welcoming way about him. Joshua really connected with him, and after y'all broke up, he asked if they could continue meeting."

"Wait, you're saying they met while we were dating too! What on earth did they pray and talk about then?" I wiped furiously at my tears.

"I think they prayed a lot for you, Naomi."

I turned and looked at her as she nonchalantly began putting the dirty utensils in the dishwasher.

"For me? Are you sure?"

"Joshua cared deeply for you and felt helpless in knowing how to help you with your struggles. Your father was a resource for him in that area, as well as in other parts of his life. His desire was to pray for more than just you, but you certainly were a topic high on their list. So, you see, your dad cares a lot for Joshua now, and hiring him would be the only option in his eyes. He didn't want to tell you all that because he thought it might make you feel uncomfortable, but I think it's important you know the whole story."

She dried a platter making slow and deliberate circles, stopping often to find her words. "No, you won't ever be fully separated from your OCD, but what God has allowed you to struggle with has also brought you to your knees, which allowed you to commit to Him alone. What a blessing! Remember, it's not impossible for God to love you. And it's also not impossible for all of us to love you like we do. Joshua loved you very much...even with all your scars. He was not unblemished, but much like the rest of us, wounded, sinful, and equally in need of a savior."

I was drowning in disbelief. I knew my mom was right, about everything. I prayed for God to help my unbelief in that moment and all the doubtful moments that would come.

"Thanks Mom, for trusting me with all this. I appreciate you telling me." I hugged her with my head on her shoulder like I used to as a girl.

"Where is dessert? We're still hungry out there!" Dad came bursting into the kitchen to find us hugging.

"We're coming, we're coming. Hold your horses." Mom brushed a few stray hairs out of my eyes then kissed my cheek.

"What are you two blubbering about?" He didn't wait for us to answer before taking the chocolate cake Mom made with him back to the dining room. The call of the chocolate cake was irresistible.

It was a cloudy and gray afternoon as I headed home from work after a particularly boring day. The truth was, I was being assigned more and more mind-numbing tasks each day. I began to wallow and could feel dissatisfaction beginning to take root. I thought when I took the job it would be a temporary situation, but since I had no idea what I wanted to do instead, I ended up staying longer than I hoped.

I drove slowly, staying in the right lane as it began to drizzle. I did my best to follow the cars ahead of me carefully. The tall food truck in front of me made it difficult for me to see very far ahead. It didn't help that the driver of the truck was inconsistent, speeding up one minute, then breaking suddenly the next. I stayed as far back as I could from their bumper, but my patience was growing thin, and before long, I found myself tailgating.

The food truck brake lights lit up, reminding me to back off, so I braked, hoping to put some distance between us. I could feel the water under my tires, so I pressed harder to keep from slipping. *I better be careful; it's slick out here.*

Just as the thought made its way down to my foot on the pedal, the driver of the food truck in front of me slammed on his breaks, forcing me to slam on mine. I braced myself for impact as my truck slid forward instead of stopping, no matter how hard I braked. At the last second, the food truck swerved to the left, changing lanes to avoid hitting the car in front of it. I kept breaking as I blew past all the cars next to me, desperate to gain back control, but since the rain had just started, the roads were like an ice-skating rink, and I was hydroplaning.

Before I could truly brace myself, my truck careened into the car that had been directly in front of the giant food truck before his sneaky escape to the left lane. My head jolted forward, and my seat belt tightened as I smashed into the bumper ahead of me. *Great. Just great.*

I shook my head in frustration and in an attempt to bring myself back to reality when I noticed the make and model of the car I hit. It wasn't a car at all, but a dirty old truck, with a familiar white paint job.

"Joshua. Are you kidding me, God?" I whispered under my breath.

He slowly emerged from the driver's side and rounded to the back of his vehicle to assess the damage. Thankfully, the impact from the crash itself wasn't as intense as it could have been. I was unharmed and hoped he was the same.

I didn't know what to do. He looked back at my car, eyes growing wide. He gave me a wave, pointing to the parking lot next to us. I saw him take in a deliberate breath, likely gathering his nerves as he climbed back into the truck and made the turn into the lot.

I followed behind reluctantly, formulating plans to escape the situation without being accused of a hit and run. No smart solutions came to mind. My knuckles were white as snow as I pulled in next to him in the parking lot. We both took our time getting out of our vehicles.

"Er...I'm so sorry about this. I totally didn't mean to hit you. It all sort of happened fast." I fiddled with my keys, looking everywhere but at his face.

"It's okay, the weather certainly isn't great for driving," he replied nervously.

"Should we, ya know, check out the damages?"

I was mortified by my current predicament as the reality of what just happened sank in and the adrenaline drastically wore off. Joshua bent down to look at my front bumper first. It was so typical of him to be more concerned with my car than his own. He was selfless like that.

A memory instantly came to mind. Once, in an attempt to perform a thoughtful act, I decided to bring Joshua's trashcan up to the side of the house after the trash collectors had come. I was rolling it with confidence when I rammed into the side mirror of his truck, leaving it dangling by one solitary wire. I stood in horror as I witnessed my own carelessness, but Joshua appeared completely calm. He quickly forgave me and proceeded to tootle around town with duct tape holding it together for weeks.

Joshua was considerably more concerned with the wellbeing of others than his own. It was a trait I used to find intimidating or guilt producing, but that afternoon, I found his thoughtfulness to be a genuine comfort.

"It looks like you have a couple of scratches on your front bumper but nothing too bad." He moved to inspect his own back bumper and took a more detailed look than his initial glance. He licked his thumb and proceeded to buff out the smudges left by my rear-ending.

"There. It's as good as new. A little spit, and the problem is solved." His smile brought out his deep dimples. Those long dimples were one of many of Joshua's characteristics that caused my stomach to drop like it did when I used to swing high as a kid. I felt my insides stir like I'd sworn they never would for him again.

"Oh, good. I'm so relieved. I can't believe I hit you! I felt myself sliding, but I kept thinking it would stop," I rambled.

"Oh, you stopped alright," He said with the familiar sarcasm I had grown to love about him.

"Well, I think you should've moved out of the way a little faster. You were driving like a grandpa, per usual, so I just gave you a little nudge to get you going," I bantered back.

It was the first time we'd conversed genuinely since the awful afternoon at Miss Corrie's house of horrors. We laughed briefly before regaining the uncomfortable silence we had recently come to know so well.

"I better get going. I've had a long day, and I really don't want to keep you from whatever you have going on. You probably have plans with your doctor friend tonight," Joshua blurted out. He seemed agitated and uneasy. He spoke uncharacteristically fast, not deliberately like usual. Before I could say a word in response, he had already hopped back into his truck and started the engine.

I stood in astonishment, digesting what had transpired as he practically flew out of the parking lot, squealing tires as he peeled around the corner.

The sky opened up and started pouring buckets. I sat in my truck, flustered and uneasy by having seen Joshua unexpectedly, yet again. I decided to do what was hardest for me. I prayed. Praying had been consistently difficult for me. It opened up the possibility for unwanted thoughts or feelings directed at God. I lived in constant fear of doing something that would condemn me. Recently, I'd been attempting to talk to Him like Miss Corrie did, like my Heavenly Father who cares for me.

Lord, why does this keep happening? Why do you keep letting me run into him like this? Literally this time. But why...how come I keep seeing him? You must know how much it hurts me to interact with him. What am I supposed to do with these feelings I keep having about him? I thought the door to that relationship was closed.

Please show me what I can do to make things right with him. I can't imagine my life without him in it, Lord, but please help me know what to do. If we're supposed to be friends, help me to put the deeper feelings to rest, and if we are meant to be together, let me know how I can be obedient as I wait for it to happen. I'm so used to thinking I can fix my fears with rituals and worry. Please help me to be wise...and to trust you. Thank you, Lord, for working in me and changing me.

I started the car after confessing my need for God's help when I got a clear prompting to confess to someone else. Oddly, I felt compelled not to confess my sins, but instead to confess my love to the one man I now knew I adored, Joshua. I wanted to be real with him, vulnerable with my feelings, and put my heart at risk, trusting that no matter how he responded, God was already the one making me whole.

I would forever wonder what could have been between us had I not squandered his love away the first time around. I had to at least ask him if he would be willing to try again. He might say no, but God had used the last few months to toughen me up. I had faced many fears now and was ready to put myself out there again. It was a risk I wanted to take.

I started out toward Joshua's house, rehearsing what I was going to say when he answered the door. I had an entire mental paragraph of things I badly wanted to tell him flowing through my mind. When I finally made it to his house, I pulled into his driveway to find his truck wasn't there, and his blinds were drawn.

My shoulders slumped with disappointment. I looked around at his beautiful garden in full bloom. It had gotten pretty hot that summer, but Joshua knew what to plant and how to care for his landscape so there was constantly something in bloom. I smiled as I thought of his detailed nature and his perfectionistic personality.

Though he and I were completely different, polar opposites even, he seemed unfazed by our uniquely contrasting struggles. I decided I was going to wait him out. He had to come home sometime, and my words couldn't wait any longer.

It was just after dinnertime, and I was hungry from having been sidetracked by the accident-turned-love-pursuit. I folded my arms and scrunched up my knees while I watched the summer sun through the passenger side window slowly go down, creating a color wave of pinks and blues in the sky. My eyes began to flag slowly, and before I knew it, I was asleep.

Only a few moments later, I awoke to a loud tapping sound on the window beside my head. I screamed out a high-pitched screech seasoned with terror. As I jolted upright, my elbow hit the horn, causing it to blast obnoxiously. The blaring horn ignited me to scream again, this time covering my ears as I shrieked.

"What in the world are you doing here?" Joshua shouted through the glass with a look of confusion.

I wobbled out of the car ungracefully, like I was getting off a boat and still finding my sea legs. I tripped on the floor mat which conveniently broke some of the growing tension.

"I, uh, well, I came here to confess something to you." My voice shook.

"You don't have to apologize anymore. You take way too much responsibility for things that aren't your fault. That accident was just that, an accident." He seemed irritated.

"You didn't let me finish. I didn't come to confess my sin. I came to confess my, well, my love," I licked my lips and rubbed the back of my neck.

He stood there looking mortified and hopeful at the same time. I thought it best I keep talking before I lost my nerve. I had totally forgotten the speech I prepared, thanks to my unexpected evening nap

"I messed up a few months ago—the way I treated you, the way I treated me. I didn't believe anyone would choose to love me, let alone tolerate all my imperfections for an extended amount of time...especially, like, forever. You always seemed so confident, so sure of how you felt about me, and I couldn't understand what I had to offer that you'd love me that much. I was consumed with worry about what you were thinking about me. I was terrified of my thoughts, so I figured you would be too if you ever knew what they were. But nothing I did seemed to faze you. You just kept being steady, faithful, quiet Joshua." I took a step closer to him, noticing his familiar earthly scent as it filled my nose. "Your silence was unnerving, even alarming for me. Truthfully, I didn't believe it was possible for these chains I'd been attached to for most of my life to ever be broken. But during our time apart, I've learned to be thankful for these chains. I'm thankful God has used them to help me trust Him more and desire His approval more than anyone else's. I can face my fears now, and right now, I'm standing here facing one more. I have no idea what you feel for me anymore. You may have a new girlfriend for all I know, but I came here to ask you if you'd like to try again. I love you, Joshua. So much. You get me and don't get me in all the right ways. So, is it possible? Do you still love me too, or..."?

"Now let me see. You say *you* love *me?*" His finger swung from me to himself.

"That's what I just said, not eloquently, but yes, I do love you."

"Okay, that does it then. I think I'll keep you." He leaned down and wrapped his arms around me into a close hug.

"What?" I asked into his chest.

"I said I'll keep you. You always were my favorite." He leaned back just an inch so he could look down into my eyes. "I never stopped loving you or praying for you. It might take me a long time to decide what I want for lunch, but I knew you were who I wanted by my side immediately. I absolutely still love you too."

"Thank you for waiting," I said softly.

"You've always said I was a patient guy, right?" He planted a gentle kiss on the outside of my ear sending a tingle through my arm.

"Yes...I have been known to say that about you," I slurred as goosebumps travelled down the left side of my body.

"I thought I'd lost you for good, Naomi. You don't know how happy I am I didn't." He pulled me in closer for a long and hard kiss on the lips.

I was up on my tiptoes with my arms wrapped around his neck and tingling all over.

"Want to go inside so we can call Miss Corrie? She'll be thrilled to know her cunning plan may not have worked in the moment but definitely played a part in getting us back together." He grinned.

"She'll be thrilled to know we landed back together. But let's wait till tomorrow to let her know. How about we sit out here on your porch swing instead. I sure could use some time with your arm around me while we catch up on the last few months. I have a lot to tell my best friend." I took his hand and lead him up the stairs, where we sat swinging and talking long into the night.

Sixteen

JOSHUA AND I spent the next few months getting reacquainted with one another. We learned about each other while we were apart and enjoyed getting to know the inner workings of our reformed hearts. Joshua worked hard to communicate better with me about his thoughts and feelings, while I learned to let the silence he brought into my life be a comfort, not a burden. We worshiped and prayed together. It was not a perfect relationship, but it was sanctifying for us both and exactly where we felt God wanted us.

Joshua never demanded to hear details about my fears. He was content knowing I was working through them in therapy, and he didn't let my anxiety change his view of who I was as a person. Not only was he committed to loving me even when I got squirrely, but he also helped me to see that he brought his own level of struggle to the table. I took him off the pedestal I'd placed him on and could sense his relief.

One Saturday morning, before heading out Christmas shopping together, Joshua and I made waffles together at my apartment. The construction for the remodel at my parents' house had finally begun to die down. Their house had been transformed into a gorgeous home where they could age gracefully. My dad kept making comments about what he wanted to do with my apartment once I moved out, but I didn't have any plans for moving…unless Joshua gave me good reason to. We sat at my island while I devoured my breakfast, but when I looked up from my clean plate to Joshua, his was still almost full.

"Are you not hungry or something?" I asked around my last bite of maple syrup covered waffle.

"I'm okay…just…you know…not starving," he answered with a mild shake in his voice.

I noticed his tone and became very aware that he had not moved his gaze off of me. I wondered if I had something unsightly on my forehead. I was a messy cook, no doubt some of the waffle flour lingered on my clothes and face.

"Are you okay Joshie?" I winked at him, knowing he hated that nickname.

As I took a long sip of my coffee, Joshua stood up, then moved onto one knee. I closed my eyes tightly and dropped my fork on my plate.

"Naomi? Naomi? Look at me…please…" He took my hand and rolled his fingers around mine, weaving us together.

"What is happening?" I slowly opened my eyes.

"I know you've always felt like getting married could be an impossible thing for you, but ever since the day I met you, I knew that fear was false. You and I are uniquely different, and it's good for both of us. Will you please do me the honor of becoming my wife and the mother of my children if God blesses us with them?" He pulled a ring from his pocket and placed it in my hand with a grin.

"Yes, *absolutely* I will!" I screamed as I jumped up, flinging my new ring onto my syrup-covered plate. I grabbed it, then jumped into his arms, knocking him down to the floor.

"Oooofff…that's an enthusiastic yes!" He pushed himself up off the floor with his elbow then kissed me quickly on the cheek as we stood up.

"Sorry, I didn't mean to knock you down. Put the ring on!" I flapped my hand in front of his face.

"It's all sticky! Don't you want to rinse it?" he asked.

"Okay okay...hang on." I stumbled to my feet and ran the treasure under the faucet. I practically ran back to him and handed him the ring.

"It's so gorgeous. It's so gorgeous," I kept repeating.

He slipped the ring onto my finger, and it was a perfect fit. I stared at it carefully as he observed my reaction.

"I hope you like it. I also wanted to offer you a job." He got back down on one knee, holding my hand tightly.

"What job? You're not going to pay me to be your wife, are you?" I giggled.

"I would love for you to come help me at my company. Really make it a family business. You're so good with people, and I figured it would be fun getting to see you every day at work. You can put that communication degree to good use! What do you say? My next job is with this really difficult family. You may know them. The Lang family? What do you say?" He raised his shoulders.

"Yes, absolutely I'll work for you!" I threw myself back into his arms and kissed him again as he laughed.

"You are a piece of work, Naomi Lang, a piece of work."

"If I had a quarter for every time you said that I'd be a rich woman."

This day was ranking high on my list of best days ever. I was learning to become content with the messiness of life and relationships. I knew Joshua and I would have hard and painful times of growth alongside the good times, but now I could see that the joy that results from trusting God and persevering together would be well worth the work.

"I'm engaged!" I bellowed out as we entered my parents' house.

Joshua followed behind me at his usual slow speed while I ran from room to room.

"Where is everyone?" I called out again when no one came immediately at the sound of my call.

"Naomi? Is that you out there?" Mom appeared from their new first floor master suite. "Oh, congratulations you two!" She gave me a hug and then quickly embraced Joshua as well.

"Where's Dad?" I asked urgently as I bounced up and down.

"Oh, he's around here somewhere. William?"

Dad almost immediately appeared too, rounding the corner from the kitchen wearing his apron.

He hugged us both gregariously and gave Joshua an overzealous slap on the back. "Good job, son. I'm glad she actually said yes."

"I can't wait to tell Shana and Beau," I said, still bouncing with adrenaline.

"They already know. I called them this morning and told them what was happening. She just texted me they're on their way over," Joshua said.

He already knew how the sister code of good news worked, and that I needed her there as soon as possible. All of a sudden, I heard a muffled bang from my parents' bedroom. They both looked in the direction of the doorway, then proceeded to look wide-eyed at one another. They were like two children caught smuggling a puppy into the house.

"What was that noise?" Joshua pointed toward the room.

"Er…well, it's uh… Should we tell them?" Mom looked at Dad, shrugging her shoulders.

"Yes! Go ahead and tell them," a voice called out loudly from the master suite. "I've already botched the surprise with this noisy wheelchair I can't seem to drive. It appears I have a new place to live! I'm living the dream now!" Miss Corrie came cruising into the living room in her electric wheelchair.

Joshua and I looked at each other, overwhelmed with amazement.

"What in the world are you doing here, Miss Corrie?" Joshua stooped to greet her.

I almost couldn't move; I was so surprised.

"Cat got your tongue, my dearest dear heart?" She made her way to where I had dropped to sit on the couch and patted my knee dramatically.

"You...you live where now?" I inquired, baffled.

"Your father and I couldn't bear the idea of Miss Corrie living so far away in a facility for people so much older than she is. We discussed the idea of her moving in with us, and after quite a lot of convincing, she finally agreed. We figure now that you're engaged and soon to be married, we'll be able to hire a full-time nurse to take care of her, and he or she can live in your old apartment," Mom explained.

"That was the only way I'd agree to impose on you, kind people. Your offer was too good to be true, and I found out that I'm not the only one who can make a good case." Miss Corrie nodded at my folks. "You two finally wore me down."

"Miss Corrie will live here as long as she's able. That's why we did the renovations so suddenly. We wanted to act fast and get her here as soon as we could," Dad continued.

"Why didn't you tell us?" Joshua asked.

"Dearest, we weren't sure how this would all turn out, and we wanted to see if it would be a fit for everyone. Plus, the looks on your faces were well worth the secrecy. This plan was in the works long before you two got back together, but now this arrangement is even sweeter with you two lovebirds tying the knot." She grabbed my hand.

"I hope you're okay with all this." Mom put her arm around me from the other side.

I felt a deep sense of peace and joy wash over me. God had not chosen to heal Miss Corrie of her disease or taken away my battle with OCD, but He continued to bless both of us and provide what we needed. I had learned so much over the past year, and it was coming full circle.

"Of course, I'm very okay with all this," I whispered with tears in my eyes. "God is answering so many prayers all at once, it seems too good to be true."

"Well, it's true, *Silsta!* You betta' believe it!" Shana shouted as she came barreling into the living room.

We hugged and jumped in unison. Then I jumped into her arms, wrapping my legs around her waist as we spun around together shouting. When she was finally out of breath, she grabbed my hand to gawk at my engagement ring.

"Congrats, man." Beau shook Joshua's hand. "Welcome to the most entertaining family on the planet."

"I think the two of us are going to need to stick together with these two." Joshua gestured toward Shana and me as we acted a fool.

"Oh please, you love us," I called out as we ceased our sister ritual of celebration.

"We sure do," Joshua answered with a content smile and his famous flirtatious wink.

Acknowledgments

There are so many people I want to thank for helping me with this book. To all my family and friends who have rooted me on, been early readers, and encouraged me in this process, thank you.

Shona, thank you for telling me I was an author when I was in the beginning stages of this book. I didn't believe you, but you gave me the bravery to keep writing.

Lacey, thank you for everything you've done for me. The hikes. The edits. The friendship. You're one of the smartest people I know.

Becky and John, thank you for taking my vision for the cover and making it happen. Most of all thank you for your constant friendship and love.

Vaneetha, thank you for endorsing my book and being a mentor for me during this process. You were a voice saying I should believe in my message and prayed for me along the way.

Su, thank you for rooting me on and making the happy heart for the back of this book! You have been a huge cheerleader for me and helped me dream big.

Joy Tanner, thank you for giving me encouragement from a counselor's perspective. You have been a promotor since day one and I couldn't be more grateful for your wisdom.

Zoë, thank you for letting me use your beautiful face on the cover.

Sarah and Lee, Lane, Tate, and Paige thank you for being my people. Sarah, you were the spark for my book dream fire. Thank you for being my first editor and for loving me well no matter what.

Marcia, Michael, Marie, Andrew, Colton, Solomon, Florence, Matt, Caroline, Lydia, Silas, Ethan, and Chloe thank you for being the best in-laws in the world. I love doing life with all of you.

Mom and Dad, thank you for raising me and teaching me about Jesus. You loved me through every single one of my days and I don't think I could ever say thank you enough for all you've done for me.

Ellis, Daphne, and Betsy, thank you for making me a mom. You're the biggest blessings and I thank God for you every single day.

Scott, thank you for growing up with me, marrying me, and being my favorite.